THE SHEPHERD'S BURDEN

By Ryan Young

For Christina and Emily

Prologue

April 7, 1995

As the clock approached midnight and the last few minutes of the day ticked away, Daniel Jefferies sat in his basement poring over comic books with his best friend, Shawn Lewis, blissfully unaware that it would be the final day of life as he knew it. For after that day, everything that he had come to understand in his short twelve years about life and death would forever change, but at that moment, such profound subjects were the furthest things from his mind.

He spent the previous five hours engaged in heated debate on such topics as the superior comic book universe, DC or Marvel, and who's favorite superhero would win in a battle. The basement was littered with empty soda cans, half-eaten bags of chips, and a greasy cardboard box with congealed cheese bits stuck to the bottom of it, the only remnants of a once fresh pizza. This was a common scene on Friday nights. Daniel and Shawn were sixth-graders at Christopher Columbus Elementary School in Utica, NY. They had been friends since the age of five when Shawn's family moved into the neighborhood four doors down. Ever since that time, they had been inseparable. They were the best of friends, but neither one would concede to the other one's point when it came to these hotly contested issues. It was a matter of pride for both of them.

"There is no superhero who is superior to the Green Lantern. He can harness all of the powers of the universe through his ring. No one can compete with that. Not only that, he has the coolest oath…In brightest day, in blackest night, no evil shall escape my sight. Let those who worship evil's might, beware my power...Green Lantern's light!" Shawn proclaimed as he stood up with his chest flexed outward.

"Oaths are for boy scouts and rings are for girls! Tell me, what does he do if he loses his ring? He's not even really a superhero because he doesn't have any superpowers. His powers are loaned to him by the Green Lantern Corps. When it comes down to it, he's nothing more than a glorified cop with a bright green suit and a mask. Heroes are born, not made. Wolverine was born a bad-ass. No matter what you throw at him, he can't be killed. He could slice right through Green Lantern's fancy magic-ring tricks with his indestructible adamantium claws," Daniel responded with both fists clenched, revealing the whites of his knuckles.

Rolling his eyes and letting out a loud sigh, Shawn hit back.

"Are you kidding me? First of all, Wolverine wasn't born with the adamantium. It was put into him. Second of all, his only real superpower is being able to heal after getting beat up. By that logic, you would be a superhero. He can't fly. He can't travel through space. There is no contest here."

Just as Daniel was about to make his next great counterpoint, he heard the familiar creak of the antique wooden door at the top of the stairs. The house had been built in 1926 and the door was part of the original construction. While it remained functional, the wood warped over time and could be heard opening from the neighbor's yard.

Daniel knew he was in trouble. He promised his mother that Shawn would leave at 11:30 pm and that he would be in bed. Jacklyn Jefferies stood at the top of the stairs. Every week, the boys promised that they would abide by a mutually agreed upon 11:30 pm curfew, and every week, she called Shawn's mother shortly after midnight to tell her that they were still in the basement and that she would be sending him home shortly. It had become an all too predictable routine.

"Are you boys still downstairs? It's after midnight," Jacklyn called down to them.

The boys immediately ended their argument. They knew that they couldn't afford to be opponents anymore. If they wanted to talk their way out of trouble, they would have to become allies and present a united front. They made their way up the stairs at a sluggish pace with their heads hung low. Once they reached the top, they stood in front of Jacklyn, lifting their heads just enough for her to see their quivering lips, but not enough to make eye contact. If they did, she would have seen right through their little performance. At least, that's what they believed. They found themselves in these types of situations quite frequently. They invested a great deal of time and energy in order to make their act believable, although their success rate left much to be desired.

Daniel was the first to break the silence.

"Mom, I'm so sorry. We got busy and lost track of time. Also, I think that the clock radio downstairs is running slow. I could have sworn it read 11:15 pm just five minutes ago. In fact, just before you opened the door, I was going to tell Shawn that it was time to go."

"He's telling the truth, Mrs. Jefferies. We were checking the clock all night to make sure that we wouldn't go past curfew. Sometimes technology can let you down, but it definitely won't happen again. We promise."

Jacklyn stood silently for a few moments, staring back at them with her best poker face. During that time, she tried to add up the number of times she had heard that same excuse. The silence was her way of making them sweat it out while they were waiting to find out if there would be any consequences. She wasn't mad, of course, but she enjoyed toying with them. As she had many times before, she let them off the hook.

"I guess I'll have to have your father check that alarm clock. Shawn, you better go. I called your mother and told her that you would be right home."

The tense, rigid looks on both of their faces brightened. Shawn waved goodbye and made his way to the door.

"Just so you know, you are both wrong. Superman is, has been, and always will be superior to any other superhero. He can fly through space and he is indestructible. Green Lantern and Wolverine wouldn't have a chance if they went up against him," Jacklyn said with a coy smile on her face.

The boys looked at each and let out a boisterous laugh.

"I can't argue with that logic. Goodnight, Mrs. Jefferies."

"Goodnight, Shawn,"

As the door closed behind him, Jacklyn turned back towards Daniel.

"OK, mister, it is past your bedtime. Get upstairs, brush your teeth, and get into bed."

"Yes, Mom. I want you to know, I really am sorry. We really tried to keep track of time but…"

"…but you are 12 years old and it is pretty much par for the course. Luckily for you, you have a very loving and understanding mother."

"I love you, mom," he said as he hugged her.

Despite breaking curfew, Daniel was a good kid and Jacklyn knew it. It had taken her so long to actually get pregnant that, at one point, she gave up hope that it would happen at all. She and his father, Donald, were considering adoption when she found out that she was pregnant with him. Even when he did something wrong, she couldn't stay angry at him for very long. The very thought of him warmed her heart. When he stared back at her, all she could think of is the smile on his face the day he was born. It was a memory that was seared into her mind and always brought a tear to her eye.

She held him for a few minutes in a tight embrace and then responded.

"I love you too. Now get upstairs. I'll come up in a few minutes to say goodnight."

Daniel headed up the stairs and into the bathroom to brush his teeth. When he was done, he walked across the hallway into his bedroom. He changed into sweat pants and a T-shirt. His room was that of a typical twelve-year old's. There were clothes on the floor and on top of the bed. There were several socks hanging out of a half-opened dresser drawer. The walls were covered with comic book and sci-fi posters. There was a nineteen-inch RCA TV facing his bed with a Sega Genesis hooked up to it. Daniel was also a big Star Trek fan. He had a life-size cardboard cut-out of Captain Kirk dressed in his original-series gold uniform against the far wall next to the window.

He threw the clothes that were on top of his bed onto the floor. He then picked up an X-Men comic from his nightstand and climbed into bed. Jacklyn entered the room a few minutes later. He didn't notice her because he was caught up in his comic book.

She cleared her throat in a distinctly obvious manner.

"Ugh-humm."

He looked up to see a look on her face that matched the tone of her attention-grabbing gesture.

"Hey, mister, I said it was time for bed and I meant it. You need your sleep. Believe me, the comic book will be there in the morning."

Thinking to himself that he already pushed his luck as far as it could go, he conceded.

"OK, Mom. I'll go to sleep. What time will Dad be home?"

Daniel's father, Donald Jefferies, worked as a custodian at the Utica City Psychiatric Center. He began working there after he was discharged from the Air Force. He was stationed in Thailand during the Vietnam War. Jacklyn also worked there in the human resources department, which is how they first met. When he started, he went into

HR to fill out some paperwork. He kept coming into her office for reasons that he claimed were work-related. It became apparent to her that he wanted to ask her out, despite doing everything he could to conceal that fact from her. After three months, Jacklyn decided to make the first move and ask him out. Although it wasn't the social norm at the time, she didn't see why a woman couldn't ask out a man that she liked. Her parents were very traditional, but they always encouraged her to be independent and to not put limits on herself simply because she was a woman. It was these strong qualities that most attracted Donald to her.

They went to see *One Flew Over the Cuckoo's Nest*, of all movies, on their first date. After only a few hours together, they felt as if they had known each other their whole lives. It was as if they could see into each other's souls. Shortly thereafter, they began dating exclusively and were married the following year.

"He is working the 11:00 pm to 7:00 am shift. He told me that he was going to pick up bagels for breakfast on his way home. He should be here when you wake up, that is, if you ever get to sleep."

With that, Jacklyn kissed his forehead, turned off the light, and walked out of the room. Daniel pulled his covers up to just below his neck and turned on his side. The digital clock on his nightstand read 12:35 am. Despite pushing the limits of his mother's patience to remain awake, he was fighting a losing battle with his own body. Before she came into the room, he read the same page three times and still couldn't remember what it was about. He closed his eyes and drifted off to sleep.

"Daniel," a voice whispered.

Still asleep, he heard the voice call his name. He didn't open his eyes because he believed that he was dreaming. The person whispered his name again. This time, he slowly opened his eyes. He was still on his side facing his alarm clock. He blinked a few times to bring his vision into focus. The clock read 3:00 am. He sat up in his bed and rubbed his eyes as he scanned the room searching for the person who whispered his name. His whole body tensed up at the unexpected site of his father standing at the foot of his bed. He was still in his work uniform. He had on a dark blue, button-down workman's shirt with matching slacks. The shirt had a white embroidered name patch with red lettering sewn on just above the left chest pocket.

"Dad? Is that you? Did you get off of work early?"

The situation was unusual. Daniel couldn't remember the last time his father took a day off of work or left early. What was even stranger is that he had never come into his room in the middle of the night to wake him up before. Also, Donald didn't respond to him. He wondered if something was wrong.

"Is everything OK? Is Mom OK?"

Donald stared back at him with an oddly calm look on his face. This time, he responded to his questions.

"Mom is fine. Everything is OK now, son."

While this still seemed unusual, Daniel relaxed the muscles in his body now that his father was responding to him.

"Did you get off of work early?" he asked again.

"My work is done. I just wanted to see you. Did you have a good night with Shawn?"

"Yes. Although, he is still so stubborn. I don't understand how he can think that DC has better comics than Marvel. We didn't even have time to get into Star Trek versus Star Wars. Hopefully, one day he will see the light, but right now he's living in a dream world. I'm a little worried about him."

"It's a good thing that he has a best friend who is so grounded in reality. Otherwise, I would worry about him too. Did you boys finally make your curfew, or did your mother have to break it up again?"

Knowing that he was caught, he tried to recreate the performance that he and Shawn put on for his mother earlier. He wondered to himself why he continued to try and fool his parents with this futile act. It never seemed to land properly. Still, he felt that there was something to be said for trying.

"We almost made it. I told Mom that the clock radio downstairs was running slow, so it wasn't even really our fault this time. She said that she was going to ask you to fix it, but I think we might need a new one."

"I'm sure a solution can be found," he said with a slight smile.

Donald paused for a moment and then began to speak in a more serious tone.

"It's late. You should get some sleep. Before I go, I want you to know that I love you more than anything in the world. You are very special in more ways than you can imagine. I want you to always remember that. Goodnight, son."

Without another word, he turned and walked out of the room.

Daniel sat alone in the dark. He had a strange feeling that something was really wrong but he couldn't think of what it could possibly be. In an effort to quell his concerns, he started to think of possible explanations for why his father might be acting so strangely. Perhaps he had a tough day at work and just needed some rest. He knew how hard he worked to support the family. Late night shifts could take their toll on anyone. He decided that he would talk to him about it in the morning. He was reasonably sure that everything would be fine until then. At that moment, he could barely keep his eyes open. He decided to lay back down and go to sleep.

Daniel awoke to the sound of music playing on his radio. His alarm was set to get him up for school during the week. He forgot to turn it off before he went to bed. The clock now read 7:00 am. The sunlight was shining through the blinds on his windows. He laid in bed for a few minutes before he got up and stretched. He looked over at the foot of his bed where his father had been standing earlier. He was unsure if the conversation with him had really happened, or if it had been a dream. He realized that the only way to know that for sure would be to ask him. Unconcerned at that moment, he made his way across the hall and into the bathroom.

He picked up his toothbrush and began brushing his teeth when he then heard the sound of a woman crying. He spat out the toothpaste and ran downstairs. When he entered the living-room, he saw his Uncle Vincent consoling his mother.

Vincent Morello was Jacklyn's older brother. He was a captain in the Utica City Police Department. The Morello's were a close-knit Italian family. Their grandparents immigrated to the United States from Italy in 1903. Most of their extended family still lived in Utica. Family gatherings were always packed full of aunts, uncles, and cousins. Vincent had always been protective of Jacklyn. He took his role as her big brother very seriously. He was always around to help out whenever she and Donald needed it. He was like a second father to Daniel.

Daniel didn't know what to make of the situation. Not only was his mother crying in the middle of the living room, but his uncle was wearing his police uniform. That meant that he was on duty. He couldn't think of a reason why he would come to the house in the middle of his shift, unless something was wrong.

When his mother saw him, she pulled him in and hugged him as tightly as she could. She continued to sob uncontrollably. He looked up at his uncle for answers.

"Mom? Uncle Vincent? What is going on?"

Vincent stared back at him with a somber look on his face. He placed his hand on his shoulder.

"Danny-boy, there is something we need to tell you. Why don't you help your mother over to the couch, so that you can both sit down?"

Jacklyn hadn't spoken yet. Daniel did what Vincent asked. He helped his mother over to the couch and sat her down. He then took a seat next to her. She grabbed his hand and squeezed it tightly.

He once again turned to his uncle.

"What happened?"

Before Vincent could answer, Jacklyn spoke.

"It's OK, Vincent. I need to be the one to tell him."

She wiped away her tears and looked into his eyes.

"Something terrible has happened. Before I tell you what it is, I just want you to know how much I love you, and that I will always be here for you."

She took a brief pause to compose herself as more tears streamed down her face.

"Daniel, your father had a heart attack. He's gone, sweetheart. I'm so sorry."

Daniel's mind went blank. He heard the words that she was saying, but he couldn't comprehend the meaning of them. He just stared back at her in silence.

After several minutes, he finally understood what he was being told, but he didn't believe it, even though it was his mother who told him. He looked to his uncle for some type of reassurance. When he didn't get it, he leaped up off of the couch and began looking for his father in the house. He scoured each room, all the while hoping that it was a mistake. Vincent and Jacklyn followed him.

When he couldn't find his father, he turned back towards his mother and his uncle.

"Where is he? Did they take him away already? Why didn't you come and get me when it happened?"

"He's not here, Daniel. He never came home from work last night. He died during his shift. One of the other custodians found him unconscious in the middle of a hallway. They called an ambulance, but it was too late. He was already gone. Your Uncle Vincent was working the night shift at the police department. The doctor on call at the hospital was a friend of his. He called him to let him know," Jacklyn explained.

Trying to make sense of what he had just heard, he once again thought about his earlier conversation with his father.

"Was it a dream? It was late and I was tired, but it felt so real," he thought to himself.

Daniel couldn't ever recall having a dream that felt so real. He wondered how his father could have been in his room if he never came home. The only rational explanation that he could think of was that he must have come home before it happened and then went back to work, but even that didn't make much sense.

"What time did they find him?" he asked as his voice quivered.

"According to the police report, they found him at 3:00 am," Vincent replied.

As Daniel listened to his uncle utter those words, an uncontrollable sense of nausea overtook him and a chill ran down his spine.

Chapter 1

July 3, 2008

The late-day sun was beating down on Sergeant Aashirya Nayar as she was inventorying supplies next to the gymnasium of a school in the city of Al Diwaniyah, Iraq. The mercury in the thermometer on the outside wall had been stuck between one hundred five and one hundred six degrees for the better part of the afternoon.

The school had been at the center of a battle between insurgents and coalition forces three months earlier. The insurgents took up refuge in it and used it as their base of operations. They took several hostages, including two American contractors. The coalition forces surrounded the building. There was a standoff for several days. Eventually, a special forces team was able to find a way in during the night. They rescued seven hostages, but three others were killed, including one of the Americans. Once the hostages were extracted, the commander on the ground called for air support and the building was bombed to take out the remaining insurgents. When it was over, thirty insurgents had been killed and the school lay in ruin.

The Army assigned a team from the 96th Civil Affairs Battalion (Airborne) out of Fort Bragg, NC to assist the city with the rebuilding effort. Civil affairs units were tasked with identifying critical requirements needed by local citizens in combat or crisis situations. They were primarily responsible for researching and coordinating activities that were needed in those types of situations. Sergeant Nayar was one of three members of the team that was sent out to the city.

Aashirya was a long way from home. She was born in Cambridge, Massachusetts. Her mother, Anura, was a cardiologist at Beth Israel-Deaconess Medical Center and her father, Sabal, had a PhD in Anthropology. Both of her parents were on the teaching staff at Harvard University. Anura and Sabal had an arranged marriage at the age of twenty-one in India. Arranged marriages were a tradition in both of their families for generations. Both of their parents also had arranged marriages. They entered into the marriage willingly and grew to love and respect one another. They moved to the United States the year after they were married. Anura was accepted into Harvard Medical School and Sabal was accepted into the Anthropology Master's program. They became United States citizens in 1986, the same year that Aashirya was born.

When Aashirya was growing up, her parent's marriage didn't seem any different from that of her friends' parents. In many cases, theirs was a much happier union. Family, hard work, and education were the three most important things that they stressed in their household. They always pushed her to do her very best at whatever task was in front of her. She was an excellent student. She spoke five languages which included Hindi, Arabic, French, Chinese, and English. She learned Hindi and English simultaneously as a toddler. She taught herself French at the age of ten.

Aashirya attended Boston Latin School for both junior high and high school. She was a popular girl. She was outgoing and had many friends. In addition to academics, she also excelled in sports as she was on the volleyball and basketball teams. She also participated in student government and was a part of several academic clubs. Anura and Sabal came from traditional Indian families, but they also loved being Americans. They encouraged their daughter to learn about her heritage, as well as embrace her American citizenship. They felt that she should enjoy all that the U.S. had to offer.

She graduated as the valedictorian of her class. She was accepted into Harvard University where she majored in Middle Eastern Studies. She learned Arabic using Rosetta Stone during her junior year in high school. The diversity of cultures and the long, rich history of the Middle East fascinated her. At the end of her freshman year, she decided that she wanted to learn more than what the classroom had to offer. She took a leave of absence from Harvard and enlisted in the Army as an interpreter and translator. The ongoing war in Iraq created a substantial demand for the services of people who spoke Arabic and understood the culture. Her parents were worried when she first told them, but they still encouraged and supported her. They felt that she was an adult who was more than capable of making her own decisions. They were proud of the fact that she was pursuing her academic interests with such vigor, while serving her country at the same time.

She left for basic training in July of 2005. Her first year in the Army was spent in training. Her first assignment was to Central Command at MacDill Air Force Base in Tampa, FL. She translated intelligence materials that had been collected at various locations around the world. She began to think that she had made the wrong decision in joining the Army. She left college because she wanted to get out of the classroom, and now, instead of being in a classroom, she was in a small cubicle inside Central Command headquarters. In spite of the Army not meeting her expectations, she always performed her duties to the best of her abilities. She was promoted to Sergeant in January of 2008 and was assigned to the 96th Civil Affairs Battalion (Airborne). It was exactly the type of assignment she had been hoping for.

The team had been in Al Diwaniyah for almost a month. They spent most of that time getting to know the city's residents and local government officials. Although they were there to help, many of the residents were skeptical of their intentions. Some of the older people were around during the first Gulf War. They remembered being encouraged to rise up against Saddam with belief that the Americans would be there to help them. When that didn't happen, many of their family members and friends were killed, which created a profound sense of distrust that could not easily be undone. Aashirya spent much of her time trying to mend those broken fences. She had a gentle and calming way about her. She was able to put people at ease. Eventually, she was able to create a dialogue between her team and the local leadership.

A plan for rebuilding the school had been devised. The Army Corps of Engineers drew up blueprints for the building. They would be supervising the construction while the local residents would be doing the actual construction. Aashirya was tasked with recruiting volunteers. It gave her a chance to get to know many of the city's residents. She enjoyed her work, although it could be emotionally taxing at times. The personal stories that she heard were heartbreaking. Most of the people that she met lost several relatives and friends in the war. Many of the children who attended the school had been orphaned and were now living in shelters set up by the city. She was struck by how many of them volunteered to help. In some ways, the school was all that they had left. Helping to rebuild it was a way to get back a small piece of what had been taken from them. She admired their strength and determination to never give up, no matter how dire the circumstances.

It was an important day. The last of the rubble had finally been cleared away and construction was set to begin the following morning. The volunteers had already left for the day, but Aashirya stayed behind to ensure that all of the materials that were needed for the construction were on site, so that there would be no delays in the morning. She had been up since 5:00 am. The temperature steadily increased throughout the day. She sweat right through her Army Combat Uniform, or ACUs, by early morning. She looked like she had been out in the rain. Working in that type of environment was difficult, but she became accustomed to it over time. She didn't let it, or anything else, slow her down.

A light tan armored Humvee pulled up beside the gymnasium. The vehicle bed was loaded up with cases of water and boxes of meals ready to eat, or MREs. Aashirya heard the familiar sound of its engine and made her way outside. The driver turned off the engine and exited the vehicle. He was wearing ACUs with matching body armor, a Kevlar helmet, and black Oakley sunglasses. The rank of Staff Sergeant was displayed on the center of his ballistic vest. He walked to the back of the vehicle and released the cargo gate to start unloading the supplies. When he saw Aashirya walking over to greet him, he removed his helmet and sunglasses. Standing before her was Daniel Jefferies, the second member of the team.

"It took you long enough. You were supposed to be here an hour ago. Did you stop to get your nails done on the way?" Aashirya asked, shaking her head with her arms crossed.

"Don't start with me. It took me an hour just to find out where those idiot contractors dropped off the shipment. They were supposed to drop it off at the police station, but, instead, they dropped it off at the fire station, which is at the other end of town. When I finally got there, they had already left, so I had to load up the Humvee by myself. I don't understand it. They get paid five times what we do. They can't drop off supplies at the right location? How hard is that?"

"Calm down. I was just messing with you. It's not the end of the world. I finished inventorying the supplies and we have everything that we need to start tomorrow. Once we unload the water and the MREs into the storage shed, we are done for the day. I'll even buy you a beer," she said with a big grin on her face.

"Beer without alcohol is not beer. It's skunky water. I might as well drink the sweat from my feet."

"OK, if you are done having your time of the month, why don't you put your big boy pants on and help me unload everything so we can get out of here? I'm sweating my ass off. I could really use a shower and a fresh pair of panties. Perhaps you could lend me a pair?"

Daniel couldn't help but laugh. Aashirya always kept him on his toes. She had a particularly raunchy sense of humor. He had heard her tell jokes that made grown men blush. As the Army became more integrated, it also became a more politically correct environment. He wasn't sure if she ever got that particular memo. If she did, she didn't care very much about it. He appreciated that about her. Working with a small team meant that the team members were together in close quarters for days or weeks at a time without a break. Trying to watch every word that one said, so as not to offend anyone, could be exhausting. It also added additional stress to an already stressful situation. Her personality was perfectly suited to the type of work that their team performed. He knew when he first met her that she would be an invaluable member of the team. Although it was her first deployment, she carried herself with the confidence and courage of an experienced veteran. He saw how eager she was to get her hands dirty and engage with the people of Iraq. She showed no fear or hesitation when it came to the missions that they were given. It was Daniel's third deployment, his second to Iraq. He had also been to Afghanistan. In all of his deployments, he couldn't ever remember serving with a better soldier than Aashirya. She was as tough and as smart as they came. He also regarded her as a close friend as he knew that there wasn't anything she wouldn't do for him and he felt the same way about her.

It took them twenty minutes to unload the Humvee. Despite the fact that evening was fast approaching, the heat was showing no signs of letting up. When they were finished, they sat on the back of the Humvee and sipped Gatorade. Daniel always kept several bottles handy, chilled in a cooler. He gulped down half of his bottle in a few seconds. He then pulled out a pack of cigarettes from the cargo pocket on his left pant leg. Aashirya was extremely health conscious and didn't smoke. She tried to make him feel guilty for smoking whenever she got the chance.

"You do realize how deadly those things are, don't you? Does your mother know that you smoke? I bet she doesn't. I bet you are too afraid to tell her. What would she say?"

"You really don't let up, do you? How is it any more dangerous than what we do for a living?"

He paused to take a drag of his cigarette.

"Besides, I'm a grown man. I could tell my mother I smoke if I wanted to. I just don't want to. I really don't think that she would care anyway."

"I see. Well, maybe I should mention it to her when we get home and I get the chance to meet her, just to be sure. We'll see how much of a grown man you are when your Mommy starts yelling at you for smoking."

As he was about to respond, a white Nissan pick-up truck pulled up beside them. The truck was one of thousands that were purchased by the U.S. government from one of their biggest private company contractors, KBR. The government purchased the vehicles for the Iraqi police forces to use in operations throughout the country. In many cases, as it was in Al Diwaniyah, the police departments had more vehicles than it had officers to drive them. The local government loaned one of the unassigned vehicles to the team while they were in the city. The driver of the truck was the third member of the team and its leader, Captain Keith Andrews.

Keith, like Daniel, grew up in Central New York. He was born in Chittenango, NY, a small village outside of Syracuse. It was the birthplace of L. Frank Baum, the author of the Wizard of Oz. Every year, the village celebrated the classic novel and film with an event called Oz-Stravaganza. It included a number of different events all related to the Wizard of Oz. As a child, Keith and his siblings attended every year. His mother sewed them all costumes to wear to the event. It was a family tradition in the Andrews' house.

He was the third of four children. The oldest was his brother, James. He had one older sister, Kelly, and one younger sister, Claire. His father, Paul, owned and operated the family business, Andrews Sporting Goods. His grandfather started the business in 1946 after he returned from World War II. Paul took over the business in 1983. His mother, Katherine, was a stay at home mom. She took a part-time job as a kindergarten teacher's aide when Claire started junior high school.

Keith's experience with the military began in high school when he joined the Junior Army ROTC program. He was one of the top cadets in the program and graduated in the top ten percent of his high school class.

He also ran cross country and played varsity baseball for all four years. His diligence and hard work paid off. He was awarded a four-year Army ROTC scholarship from the State University of New York at Oswego. After graduation, he was commissioned as a Second Lieutenant. He began his career in the Army as an intelligence officer. He completed two tours in Iraq with the 504th Parachute Infantry Regiment of the 82nd Airborne Division at Fort Bragg, NC. After returning home from his second tour, he transferred to civil affairs and was eventually assigned to a team leader position within the battalion.

Daniel and Keith met during their first tours in Iraq. Their units worked together on several missions. They initially bonded over the fact that they grew up forty-five minutes away from one another but didn't meet until they were stationed half way around the world. They worked well together. When Keith was assigned as the team leader, it made the transition all that much easier. As time went on, they struck up a friendship. Normally, socialization between officers and enlisted members was frowned upon. In traditional units, it could be regarded as supervisors showing favoritism towards subordinates. However, civil affairs units were structured somewhat differently. They were much smaller and the team members worked much closer together. It was not uncommon for officers and enlisted members to form closer friendships. There was still a clear chain of command. Neither Keith nor Daniel ever had any issues following it, or conducting themselves in an appropriate manner. If anything, it made their professional relationship even stronger. They trusted one another and the other one's ability to get the job done.

The team usually had a huddle at the end of each day. On most days, they were split up to complete different tasks. Time was set aside to go over progress from that day and to coordinate efforts for the following day. Keith just got off of a teleconference with their battalion leadership. Their main headquarters was located at Camp Victory in Baghdad. The battalion had teams deployed all across Iraq. Teleconferences were their main source of communication. It could be challenging to coordinate activities. In some cases, teams were sent to areas that didn't have electricity, let alone working telephone or internet lines. It required the team members to be extremely self-sufficient.

Keith stepped out of the truck. He was also wearing his ACUs, but unlike Daniel, he wasn't wearing his body armor or a Kevlar helmet. He had on his soft cover patrol cap and a pair of sunglasses. It was standard operating procedure to be wearing protective gear when traveling outside of fortified bases, but he tended to overlook such guidance on occasion. For Keith, the best part of being the only officer in the area was that there was nobody around breathing down his neck. The ballistic vest and the Kevlar helmet were cumbersome. They weren't anyone's friend in the relentless desert heat.

Iraq was a dangerous country. There were constant threats from insurgent attacks and hidden improvised explosive devices, or IEDs. The insurgents were highly adaptable and they changed their attack strategies faster than the military could find ways to combat them. Most military members operating in the country were worried about these types of attacks and it put them into a constant state of anxiety and fear, but not Keith. As far as Daniel could tell, the situation never bothered him. He didn't seem any more concerned about driving through crowded cities in Iraq than he would be driving to the supermarket in his own hometown. They had been in multiple fire-fights over the years and even that didn't seem to faze him. The lack of fear seemed strange to Daniel, but he thought of it as an asset, especially for a military leader. Keith's lack of fear helped both he and Aashirya deal with their own fears. Fear and confidence were infectious. Both could easily spread throughout a team, depending on which one the team leader possessed.

Keith took a seat next to Aashirya on the Humvee gate. Daniel handed him a bottle of Gatorade. He took a few sips before he spoke.

"I have some bad news. Battalion is pulling us out. We have orders to pack up and head back to Camp Victory tomorrow."

"Why? I don't understand. Construction on the school starts tomorrow morning. That is the whole reason that they sent us out here. We have spent our entire month doing nothing but planning for its rebuilding. Why would they pull us out the day that it is supposed to begin?" Aashirya asked.

"It has nothing do with the mission. They are recalling all teams until further notice. There has been a substantial uptick in insurgent violence throughout the country. The top brass has decided that all civil affairs activities are to be put on hold until the situation can be brought under control."

She jumped up off the cargo gate, turned, and planted herself directly in front of Keith as she continued her line of inquiry.

"Put on hold? These are people's lives. They can't be put on hold. They need our help. This school is all that many of these children have left. They were counting on us. We can't just abandon them because it is too dangerous for us to be out here. When has it not been dangerous? How will that look to them? Does the brass realize how hard it was for us to gain these people's trust? The whole reason that they didn't trust the American military is because they abandoned them when the threat against their lives was at its worst. We promised them that we would stand by them this time and now we are breaking that promise again. How are we supposed to make any progress in this country when we turn tail and run every time the going gets tough?"

Sensing her frustration, Daniel chimed in.

"Keith, we are willing to accept the risk. Maybe we can request an exception from battalion to stay here until the school is finished. They might grant it. It hasn't been as bad down here as it has been up north."

"It's not battalion's call. This is coming straight from the commanding general in Iraq. Additional combat units are being deployed across the country to take on the insurgency. All non-combat, non-essential units are being pulled back and their missions are being put on hold. The battalion commander already asked for exceptions to keep units out in the field in areas with lower levels of enemy activity. That included us, but the answer was no. There will be no exceptions. The engineers' mission here has been canceled as well. Even if we stayed, it wouldn't matter. There wouldn't be anybody to oversee the construction. The strategy now is to fight. Rebuilding will have to take a back seat.

I'm sorry, but we have been sidelined and have no choice but to follow our orders. I'm sorry, Aashirya. I know how much this means to you, but it's out of my hands."

Keith turned to Daniel.

"I need you to get all of our gear packed up. Anything that is non-essential can be left behind. We have been given broad discretion to leave any equipment and supplies that the city might need with the local government. It could be a while before we get back here and we have been told to give them all the help that we can. The only exception is weapons and communications equipment."

He then turned back to Aashirya.

"I need you to make a detailed inventory of all of the equipment that is left here so that it can be turned into battalion supply. We are pulling out in eighteen hours, so we need to work quickly. I have a meeting scheduled with the city leadership in an hour to bring them up to speed on the situation. Once I'm done, I'll be back to help. It's going to be a long night, so make sure that you get some caffeine and chow in you before you start."

Just as he was finished issuing orders, his satellite phone rang. He stepped away to take the call. Daniel and Aashirya waited silently as the prospect of leaving sank in. They had grown quite fond of the residents and they deeply empathized with all that they had been through. Leaving was going to be easier said than done.

When the phone call ended, Keith returned to the group and issued new orders.

"Packing will have to wait for now. Grab your gear and your weapons. We need to mount up in full battle rattle and pull out in five mics."

"What happened?" Daniel asked.

"That was the city police chief. There has been a murder. A young woman's body has been found at the edge of town."

Chapter 2

Chief of Police, Amir Rashid, was driving home after being on duty for thirty straight hours. It was not unusual for him to work such long shifts. His department was severely understaffed and he had to take on more duties than that of a typical police chief. On most days, he spent more time performing the duties of an entry-level patrolman than that of the department's chief. The day had been relatively uneventful, which meant that there had been no violence. For an Iraqi police officer, it was a good day. He pulled into his driveway with only the thought of his head hitting the pillow on his mind, when he received an all too familiar phone call from one of his officers. A resident of his city had been killed. The body of a young woman was discovered at a waste disposal site on the outskirts of the city.

The city had been without sanitation services since the initial invasion of Iraq. The site was one of several where the residents would dispose of their trash. Since there were no pick-up services, people drove out to these sites on their own to unload their trash. There was constant traffic to and from these areas. Three young boys were playing soccer in the area when they found the body. One of the boys accidentally kicked the ball into a mound of trash where the woman had been left. They flagged down two police officers who were on patrol in the area.

Once Amir arrived at the scene, he instructed his officers to section off the area with police caution tape and cover the body.

Amir was a Shia Muslim and born in Al Diwaniyah, Iraq. He had three brothers and two sisters. His parents owned a local café and he started working there at the age of eight. He was the eldest son and stood to inherit it from his father. In 1988, at the age of twenty, he was drafted into the Iraqi Army. He was forced to leave his home and his family.

Life in the Iraqi Army was difficult, especially for Shias. They were treated like second-class citizens by the ruling Sunni dominated regime. Saddam Hussein was a Sunni and notorious for treating Shias with extreme cruelty. Despite the challenges, Amir excelled at being a soldier. He was physically fit, disciplined, and never questioned his superiors. The Sunni officers recognized that he could be an asset and that he was not being fully utilized in his current position. In 1989, he was assigned to the Republican Guard. The Republican Guard were the elite troops of the Iraqi army who reported directly to Saddam. Shias rarely served in this branch of the military, but Saddam was preparing for a showdown with the West. He needed as many competent, able-bodied soldiers in his ranks as he could muster.

Amir's unit was stationed in Kuwait during Operation Desert Storm. They experienced some of the bloodiest fighting of the war.

They were eventually driven back into Iraq after suffering extremely high casualties. When the war ended, he was released from service and returned home to Al Diwaniyah. The city was badly damaged. A separate unit of the Republican Guard had taken up refuge in the city. The Americans dropped several bombs on it in an attempt to kill them. Most of the soldiers were killed, but there was also a significant amount of collateral damage. Many of the city's residents perished in the attack, including Amir's family. His younger brother, Abdul, was the only one of his family members who survived. The family's home and café lay in rubble. They had nothing left.

Abdul tried to convince Amir to leave the country with him. Saddam was re-organizing his forces. There was tremendous fear throughout the country that he would target Shias whom he suspected of collaborating with the enemy during the war. Amir decided that he didn't want to run. He felt that if he was going to die, then he wanted to die in his homeland. He did, however, encourage his brother to leave. Abdul was only fifteen years old. They said their goodbyes and Abdul left with a group of friends and neighbors. Amir never saw him again.

Amir returned to his family's home and began to clear away the rubble. He eventually rebuilt it. In the month following his return, the police force began recruiting male residents in the city. The city's police force had been called up for service during the war. Many of them were killed or captured. Others simply left the country, never to return. Like many cities in Iraq at the time, Al Diwaniyah was in chaos. It didn't have water, electricity, or a functioning local government. It was up to the city's residents to rebuild it for themselves. Amir felt that it was his duty to help return his city to some semblance of normalcy. He joined the police force. He believed that law and order had to be restored before any rebuilding efforts could take place.

He was not able to rebuild his father's café as it was too badly damaged. It was in a small shopping plaza in the downtown area. The whole structure had to be bulldozed to the ground. He decided to make a career as a police officer. Many of the initial recruits didn't last past the first year, but Amir proved himself to be a capable officer, much like he did in the military. He was promoted to captain and was responsible for the southwest section of the city. He had forty subordinate officers that were assigned to his prescient and was respected by the city's residents and his fellow officers. He was a fair and honorable man.

In late 2002, it became apparent to all Iraqis that the Americans were coming back. It was only a matter of time. This time, they would not be stopping at the border. They would be going all the way to Baghdad. There was a great deal of fear amongst the Iraqi population. In the previous conflict, many of them had risen up against Saddam, only to be abandoned by the American Army once Kuwait was liberated. Once the war was over, Saddam unleashed terror upon all those who stood against him. For those who escaped his wrath, the thought of reliving that horror was terrifying.

Amir understood the fears of his fellow Iraqis. He suffered a tremendous amount of loss himself, but he also knew that it could be Iraq's last opportunity to rid itself of Saddam and his regime. He organized an underground resistance cell to fight on the side of the Americans in the pending invasion. He also helped to organize safe havens for the city's non-combatants. When the invasion came, the city once again suffered heavy casualties and widespread destruction. The difference this time was that the Americans stayed and fought beside the Iraqis. His resistance cell quickly allied itself with the American combat forces. They offered their assistance in securing the city and routing out any sympathizers of the regime.

When the initial combat operations ended, Amir was one of only three career police officers remaining in the city. Several were killed in the fighting and many more fled before it began. He was the most senior officer, so he assumed the responsibility of chief of police. Most of the law enforcement responsibilities fell to the Americans during the first year following the invasion. He served as the primary liaison between the Americans and the city's residents until a new local government could be formed. He was also tasked with recruiting a new police force. There were many volunteers in the beginning. Most people lost their jobs as a result of the war. They were willing to take any job to survive. The job of police officer paid better than most. Most of the volunteers had no experience in law enforcement and even less discipline. Turn-over in the ranks was a substantial challenge. The situation became even worse when the insurgency took hold across the country. Police officers and their families became primary targets for assassination. Most of them were no longer willing to accept the risk to their lives, or to that of their families' lives, regardless of the amount of money being offered. Amir was targeted several times himself and was almost killed on a few occasions.

Amir turned his attention away from the crime scene when he heard the sound of a vehicle approaching. An American military Humvee pulled up beside him carrying Keith, Daniel, and Aashirya. Aashirya was in the gun turret manning the fifty-caliber machine gun. It was mounted to the roof of the vehicle. Daniel was driving and Keith was in the front passenger seat. Keith was the first to exit the vehicle. He stepped out and greeted Amir. Daniel and Aashirya followed him with their M4 assault rifles in hand, held at the ready position.

"We came as fast as we could. What is the situation?" Keith asked as he shook Amir's hand.

"I received a phone call from one of my patrol officers about an hour ago. Three young boys were playing soccer near the trash and one of them kicked the ball into one of the mounds. When they went to retrieve the ball, they saw the body of a young woman underneath a thin layer of trash. They saw my officers in the area and ran to tell them what they found."

"Do you suspect that this is insurgent-related?"

Amir shook his head.

"I can't rule it out, but it seems unlikely. When the insurgents kill someone, they want people to know it's them who did it. It's their way of instilling fear in the civilian population. They haven't claimed any credit for any recent killings in the area. It appears that this killing was done quietly, well out of the sight and sound of anyone. Also, there doesn't seem to be any particular reason why this woman would have been targeted by any of the known groups, at least none that I'm aware of."

"Did you know the woman?"

"Yes, and I believe your team knew her as well. Come. I will show you."

Amir led the team towards the trash mound. He lifted up the caution tape so that they all could pass under it. Once everyone was through, he walked over to the body. With the team looking down, he knelt beside her and pulled back the plastic tarp. He pulled it down to just below her shoulders, revealing her identity. Aashirya gasped out loud. She recognized her immediately.

"It's Nella!"

Keith didn't recognize her.

"Who?"

She paused for a minute to compose herself before she replied.

"Her name is Nella Kassab. She was one of our volunteers. Her parents and her sister were killed during the invasion, she was only fourteen when she lost them. She was living in a shelter that the city set up for children who had been orphaned by the war and she stayed on after her eighteenth birthday as a volunteer to look after the children who lived there. She was one of the first people to volunteer to help rebuild the school. She helped me convince others to volunteer as well. Despite all that she had lost, she was one of the kindest and gentlest souls that I have ever met. She didn't harbor any ill-will towards anyone. All she wanted to do was help people. I can't understand why anyone would want to harm her."

"That is one of the reasons why I have my doubts that this was insurgent-related. They are not above killing innocent civilians, but they usually have a reason for targeting them. In most cases, it is because their family members are working for the police or the government. This girl's family was killed years ago. She wasn't political and she wasn't connected to anybody who was. Her death would be of very little value to them," Amir explained.

Daniel had also gotten to know Nella. The sight of her corpse gave him a sickening feeling in his stomach, similar to the one that he felt when he learned of his father's death. He too couldn't think of a reason why someone would kill her.

"If it wasn't insurgents, then who do you suspect it was?" he asked.

"I don't know. My police force is little more than a skeleton crew at the moment. We don't have enough resources to patrol the city, let alone investigate crimes. Record keeping has been virtually non-existent since the invasion. In all honesty, I don't have a good handle on who is living in the city. People can come and go as they please, and there is no way for me to track their movements. When a society falls, its criminals have a distinct advantage over its law enforcement. The killer could be living in the city or be long gone by now. I have no way of knowing."

"You said killer. Do you believe that there was just one killer?" Keith asked.

"I can't be completely certain, but the evidence suggests that only one person was involved."

Amir pulled the tarp completely off of the body so that he could explain his theory to the team.

"As you can see, the only wounds on her body are the bruises around her neck. That suggests strangulation. There are no other signs of a struggle, or of a sexual assault. Strangulation is an intimate crime. It usually doesn't involve more than one killer. If another person was involved, you would expect to see marks on other areas of the body from restraining her or assaulting her. If someone is sick enough to be a party to this type of murder, they usually don't just show up to watch. They would most likely want to participate. I'm fairly confident that it was one person who committed this crime. I also believe that killer was male and that she knew him. He likely killed her in another location and dumped her here after it was over."

"Why do you think that?" Aashirya asked, trying to hold back her tears.

"Since there are no other signs of a struggle, that suggests that she knew and trusted the killer. She probably didn't know what was going to happen to her until it was too late and he had already began strangling her. If he was a stranger, she likely would have tried to fight back when he started to get close to her. The lack of additional wounds also suggests that the killer was larger than she was, making it extremely difficult for her to fight back. In addition to that, most women who are strangled to death are strangled to death by men. It's very rare for a woman to kill another woman using this method. Based on the time that the body was discovered and the amount of rigor mortis, I would say that the killing took place during the night or early morning. I can't think of any reason why she would be out here alone at night. If she did trust the killer, it would have made her suspicious if he decided to drive her out to a trash dump in the middle of the night. He would have lost that trust and the advantage that it gave him. There is one other reason why I believe the killer drove her out here after he killed her."

"What is that?" Daniel asked.

"Our motor pool was broken into last night. We had fifteen white Nissan pick-up trucks parked inside of it, just like the one we lent your team. Someone broke in, stole one vehicle, and slashed the tires on the remaining fourteen. The stolen vehicle was found this morning abandoned a few miles away. The tires on it were also slashed after the thief finished driving it."

"That sounds like simple vandalism. There are many people in the city who are unhappy with the police department for one reason or another. What makes you think that these crimes are connected? It could just be someone's way of getting back at the police or bored teenagers blowing off some steam," Keith said.

"I don't have any hard evidence to connect the two. It's just a hunch. Most of the people around here can't afford to own their own vehicles. The people that can, usually do so by splitting the cost with several of their family members. The killer went out of his way to carry out this crime in the darkness of night. It makes sense that he wouldn't want to draw attention to himself by taking out a shared vehicle in the middle of the night. While it might not seem suspicious to anyone initially, someone might connect the dots when news of the murder spreads throughout the city. Word travels fast when it comes to something like this. At the very least, it would put him in the position of trying to explain where he was at the time Nella was killed if someone inquires. It would be much easier to sneak out of the house when everyone is sleeping and steal a vehicle."

The group stood silently for a few moments as they absorbed all of the information they just heard.

Keith broke the silence.

"I'm very sorry. This was a terrible crime. She seemed like a lovely young woman. I wish I had gotten the chance to get to know her. Unfortunately, I have some more bad news. We have just received orders to pull out of the city tomorrow."

"I don't understand. Construction on the school was supposed to begin tomorrow morning. Why are you leaving?" Amir asked.

"I was going to inform you and the other city leaders at the meeting this evening. The commanding general in Iraq is putting all non-combat, non-essential missions on hold for the time being. They are expanding the combat mission against the insurgency and all available resources are being re-allocated to support that mission. All of our teams are being recalled back to Camp Victory tomorrow."

"That is unfortunate. The people of this city were counting on that school. We have no way to educate our children until it is rebuilt. I certainly understand the military decision-making process. I was just hoping that those who are in charge of this war would eventually realize that the best way to fight it is with more education and less bullets. Until we break the cycle of violence, we will never be able to move forward. My people will never truly be free until we do."

"That will be the day! It's always easier to destroy something than to build something," Aashirya shouted.

Sensing that everyone's emotions were taking over, Keith knew that it was his duty as the team's leader to refocus their energy and attention on the tasks at hand.

"I know everyone is upset. A lot has happened today, but we are all professionals and we have a job to do. The fact is that I agree with both of you to an extent, but we still have to acknowledge the reality of the situation. We can't provide education to anyone when terrorists are murdering people and destroying the places where they live. Who is to say that if we rebuild the school today, it won't be blown up again tomorrow? We are committed to rebuilding this city and this country, but right now we have to take a step back and eliminate the people who are trying to stop us from doing that. In the long run, educating people and showing them a path to a better life is the right answer. In the short-term, more bullets are the right answer. As hard as it might be for us to admit, now is the time for violence. The fight must be taken to our enemies before it is too late. Nobody expected any of this to be easy. We all knew what we were signing up for. We have to forge ahead."

After giving everyone a minute to calm down, he changed the subject.

"Amir, we will be leaving most of our supplies behind. You are welcome to them. If you can find people in the city who have knowledge of carpentry and architecture that we haven't already identified, then you can begin the construction on your own. We only had a limited amount of time in which to recruit volunteers. There could still be a substantial number of qualified people out there. Many of the people that we spoke to were reluctant to help us because of their distrust of the American military, or out of a fear of retribution for working with us. They might be more likely to volunteer now that we will be out of the picture for a while. We will try to get back here as soon as possible."

"Yes, of course. I know that this isn't your decision and that you would all stay if you could. Soldiers don't have the luxury of questioning orders, whether we agree with them or not. I'm sorry to see you go, but you have helped us tremendously while you were here. I will help you explain the situation to the rest of the city's leadership. Hopefully, they can make the residents understand that this is only temporary so that the progress that we have already made isn't undone. It is of the utmost importance that we continue in our partnership and trust one another."

"Thank you. I appreciate that. We need to head back so that we can begin packing up for tomorrow. I will drop these two off and then I will head over to the meeting. I wish we could have been of more assistance with Nella."

As Keith was about to turn and leave, Amir stopped him.

"Perhaps there is something that you can do. I was hoping that you could put in a request to the Army to send out investigators from their criminal investigation division. As you are aware, I don't have the resources or the expertise within my department to conduct a proper investigation. This young woman deserves to have her killer found and brought to justice."

"I will put in the request. That much I can promise you. Beyond that, I can't promise anything. CID only has a handful of agents in the country right now. Most of the cases that they are assigned to directly involve Army personnel. It's not out of the realm of possibility that they would assist on a case involving an internal Iraqi matter, but it is unlikely. It is simply a matter of availability and priority. Given the current mission priority, it seems even more unlikely. That being said, I will do what I can to push it up the chain of command, if that is worth anything to you," he told him, knowing that the request would likely be turned down.

Amir smiled and shook Keith's hand once again.

"It is worth a lot. Thank you for your time and for that of your team's. I won't keep you any longer. I know that you have a great deal to accomplish before you leave tomorrow."

Keith raised his right arm and waved his hand in a circular motion as a signal to Daniel and Aashirya to mount up in the Humvee. They took the same positions in the vehicle that they were in when they arrived.

Daniel turned on the engine.

"When do you think we will be back?" he asked Keith before he shifted it into drive.

Keith replied without any emotion or pretense.

"We won't, Danny. The battalion is redeploying us back to Bragg in two weeks. There are other priorities and other missions to prepare for. These people are on their own now."

Chapter 3

Daniel was enjoying some much-needed solitude and peace as he was loading up the Humvee for the team's journey back to Camp Victory. The temperature outside was uncharacteristically mild and there was a slight breeze in the air. While being in Southern Iraq couldn't seem farther away from life in Upstate NY most of the time, it was days like this where it didn't seem like they were that much different.

He decided to take a break to eat some lunch. As it had for most days during that deployment, his lunch consisted of an MRE and a large bottle of water. The MRE included chili macaroni, crackers, a packet of jalapeno cheese spread, and a brownie. It was one of the better meal options that one could hope for in the field. He'd been saving it for the past few days and decided that he might as well eat it before they headed out. Once the team got to Camp Victory, they would all be enjoying three hot meals a day. MREs would be nothing more than an unpleasant memory. He didn't want to leave before the mission was complete, but he couldn't help but daydream about dinner that evening. The last time that he was there, the dining facility was serving steak, lobster, pasta, and just about every other food item that could be imagined. His personal favorite was the Mongolian style barbeque. A variety of meats, vegetables, and spices were offered to choose from. The chef would then grill it all up fresh on the spot. It seemed a little excessive for a combat zone, but there was an unusually high number of general officers that were headquartered at Camp Victory. Most of them had been in the military for more than thirty years. Daniel figured that they probably weren't willing to settle for MREs by that point in their careers, and that whoever planned the daily menus wanted to win favor with them. When he was outside the wall, it seemed terribly unfair and it was a constant source of resentment. When he was back on base, those feelings quickly faded away. After living out in the desert for so long, it was hard for him to be angry about anything when his belly was full of hot food.

Aashirya emerged from the building where they had been staying since they arrived. At one point, it was a hotel. There wasn't any room service, but it beat sleeping in the Humvee or outside on the ground. She silently walked past Daniel and opened the front passenger door. She pulled out the vehicle's operating manual and a clipboard with a checklist attached to it before performing a preventive maintenance check. It was a standard operating procedure with the expressed purpose of ensuring that vehicles were in proper working order before being used on missions. Being stranded on the side of the road in Iraq with a disabled vehicle is not a situation that anyone wanted to find themselves in.

Daniel finished his lunch and pulled out a cigarette. When he lit it, Aashirya didn't say a word. It was no secret that she was troubled by the events of the past twenty-four hours. She was not the type of person who easily backed down from anything, especially when she believed in it so wholeheartedly. He had nightmares about having to drag her out of town kicking and screaming. She had barely said a word since they left the murder scene the previous evening. Nella was the first person that she knew personally who was killed in Iraq. That would bother anyone. Daniel remembered how hard it was for him the first time that he lost somebody in combat. It was his team leader during his first tour who was killed by a sniper. They were only three weeks away from redeploying home. He had a wife and two young sons. At the time, he didn't think that he would be able to cope with the loss. He seriously contemplated leaving the Army but decided to stay. As hard as it was to accept, he realized that death was a part of war. There was no way to avoid it. He came to feel that when your time was up, it was up. He also felt that those who survived had a responsibility to carry on with the mission so that those who were lost had not died in vain. It was a heavy burden to carry. It didn't make the loss any easier, but it did put it into perspective. It allowed him to keep moving forward.

He wanted to talk to her before they left so that he could be sure that she was in the right state of mind. If she wasn't thinking clearly, she could become distracted on the road. That could put the lives of the whole team in jeopardy.

"We need to talk," Daniel said.

"I'm fine. There is nothing to talk about," she responded in a monotone voice.

"I didn't ask you if you were fine. I told you that we need to talk. It wasn't a request. Luckily for me, the Army has this whole rank system in place. If I need you to do something, I don't have to ask you. I can just tell you."

"Are you fucking serious, Daniel!? You are going to pull rank on me? Would you like me to stand at attention while you lecture me?"

Seeing how upset she was, he took a step back and spoke in a softer tone of voice.

"Relax. I'm just joking with you, but I am serious when I say that we need to talk. I know that you are upset and you are far from fine. If you were truly OK, you wouldn't have let me smoke a cigarette without laying some type of guilt trip on me. Whether you believe this or not, we are in this together. I'm not giving you an order. Still, I have a responsibility to you and to this team. We have to talk this out. Keeping all of this bottled up is the worst thing that you can do. I need to know where your head is at. If something happens out there and you aren't thinking straight, we could all end up dead. There are no do-overs. We have to work this out now."

"I don't know what you want me to say. I thought that we were here to help these people. I thought that we were here to make a difference. Now someone, who probably has no idea what we actually do out here, has pulled the rug out from under us just as we were about to make some real progress. Not to mention the fact that an innocent young girl has been murdered and we aren't going to do anything to help find her killer. We don't even have the decency to be straight with these people. Keith lied to Amir about us coming back here. It doesn't seem to bother him, and I don't know if it bothers you either. How am I supposed to feel? How am I supposed to be OK with all of this?"

Tears began to well up in her eyes. She turned away from Daniel, hoping that he wouldn't notice. She didn't want him to see her in such an emotional state. She worried that he would think she wasn't strong enough to handle the situation. He didn't think anything of the sort. It was just the opposite. He gave her a few minutes to pull herself together before he continued the discussion.

"Everything you are feeling is normal. We all wrestle with these types of emotions and it's not easy. I feel the same way. I don't like leaving a job unfinished any more than you do. I know how much what we do means to these people but, at the end of the day, we are soldiers. We have to follow orders. That is all that we are doing. That is all that Keith is doing. He is in charge and he has to show strength. That could be easily mistaken for indifference, but I know that he cares about what happens here. He's not lying. We might not be back, but another team might be. There is no way to know what the future holds. He's just trying to keep them from giving up hope."

He put his hand on her shoulder.

"Look, we put so much of ourselves into our work. We invest heavily in the people that we help. We work day and night to accomplish our mission, and then one day, it's suddenly over. Leaving under these types of circumstances can feel like amputating one of your own limbs. Unfortunately, it's the price of doing business. We can't always control the circumstances that we find ourselves in. The only thing that we can control is how we react to them."

She found his words surprisingly reassuring. She felt as if he truly understood how she was feeling.

"How do you control it?" she asked.

"Alcohol."

They both shared a laugh.

"You have to find your own way to make peace with it. For me, personally, I remind myself of all the good that I have done, rather than all of the good that I can't do. You have to remember that you are only one person. You can only do so much. It might not always be enough, but at least it's something. Doing some good is better than doing none at all. Making a difference in people's lives is what's important, not the size of that difference."

"Do you think we made a difference here?"

"Absolutely!"

"Thank you, Daniel. You've looked out for me since day one. I don't know what I would do without you. I want you to know how much that means to me and how much you mean to me," she said as she hugged him.

Daniel kissed her on the forehead and smiled at her.

"You've done just as much for me. You've had my back out here too. We are going to get through this. We have to look on the bright side. We'll be home in a couple of weeks. Once we get home, we can finally kick back and drink some real beer. You'll get the chance to come to Utica and NARC on me to my mother for all the cigarettes that you've witnessed me smoking. I'll get the chance to come to Boston and meet that girlfriend of yours that you haven't stopped talking about since we got here. It will remind us both that there is more to life than all of the madness we have witnessed over here. Are you still planning on asking her to marry you?"

"Yes"

"Good. It's good to think about things like that. It's good to have something to look forward to. It will get you through the bumps in the road. You'll be with her before you know it. In the meantime, do one last check of the 50-cal before we roll out. I'll put the last of the gear into the Humvee."

Just as they were finished talking, Keith walked out of the building. He was carrying his rucksack, packed up with all of his personal gear. He loaded it into the back of the Humvee. Daniel finished loading the remaining team gear and locked up the cargo gate.

Keith pulled Daniel aside

"How are we doing?" he asked.

"We are good to go. Aashirya should be done checking the 50-cal in a few minutes and then we can hit the road as soon as you give the word."

Keith pulled out a pack of cigarettes. He took one for himself and then offered one to Daniel. Daniel checked to see if Aashirya could see him. He noticed that she was focused on her task and wasn't paying any attention to the two of them. When he was confident that she couldn't see him, he accepted the cigarette and pulled out a lighter. As a thank you, he lit Keith's first.

"Did you get a chance to talk to her?" Keith asked as he took a drag.

"Yeah, she'll be fine. She's tough. It's her first time in the sandbox. She just needed someone to help her sort it all out. It will take some time, but she will adjust. It's probably a good thing that we will be heading home soon. She could use a break."

"So could I. I've had enough of this sewer of a country to last a lifetime. This will be my last dance, Danny."

"Are you planning on leaving the Army?"

"I turned my paperwork into the Colonel two weeks ago. It's been approved. In thirty days and a wake-up, I will be a civilian."

Daniel was caught off-guard. Keith never mentioned a desire to leave the Army before.

"I thought you were a lifer. What changed your mind?"

"Nothing. I've gotten all that I can out of it. Now it's time to move one. Change is a part of life, Danny. Nothing lasts forever. You should give it some thought yourself."

Daniel was about to respond when Amir pulled up beside them. He was driving a white Chevy Tahoe with the words, *Al Diwaniyah City Police Department,* painted in black Arabic letters on the side doors. It also had red and blue police lights mounted to the roof.

"I wanted to wish you all well before you left," Amir said after stepping out of the vehicle.

"Captain Andrews, I would also like to apologize to you for what took place at the meeting last night. Many of the city's leaders were angry, but they should have understood that you were not to blame. Your team has been a great asset to this city. That should have been acknowledged."

Keith took another drag of his cigarette.

"There is no need to apologize. It's nothing new. I'm a big boy, I can handle it."

"Nonetheless, I would still like to extend an apology to you on behalf of my city. I would also like to thank each one of you for what you have done for us. You have put your own lives at risk to help us reclaim ours. You have my deepest appreciation."

Amir's words validated Daniel's own beliefs that he was making a positive impact on the lives of the people of the city.

"Thank you, Amir. It means a lot to hear that. It was an honor working with you. I hope we see each other again someday."

"As do I, Daniel."

"Before we go, I should let you know that I sent up your request for CID assistance last night. Our battalion commander got back to me this morning. As I suspected it would be, it was denied. CID is stretched too thin right now. They have a full caseload and don't have any available agents to spare at this time," Keith explained to Amir.

"I see. It wasn't the answer that I was hoping for, but I understand. Thank you for trying. Well, I'm sure you are anxious to get going, and I have a staff meeting shortly. I won't take up any more of your time. Have a safe journey."

Amir waved goodbye and got back into his vehicle. Keith and Daniel finished their cigarettes as they watched him drive off. When they were done, they walked towards the Humvee. Aashirya was finished checking the 50-cal. She was in the gun turret drinking a bottle of water. When she saw them approaching, she put on her Kevlar helmet and protective goggles. The goggles shielded her eyes from the sand and wind on the road.

Daniel started the engine and Keith radioed their battalion headquarters to let them know that they were pulling out. All units required their personnel traveling throughout the country to report the times that they departed their locations and the times that they arrived at their destinations.

"Let's move out," Keith said once he finished his report.

Daniel took the main route out of town. It took them through the city center and back to the site of Nella's murder. As they approached the site, they saw a man and his young son crossing the road with their donkey. The donkey was towing a wooden cart full of produce. There was an open-air market in the city center. People traveled there to sell their goods. For many of them, it was their only source of income. The boy was four or five years old and the cart was fully loaded, so they were moving slowly. Daniel pulled to a complete stop to allow them to cross.

"Keep an eye out," Keith yelled up to Aashirya.

It was always dangerous to be stopped in the middle of a road in Iraq. Instead of the vehicle being a moving target, which could be hard to hit, it became a stationary target, which was much easier to hit. The chances of an ambush greatly increased.

It was Keith's job to keep his team on alert, but the heightened state of awareness didn't change his demeanor. He was perfectly calm. He pulled out another cigarette and lit it while they waited for the man and his son to cross the road. He offered one to Daniel, but he turned it down.

"I can't understand how nothing seems to bother you. I've been doing this just as long as you have. No matter how many times I'm out here, I still get nervous. I wish I knew your secret," Daniel said.

Keith laughed it off.

"There is no secret, Danny. I told you before, nothing lasts forever. Everyone dies at some point. It's a foregone conclusion. It's not a question of if, but when. What's the difference if we die now or fifty years from now? We shouldn't fear death. We should embrace it."

"I think you have been out here too long. You are really starting to trip me out. I think you need a long nap and a cold beer. After that, you need to get laid and seriously rethink that no-fear, embrace death bullshit. Personally, I would much rather be afraid and alive than calm and dead."

Daniel turned his attention back towards the road. The man and his son were now directly in front of the vehicle. The boy stopped walking and turned to look at him. When they made eye contact, Daniel got an eerie feeling that something was wrong. Before he could react, a large explosion went off underneath the Humvee. The blast tossed the vehicle fifteen feet into the air, landing it on its side.

Daniel was pinned down against the driver's side door with Keith on top of him. The blast momentarily disoriented him, but he remained conscious. The only thing that he could hear was an intense ringing in his ears. He couldn't see anything in front him. A thick cloud of smoke and dust enveloped the cab of the Humvee. It took him several minutes to get his bearings. He felt a warm liquid running down the left side of his face. When he put his hand in front of his face, he saw that it was blood. He knew that he was wounded, he just wasn't sure how badly. His body was in shock, so he wasn't feeling any pain. He could smell smoke and knew that the Humvee could explode again at any minute, so he had to free himself immediately. Keith was unconscious. He tried to wake him up but was unable to. He wasn't sure if he was dead or alive. As the smoke and dust began to dissipate, he could see that the windshield had been shattered, although it was still attached to its frame. He was able to free his legs and then began kicking it. It gave way after a few strong kicks, then he wiggled out from under Keith's body and pulled himself out of the vehicle.

He stood up and surveyed the area. The only sign of the boy and his father were a few charred, bloody remains scattered on the ground in front of him. He looked around for Aashirya but couldn't locate her. He saw bright orange flames coming from the section of the vehicle near the gas tank, which confirmed his earlier fear; he had to get Keith and himself clear before it went up. He grabbed Keith from underneath his shoulders and dragged him out as fast as he could. He carried him almost one hundred feet and then fell to the ground from exhaustion.

He caught his breath and got back up to go look for Aashirya. As he was about to leave, he noticed that Keith was missing his left foot. He was bleeding profusely. Daniel took off his belt, picked up a small stick nearby and constructed a makeshift tourniquet to stop the bleeding. He worked quickly. When he was finished, the bleeding stopped, but Keith still needed immediate medical attention if he was going to survive. He had to call for help, but the radio was in the Humvee, so he would have to try and retrieve it before it exploded. Daniel ran in that direction as fast as he could and made it half way there when he heard a faint voice call his name. He stopped and looked around. He saw Aashirya lying on the ground just to his left. He rushed over to her. Her body was badly burned and she was missing both of her legs. She was also bleeding from her head, even though she still had her helmet on. He dropped to his knees and removed her helmet. Miraculously, she was still conscious.

"I got you. You are going to be OK. I have to get back to the Humvee to get the radio so I can call for help. I need to you to hang on. Can you do that for me?"

She tried to speak but it was difficult. She coughed several times as she tried to get her words out.

"Daniel," she finally said in a muffled voice.

She touched his cheek with the palm of her hand. Tears streamed down from her eyes and then she stopped breathing.

"Aashirya! No! Please, just hang on! It's going to be OK. Just hang on!"

He pulled her lifeless body up into a brief embrace before gently laying her back down. He knew that he was running out of time, but despite the fact that she was unconscious, he tried to reassure her for a second time.

"You are going to be OK. I'll be right back. I'm not leaving you."

He got back up and ran towards the Humvee. He made it to within a few feet of the wreck when it exploded into a tremendous ball of fire.

The force of the explosion blew him backwards onto the ground. His only hope to call for help was gone.

He managed to get up onto his knees and then desperately began shouting.

"Help! Help! Somebody, please help us!"

After a few minutes, he noticed two people in the distance. Clinging to his last bit of hope, he ran towards them. He stopped ten feet short of where they were standing, out of breath. He could see that one of them was a man and the other was a woman, but they had their backs turned to him.

"Please, I need your help! We were attacked. I need to call for help. My friends need medical attention. Please, I'm begging you. Help us!" he pleaded.

The woman turned around. Daniel couldn't believe the face that was staring back at him. It was Nella Kassab. He began to feel dizzy and dropped to his knees. A bright light appeared behind her. She turned back around and walked into it. The light disappeared and she was gone. The man who was with her never turned around. When she disappeared, he walked away. Daniel tried to call out to him, but couldn't form the words. His vision became blurry and he passed out.

Chapter 4

December 19, 2011

As a light snow began to fall and a thin layer of frost began to form on the windows of his 1999 Forrest Green Toyota Camry, Shawn Lewis sat with a cup of coffee perusing the latest issue of *The Green Lantern* in the parking lot of the VA outpatient clinic at the Griffiss Business and Technology Park in Rome, NY. Griffiss was formerly an Air Force Reserve base until it was closed and repurposed in 1995. He'd been waiting there for over an hour. This had become his weekly routine over the past six months. Every Monday, he would close up his comic book shop at noon and drive his best friend, Daniel Jefferies, to his counseling appointment at the clinic. He would wait in the parking lot for him until his appointment was finished.

Shawn purchased 315 Comics six years earlier. The shop was located on Genesee Street on the same block as the historic Stanley Theater in the heart of downtown Utica. He and Daniel first began buying comics there when they were six years old and Shawn started working there during his junior year in high school. It helped him pay for college. He attended Utica College and earned a degree in business management. After he graduated, the owner informed him that he was retiring and offered to sell it to him. He bought it with some money from his parents and a small business loan. He couldn't think of anything else that he would rather devote his time and energy to. To him, it was more than just a store that sold comics. It was the place where his dreams came true and anything seemed possible. When he took over, he didn't change a thing. He wanted to preserve everything the way it was so that everyone could have the same experiences there that he had.

He hoped that Daniel would become his partner. Daniel left for the Army after they graduated high school. They kept in close contact at first and when Shawn told him that he bought the store, Daniel seemed more excited than he was. He told Daniel that he could buy in at any time and then they could run it together once he was discharged from the Army. At the time, Daniel was getting ready to deploy to Iraq for the first time. He told Shawn that they could discuss the details when he came home on leave. When Daniel finally did come home, he didn't mention it. To Shawn, he didn't seem like the same person that he'd grown up with. He was disengaged and didn't take pleasure in the things that he once did. He never discussed what went on when he was deployed. He didn't discuss much of anything. Shawn didn't press the issue. He felt that Daniel would talk to him when he was ready.

After that first visit home, Shawn didn't hear from him as much. Daniel came home a few more times over the years and they still got together, but he seemed more withdrawn each time. Shawn could still remember the phone call that he got from Daniel's uncle when his team was ambushed in Iraq. He couldn't shake the memory of all the thoughts that passed through his mind in those few seconds before he was told that Daniel was alive, although injured. Daniel had shrapnel lodged in his right shoulder from the IED explosion. He was flown to Germany where he underwent surgery and was then transferred to Walter Reid Medical Center in Washington D.C. for his recovery. Six months after that, he underwent a second surgery, but it was unsuccessful. The doctors determined that his shoulder would never be fully functional again. There was too much nerve damage from the shrapnel. As a result, he was medically discharged from the Army.

There was a vacant apartment above the comic book shop which was included with the purchase of the building. Shawn offered it to Daniel when he returned home, rent free. He also offered him a job. It was clear to Shawn that Daniel needed some time to work everything out. He was willing to do whatever it took to help out his best friend. It also became clear to him that the physical wounds of war were not the only thing that he was dealing with. Shawn and Daniel's family became increasingly worried about him. After some convincing, Daniel reluctantly agreed to go for counseling at the VA. Shawn volunteered to be the one to drive him there each week. He wanted to make sure that he was keeping his appointments.

Shawn took a sip of his coffee and glanced at his watch. Daniel's appointment was almost over. Five minutes later, he saw Daniel walk out of the clinic's front entrance. He was wearing a pair of faded blue jeans, a vintage Star Trek T-shirt, and a black leather bomber jacket.

His hair was wavy and unkempt and he was unshaven with several days-worth of stubble on his face. He made his way over to the car and got into the front passenger seat. Shawn didn't take his eyes off of his comic book. He handed him a cup of coffee that was sitting in the passenger side cup holder in the center console. Daniel accepted it and took a sip.

"Did it ever occur to you that sitting in your car alone in this parking lot every week might make someone suspicious? I'm surprised that nobody has called the cops on you yet," Daniel said.

"Are you saying that a black man can't sit alone in a car without it being suspicious? That's a pretty racist thing to say. I really thought I knew you," Shawn said with his gaze still fixed on his comic book.

"Are you done?"

Shawn let out a brief chuckle and closed his comic book.

"I think so. How was your counseling session?"

"It was wonderful. I feel like all of my problems have been solved. They told me that I'm cured, so I don't have to come back here anymore."

"That's good to hear. It frees up more of my time. And now that you are a fully functional human being again, you can start paying me rent. I will finally be able to afford to buy that second private jet that I've had my eye on."

"I should remind you that it was your idea to drive me here each week. It was also you who wouldn't leave me alone until I agreed to move into that rundown dungeon that you claim is an apartment. If you don't want to drive me here anymore, that's perfectly fine with me. As far as moving out, that also won't be a problem. I'm sure I can find a comparable place to live. I think the dumpster behind the coffee shop across the street might be opening up."

Daniel paused to take another sip of his coffee before he continued.

"And just FYI, I would be more than happy to pay you rent if you paid me a living wage."

"I love you, man. Really, I do. I love you," Shawn said with a big grin on his face.

Daniel shook his head and let out a deep breath.

"Once again, are you done?"

"I'm done. I was just messing with you. Seriously though, how did it go today?"

"It went the same as it always does. She asked the same questions and I gave the same answers. I really would like to meet the person who came up with idea that the way to get over the most terrible things in your life is to keep reliving them over and over again by discussing them with a perfect stranger."

"Look, I know how worried you and my family are about me. You have to realize that there are some things that just can't be fixed. That being said, I really do appreciate what you have done for me since I've been back. I know I don't say it enough. And as much as I don't think that the counseling is helping, I'll keep going if it keeps everyone from worrying about me so much."

"I can't pretend to know what you are going through, because I really have no idea. And I know that you think things won't get any better, but you should never give up hope that they could. Maybe this whole counseling thing seems like a waste of time right now, but you never know, it might actually be helpful at some point. You just need to give it some more time. Don't push yourself. It takes time to heal. It doesn't happen overnight. I will always have your back and you will always have a place to live and, more importantly, a place to read free comic books."

"Thanks, man. You are a good friend. And since you are in such a giving mood, do you mind driving me to my mother's place before we head back to the shop?"

"Sure, no problem. Is everything OK?"

"I'm not sure. I know her MS has been getting worse. She can't get out of her wheelchair now and it's getting harder for her to speak. My uncle Vincent called me last night and told me that her doctor wanted to talk to me. He wasn't any more specific, but he did say that we have some things that we need to discuss as a family after I speak with him. I can't imagine that any of it is good news."

Fourteen years earlier, Jacklyn Jefferies began feeling more rundown than usual. After Donald died, she had to work longer hours to make up for the loss of his income. At first, she thought that all of the extra hours and the stress of being a single mother were just catching up with her, so she didn't get checked out right away. She continued to feel worse and then her hands began to shake periodically. By then, she knew that something was wrong. She finally went to see a doctor. He performed several tests and diagnosed her with multiple sclerosis. Her first thought, as always, was for her son. All she could think was that he had lost his father and now he would have to face the possibility of losing his mother. When she told Daniel, he didn't show any emotion. He just hugged her and told her that it would be OK. She wished that she could have believed that.

At first, the medication helped relieve some of her symptoms and she was able to continue working, although she couldn't keep up the same pace as before. She could no longer work the extra hours that were needed to pay all of the bills, so things became much tighter financially. Vincent and his wife, Deanna, helped out as much as they could. When Daniel turned fifteen, he got a part-time job at a supermarket. He gave her his whole paycheck each week. Still, the bills continued to pile up, especially the medical bills. Her condition began deteriorating more each year. By Daniel's junior year in high school, she could no longer work. Everyday activities like getting dressed and bathing became increasingly difficult. She was forced to quit her job and go on disability. Vincent and Deanna paid for an in-home nurse to come by each day to help her with her daily routine. By Daniel's senior year in high school, she could no longer afford to pay the mortgage on the house. She also began needing around the clock care. The nurse only came to the house for a few hours in the afternoon, so the family divided up the rest of the day amongst each other. It got to the point where it became unmanageable. Eventually, Vincent arranged for her to go and live in an assisted living facility. They moved her into the Masonic Care Community, a non-profit, elder-care facility run by the Shriner's organization. Her house was sold and Daniel went to live with Vincent and Deanna while he finished high school.

Shawn pulled up to the entrance of the Masonic Care Community Campus. The campus consisted of several buildings. Each one was designated for a specific level of care. Jacklyn initially moved into the assisted living building. The residents there were closely monitored, but they still enjoyed some degree of independence. They were able to get around on their own or with some minor assistance. As her condition got worse, she was moved into the nursing home building. The residents there were severely disabled. Many of them had severe dementia or were incapable of moving around without assistance. She had been there for the last three years.

Shawn pulled the car into the nursing home parking lot and they both got out. Shawn started to walk towards the building's entrance when Daniel told him to hold up. Daniel pulled out a pack of cigarettes from his jacket pocket and lit one up.

"I thought you quit," Shawn said.

"I cut back. I just need a minute."

Shawn understood. Jacklyn was like a second mother to him and seeing her decline over time wasn't easy. He could only imagine how Daniel was feeling. When Donald died, she stepped in to fill the void. In effect, she became both of Daniel's parents. She did everything from comforting him when he was sick to teaching him how to hit a curveball. She was a pillar of strength. For boys who admired superheroes, she was just that. She seemed invincible, until she wasn't.

Daniel smoked half of his cigarette and then flicked what remained of it onto the ground. He stepped on it to extinguish the flame as he walked towards the building's entrance. Shawn followed close behind him.

There was a nurse on duty behind the front desk at the entry-way. She smiled at them as they walked past her and they made their way down a long hallway. There were pictures on the walls of doctors, nurses, administrators, and residents dating back to the 1930's.

They came to the entrance of the residence wing where Jacklyn lived. There were two large double doors that opened up automatically. The automatic doors allowed the staff to pass through when they were transporting residents who were confined to wheelchairs or hospital beds. As they walked through the doors, the resident's rooms were on their left side. The rooms stretched down another hallway. The right side of the hallway opened up into a large common area, where there was a kitchen for the staff to prepare meals in and a dining area in which to serve the meals to the residents. The far end of the room was designed to function as a living room as there were three couches arranged around a television set with end tables and a coffee table. The coffee table had several magazines and newspapers scattered on it. There was a large plate glass window on the far wall which looked out onto a courtyard and provided the room with an abundance of natural light.

When they arrived, the residents were finishing their lunches. They were sitting around a large wooden table. There were two male staff members who were picking up their plates and serving them dessert. Jacklyn was not at the table. One of the staff members recognized Daniel and pointed towards the far end of the room where she was sitting in her wheelchair, staring out the window.

Daniel and Shawn made their way over to her. Jacklyn was wrapped up in a blanket. She looked thin and pale. Her hair was thinning and she had dark circles under her eyes. To them, she was almost unrecognizable. They never got used to seeing her in such a state.

She was lost in thought and didn't hear them approach. Daniel gently touched her shoulder to get her attention. She looked up and smiled at him as best she could. All of the muscles in her body were extremely weak that even movements as simple as smiling were strenuous. Despite her physical limitations, her mood always brightened when Daniel visited.

Daniel wheeled her over to the couch that was closest to the window and placed her in front of it. He and Shawn then took a seat on it.

"Hi, mom. How are you feeling?" Daniel asked.

Her response was difficult to understand. She had scanning speech, which was when a person's normal speech pattern was disrupted with long pauses between words or syllables. Daniel had become accustomed to it. In order to understand her, it required a more focused style of listening on his part.

"I'm OK...but I...think my...break dancing...career is...over," Jacklyn replied.

The one thing that her disease hadn't robbed her of was her sense of humor.

"That's because break dancing ended in the eighties. Maybe you should try becoming a rapper," Shawn suggested.

"As you can see, not much changes. Shawn is still a wise ass. Ass, being the operative word."

"Be nice...Daniel. He can't...help himself. He was...just born ...that way."

They all shared a laugh

"How are you feeling, Mom? Seriously, are they taking good care of you? Do you need anything?"

"I'm doing...how I...am doing. The staff...here is...wonderful. They keep...me as...comfortable as...they can. I've been... more tired...than usual...lately. They changed...my medication...a few...weeks ago. My doctor... said that...the fatigue...is one...of the...side effects. All I...can do...is take...it one...day at...a time."

She paused for a moment to catch her breath.

"How are...you doing? Have you...been going...to counseling?"

Shawn jumped in and answered for him.

"Every week, Mrs. Jefferies. I drive him myself and he has been very appreciative of my help."

"Yes, he has been quite a help. Not only does he drive me to counseling, he lays out my clothes in the morning and cuts up my food so I don't choke," Daniel added.

"You should...feel lucky...to have...such a...good friend ... looking out...for you," "That's what I've been telling him." Shawn said.

"Lucky is definitely one way of looking at it," Daniel commented.

"You don't need to worry about me. I'm going to counseling and I'm doing OK."

"I'm your…mother. I will…always worry…about you. Speaking of…which, you… aren't smoking…anymore, are…you?"

Shawn once again replied on Daniel's behalf.

"No, I made sure he quit. I flushed all of his cigarettes down the toilet. I also threatened to evict him if he smokes in the apartment."

Although he just witnessed Daniel smoking a cigarette a few minutes earlier, Shawn didn't want to give Jacklyn any other reason to worry.

Jacklyn's doctor, Dr. John Spencer, was making his daily rounds. He was a graduate of Boston University's School of Medicine. He grew up in Rome, NY and moved back to the area after a residency in Boston. He'd been her doctor for the last six years.

Dr. Spencer walked up to the group and greeted them.

"Daniel, Shawn, it's good to see you. I know how much your visits mean to Jacklyn. I'm glad that you had the time to come by today."

He then turned his attention to Jacklyn.

"How are you feeling today?"

"I'm doing…OK. I'm just…very tired. It's hard…to keep…my eyes…open."

"Unfortunately, that is one of the side effects of the new medication that we discussed. The best thing to do is to rest and not over-exert yourself. You need to allow your body time to adjust to the medicine. Have you noticed any changes in your muscle strength since you started the medication? Is it any easier to flex your fingers or toes?"

"I haven't… noticed any…difference yet."

"Well, it can take some time. Everyone responds differently. We might have to adjust the dosage if we don't see the results that we want. We will keep on it. If you wouldn't mind, I would like to talk to Daniel alone for a few moments. Could I steal him away? I promise that I won't keep him too long."

"Yes, that...will be...fine."

"I'll stay here with her. You go ahead," Shawn said to Daniel.

"Why don't we speak in my office? It's right around the corner," Dr. Spencer said to Daniel.

Dr. Spencer led Daniel out of the common area and down the hallway where the resident's rooms were located. His office was at the end of that hallway. He entered his office and took a seat behind his oversized mahogany wood desk. There were two leather high-back chairs in front of the desk. Daniel took the seat on the right.

"Are you thirsty? Can I offer you a drink of water?" Dr. Spencer asked.

"No, thank you. I'm fine," Daniel replied.

"I spoke with your Uncle Vincent earlier this week. During our meeting, I told him that I also wanted to speak with you."

"He mentioned that the last time we spoke."

"Did he mention any specifics about our discussion?"

"No, he didn't."

Dr. Spencer paused for a moment in order to find the right words.

"I see. I did tell him that it was up to him if he wanted to discuss anything with you before we had a chance to talk. When patients have complications such as your mother does, their family members often have many questions that they want answers to. It can be difficult to get those answers from another family member given the complexities of the disease."

The tone of his voice began to make the muscles in Daniel's forehead and jaw tense up.

"What are you getting at? Has something changed with my mother's condition? She doesn't look good. Is she getting worse?"

"I apologize. There is no easy way to say this. In the past six months, we have tried several different combinations of medications. She hasn't responded to any of them as we had hoped. She hasn't shown any substantial progress that would lead me to believe that her condition will improve in any meaningful way. As you saw for yourself, the medication that we have her on now has its side effects. She has been increasingly weak and fatigued over the past few weeks and we are at the point now where aggressive medical treatment is doing more harm than good. Her quality of life continues to deteriorate because of that treatment, and it's not resulting in any added benefit to her overall health."

"So, what do we do now?"

"It's now up to you and your family to decide how you want us to treat her moving forward. We can continue to treat her with her current medication regiment with the hope that it might improve her condition, or we can focus on making her comfortable with the time that she has left. The other decision that has to be made is whether you would like her to remain here or if you would like to have her transferred to a hospice facility. While we certainly have a competent staff that can care for her here, a hospice facility is more equipped to focus on patient comfort at this stage of the illness."

"A hospice facility is for people who are dying," Daniel remarked.

"MS is a degenerative condition. There's no cure. The life expectancy of patients who are diagnosed with it varies greatly. Some patients enjoy a relatively high quality of life for many years, but in the end, they all succumb to it. It's not a question of if, it's a question of when."

"How long does she have?"

"While there is no way to be completely sure, I would estimate that she only has six to nine months left."

Chapter 5

Closing time at 315 Comics was ten minutes away. Daniel was on the sales floor arranging a box of superhero figurines on a shelf and Shawn was in the back room catching up on some bookkeeping. The only customers in the store were two young boys, Jordan and Sam. They were regulars who came in three to four times a week. The latest issues of most comics were released on Mondays. Every week, Jordan's mother would drop them off at 8:00 pm and Sam's mother would pick them up at 10:00 pm. They spent that time perusing through their favorite comics and discussing their insights and philosophies about them. Often times, those discussions would lead to heated arguments. On occasion, Daniel and Shawn would have to step in and mediate the situation. It felt strange to both of them to play the role of peacekeeper, given the fact that they'd had so many of the same arguments with each other over the years. The irony was not lost on Daniel. When he watched Jordan and Sam argue, he couldn't help but see himself and Shawn at that age. It transported him back to a much simpler and happier time in his life.

When Daniel finished stocking the figurines, he walked behind the sales counter and began counting the cash in the register to tally up the days' receipts. Jordan and Sam approached the counter, each with one comic book in hand. Typically, they would read dozens of comics while they were in the store, but they would only purchase one or two issues to take home. It didn't help business, but Shawn didn't mind. He and Daniel used to do the same thing and the previous owner never seemed to mind. He felt that letting them read comics for free was his way of paying it forward.

"Do you have any more copies of *The Walking Dead* issue fifty? There was only one copy on the shelf," Jordan asked.

"Nope. Sorry, fellas. They sold out quickly," Daniel replied.

"You sold out last week too. Shawn said that he would put aside a copy for both of us," Sam said.

"We both need the issue to keep our collections complete. Now one of us will be one issue short," Jordan added.

"Sorry, that's my fault. He told me to put the issues aside, but I forgot. Those two blond girls from your school were the last customers to buy that issue. Why don't you give them a call? They might be willing to sell it to you. It would be a good way to get to know them."

"Why would we want to get to know them?" Sam asked.

Daniel shook his head and laughed.

"Fellas, you really have a lot to learn. You don't even know how lucky you are. When I was your age, most girls weren't into comics. They thought that guys who read them were nerds. Now, all of a sudden, they think that it's cool for some reason. On some days, more girls come in here than guys. Don't let this opportunity slip through your fingers. Believe me, you will regret it."

"They only think comics are cool because they watch the *Big Bang Theory*. They aren't true fans like us. Next month they will be into something else. Why should we even waste our time with them?" Jordan remarked.

"I can see that my words are falling on deaf ears. Why don't we table this conversation until puberty kicks in? I'm fairly confident that you will understand my point by then. In the meantime, those issues are on me tonight. I'll order another copy of *The Walking Dead* and set it aside for you. I promise that even if Kaley Cuoco herself comes in, I will not sell it to her. However, if Gillian Anderson comes in, that promise is null and void."

"Who is Gillian Anderson?" Jordan asked.

"Are you kidding me? Haven't you ever heard of the *X-Files*?"

Both boys looked at him with blank expressions on their faces.

"She was the number one nerd crush of the nineties," Daniel said.

"Dude, we aren't nerds. We are comic book aficionados," Sam stated.

"OK, Mr. aficionado, it looks like your Mommy is waiting for you outside. You better hurry before she gets upset and gives you a spanking. When you get home, you can look it up on the internet before she tucks you into bed."

"Will it be on the same website as cassette tapes and Blockbuster Video?" Jordan asked with a sly smile on his face.

"You are really pushing it, little man."

"He's right, man. We should respect our elders," Sam said to Jordan.

Both boys burst out into laughter and walked out the front door. Shawn heard the commotion as he walked in from the back room.

"Was that Dumb and Dumber?"

"Yeah. Kids today are hopeless. Were we ever so clueless about life?"

"You were. I always had it figured out. As you can see from my billion-dollar business empire, I still do."

"That's good to know, Mr. Rockefeller. I guess that means I will finally be getting that raise you have been promising me."

"I might need a little more time on that. Our third quarter sales figures were slightly lower than the projected estimate. I can, however, offer you a little something in the meantime."

Shawn opened the door to a black mini-fridge underneath the counter. He pulled out two bottles of beer and handed one to Daniel.

"Hmm, Miller Genuine Draft," Daniel remarked.

"Truly the champagne of beers. Only the best for my employees."

"Employee, singular. Did you really buy these?"

"No. My Dad called me from Florida and told me that they were in the back of the refrigerator in the garage and were about to expire."

"I guess almost expired free beer is one of the many benefits of still living with your parents."

"Hey, I only live with them six months out of the year. The other six months, they are snow-birding down in Florida. At the very least, that makes me a part-time adult."

Both of Shawn's parents were teachers in the Utica City School District. His father, Walter, taught physics at Proctor Senior High School and his mother, Sandra, taught math at John F. Kennedy Junior High School. They were everyone's favorite teachers. Daniel and Shawn were in both of their classes when they were in school. They retired two years earlier. They owned a condo in Port Charlotte, Florida and spent the winter months down there. As much as they loved living in Utica, winters in upstate New York were unforgiving. It was a relief for them to finally have the luxury of avoiding the snow after all of the years of shoveling and plowing. Shawn continued to live with them after he graduated college. It was a mutually beneficial arrangement that helped him save money so he could invest in his business, and it reassured them to have someone at the house when they were away.

Daniel took a sip of his beer. The taste was unexpectedly harsh.

"Did you say, about to expire?" he asked as he choked it down.

"Sorry about that. I was hoping you wouldn't notice. At least the alcohol is still good."

Daniel put down his beer and returned to counting the money in the cash register. Shawn continued drinking his in silence. He was trying to figure out the best way to ask Daniel about what Jacklyn's doctor had discussed with him earlier that day. Daniel hadn't said a word about it since they left the Masonic campus and Shawn knew that Jacklyn's condition was getting worse, but he didn't know the specifics. It was hard to get information out of Daniel because he kept everything so bottled up inside. Still, he thought that it was important to bring up the subject with him as he didn't want Daniel to shut down completely.

"Speaking of my parents, they have been asking about your mom. They are concerned about her."

Daniel continued counting the money without looking up to acknowledge Shawn's statement.

"She is sick. She has MS. You've seen her for yourself."

"You know what I'm getting at. What did her doctor say to you today? I know that it's not good news, but I want to know. She is your mother, but she means a lot to me too."

"Dr. Spencer said that she is dying. She has six to nine months left to live."

Shawn wasn't expecting good news but hearing it in such blunt terms put it into a different perspective. He bowed his head and placed his hand over his eyes to fight back his tears. Daniel placed his hand on Shawn's shoulder.

"This has been a long time coming. Death is a part of life. I've faced it more times than I would have liked, but there is nothing I can do about it. There is nothing you, or your parents, or anybody can do about it. We all try to fight it at one time or another. It's a futile effort. Death is an undefeated opponent. It will beat us all eventually. As hard as it might be to accept it, that is all we can really do in the end."

Shawn took a few minutes to compose himself before he responded.

"I know that we are going to lose her eventually, but as long as she is alive, there is still hope. They are always coming up with new treatments. Anything is possible these days. Did Dr. Spencer say there was anything that could be done for her?"

"I'm sorry. I wish I could tell you that there was a cure out there and that she will get better, but that's not reality. Whatever treatments are out there, aren't going to help her at this point. She is too far gone. You have seen her yourself. She is in excruciating pain. I can't put her through any more of it. I have to let her go and so do you."

"What are you planning on doing with her for the time that she has left?"

"The only thing that I can do, make her comfortable. Dr. Spencer suggested putting her in a hospice facility. He said that they are more equipped to deal with end of life care. I'm going over to my aunt and uncle's house for dinner tomorrow night. Dr. Spencer talked to them about all of this too, so I'm sure that they already have some ideas in mind."

"Does your mom know? Have they told her?"

"I'm not sure if my uncle has said anything to her yet. On some level, I think that she knows. She might not know exactly how much time she has left, but she knows that it is running short. I can see it in her eyes. To tell you the truth, I think she wants to let go. I think the only reason that she is still holding on is because she is worried about me. I wish there was a way that I could help her. I wish there was a way that I could take away her pain."

"She loves you. All you need to do is be there for her. That's all any mother really wants from her son."

Not wanting to discuss the matter any further, Daniel changed the subject.

"I meant to ask you earlier, but it slipped my mind. I need tomorrow off. I'm going to Syracuse to see Keith. Do you think you can get along without me?"

"Yeah, no problem. Keith, that is your buddy from the Army, right? How is he doing?"

"As far as I can tell, he is perfectly fine. Nothing ever phases that guy, not even losing a foot. After the IED explosion, I didn't know if he was dead or alive. I woke up in the hospital in Germany eleven days later. He was in the bed next to me reading a newspaper like it was any other Tuesday. I found out later that he regained consciousness and called for help after I passed out. If he hadn't, I probably would have died out there. Luckily for me, he is a hard man to kill."

After the ambush in Iraq, Daniel passed out from a severe concussion as a result of the IED blast. A short time later, Keith woke up. He had a hard time trying to stand up at first. When he looked down, he saw that his left foot was missing. He also saw the makeshift tourniquet that Daniel had fastened around his leg. It saved his life. Doctors later told him that without it, he would have bled to death within a matter of minutes.

He rolled onto his stomach, planted his right foot on the ground, and pushed himself up with his arms. He managed to balance all of his weight onto his one foot and stand up. When he was finally up, he saw the metal frame of the Humvee engulfed in flames. He looked around and found a large stick on the ground that he used as a cane. He hopped towards the fiery vehicle and made it halfway there when he heard the sound of coughing. He turned to his left and saw a body on the ground, badly burned and missing both legs. When he got closer, he could see that it was Aashirya. The coughing suddenly stopped. He knelt down beside her to listen for breathing sounds. When he didn't hear any, he checked for a pulse. There was none. She was dead.

He got back up and surveyed the area. He knew that Daniel must have survived. It didn't seem plausible that a random stranger would have happened to pass by, pulled him out of the vehicle, and then treated his injury. There was a great deal of smoke emanating from the vehicle fire, so visibility was low. It took him several minutes before he spotted Daniel. He was lying face down in the sand. It appeared that he had been moving in the direction of the city before he passed out. Keith guessed that he must have been going to get help. He made his way over to him and checked him out. Unlike Aashirya, Daniel was breathing and had a pulse, albeit faint. He also saw blood dripping from his head and his right shoulder. He removed his helmet and found a small piece of shrapnel lodged in the side of his forehead, just above his temple. He had multiple pieces of shrapnel in his shoulder. He pulled out the shrapnel from his forehead and the blood flow increased slightly. He decided to leave the shoulder wounds for the medics. He pulled out his knife and cut off a piece of Daniel's ACU jacket and wrapped it around his head to slow the bleeding.

Once he was satisfied that Daniel was stable, he pulled out his satellite phone that he had packed in one of his ammunition pouches before they left the city. Miraculously, it had not been damaged in the explosion. He called their battalion headquarters to report the attack. A nearby quick reaction team and medical evacuation helicopter were dispatched immediately. The quick reaction team arrived on the scene first. They had to secure the area before the helicopter could land. They formed a perimeter around Keith and Daniel. They then sent out a reconnaissance team to scout the area for enemy combatants and additional explosive devices. Once they were satisfied that the area was secure, Keith and Daniel were evacuated out on the helicopter. Aashirya's body was placed in a body bag and put in the back of one of the quick reaction team's vehicles.

Keith and Daniel were both treated and stabilized in Baghdad. Daniel had to be placed into a medically induced coma so that his head injury could heal properly. They were then flown to Landstuhl Regional Medical Center at Ramstein Air Force Base in Germany for surgery. It was the largest military hospital outside of the continental United States, and it served as the nearest treatment center for wounded service members coming from Iraq and Afghanistan.

Daniel and Keith maintained their friendship after being discharged. They agreed to get together at least once a month. As much as he wanted to put the past behind him, Daniel did not want to abandon his teammate. Seeing Keith on a regular basis was also one way of keeping Aashirya's memory alive. He felt that he owed her that much.

"Why don't you get out of here? I'll finish counting the money and lock up," Daniel said.

"It's no problem. I can help you and then we can go get a real drink."

"I appreciate it, man, but if you don't mind, I'll take rain check. I'm a little wiped. It's been a long day."

"Sure, no problem. I'm a little beat myself. I'll just go home and play some Call of Duty. If you need anything, just give me a call."

Shawn walked into the back room and grabbed his coat. There was a back door that opened up into a small parking lot behind the building. He walked through it and got into his car, leaving Daniel alone in the shop.

When Daniel finished counting the money, he placed the day's profits, along with a daily count sheet, into a blue leather pouch. He then put the pouch into a small combination safe in the back room. Once the safe was securely locked, he turned off the lights on the sales floor and made his way to the front entrance.

He decided to have a cigarette before he locked up for the night. Shawn didn't want cigarette smoke in the store, so he had to go outside. Normally, he would smoke out back, but since the store was closed, he went out onto the front sidewalk.

During the day, Genesee street was a bustling boulevard with people and cars coming and going. It was the main commercial street that ran through the center of the city. At night, it was much more peaceful. One could observe and appreciate the history of the city. The bright lights of the Stanley Theater's Marquis lit up the entire block.

Most of the surrounding buildings were built in the early 1900s. While they had been renovated over the years, they still maintained their original look and feel. It was as if the area was frozen in a time that had long since passed. Daniel always enjoyed the quiet nostalgia. Standing outside on nights like that provided him with a few moments of peace that were all too fleeting in his life. He was grateful for any time that he could detach himself from the stresses in his life.

There was a small coffee house across the street called Sweet Escapes Café. They specialized in gourmet coffee and homemade Italian pastries. On Monday nights, they hosted an open-mic. People would come out to read poetry, play music, and perform stand-up comedy. It was primarily a poetry audience, so most of the jokes tended to fall flat. It wasn't Daniel's scene, but he did enjoy the coffee and pastries, especially coming from an Italian family.

He watched several groups of people enter the café while he was smoking. The open mic started at 10:30 pm. The room usually filled up to capacity. As he was taking the last puff of his cigarette, he noticed a woman that was standing at the back of the line waiting to be let in. She seemed familiar to him. She had dark black hair and was wearing a long white overcoat. The light from inside the café was shining onto the sidewalk, but it didn't extend all the way out to the area where she was standing. He couldn't see her face in the dark. When the door opened, the light extended out further, but it still didn't go all the way to the back of the line. As the line started moving, the people in front of her walked through the door one by one. She followed close behind them. When she finally stepped into the light, she turned and made eye contact with him.

He finally saw her face clearly. He couldn't believe who was staring back at him. It was Aashirya.

His jaw dropped and his cigarette fell out of his mouth onto the sidewalk. He tried to call out to her, but he couldn't seem to form the words. Before he could say anything, she turned away and walked into the café. Instinctively, he ran across the street without looking. An oncoming car, which he didn't see coming, slammed on its breaks just a few inches in front of him in the middle of the street. He apologized and continued across the street.

His heartbeat and his breathing increased substantially as he entered the café and began searching the room for his fallen comrade. It was crowded and there was very little room to maneuver. He spotted the group of people that were in front of the woman. They were at the counter ordering, but she wasn't with them. He continued searching for her. As he focused his glance towards the bathrooms at the back of the café, he saw a woman with the same build and dark black hair walking towards the women's room. She was no longer wearing the white coat, but he was sure that it was her.

He pushed his way through several people in order to reach her.

"Aashirya! Aashirya, wait!" he called out to her.

She didn't turn around. He reached her just as she was about to enter the women's room. He grabbed her arm.

"Aashirya!"

The woman jumped back as he swung her around.

"Do I know you?"

Daniel felt as if his heart stopped. The woman standing in front of him was not Aashirya. It was a young Indian woman. There was a slight resemblance, but it clearly wasn't her. He stood there in silence. He was sure that he had seen her. He didn't know what to say.

"Are you OK?"

"Yes. Yes, I'm fine...I'm very sorry. I thought that you were someone else. I'm sorry if I frightened you."

"It's OK. Who did you think I was?"

"Just an old friend. It was somebody that I haven't seen in a while. You look like her. I saw you come in from across the street and I thought that you were her, but you are obviously not. I guess the light was just playing tricks on me."

She could see that he was sweating and his hands were shaking.

"Are you sure that you're OK? You look like you are not feeling well. Did you want to sit down for a minute? I could get you a glass of water."

"No, thank you. I'm fine. It's just been one of those days. I'm just tired. I'm sorry for bothering you."

Daniel ran out of the café and back into the comic book shop. He locked the door behind him before rushing into the back room and up the stairs into his apartment. When he entered his apartment, he went right into the bathroom and pulled out a prescription bottle from the medicine cabinet. He opened it up and swallowed two pills without bothering to get a glass of water to help them go down. The prescription was for Risperdal, an anti-psychotic medication used to treat hallucinations.

Chapter 6

After a long, sleepless night trapped in the confines of his own thoughts, Daniel pulled into the parking lot of the Colonial Village apartment complex in Syracuse, NY in a red 1998 Jeep Cherokee. It was his mother's car before her MS prevented her from driving. He rang the doorbell to apartment 107.

"Come in. It's open," a voice said from inside the apartment.

Daniel entered the apartment. It was a basic one-bedroom, one-bathroom unit. The walls were white and the carpets were light beige. The front door opened up into a living room that had a small kitchen attached to it, which was separated by a breakfast bar. There was a short hallway off the living room with a bedroom on the left and a bathroom on the right. At the end of the hallway was a closet, which housed a stacked washer-dryer combination unit. The walls were empty. There were no pictures or decorum of any kind. The only furniture in the apartment was a brown leather couch, a wooden coffee table, and a black metal TV stand with a flat screen TV on it.

Keith Andrews was watching TV on the couch with a Corona in hand. He was dressed in khaki pants and a dark blue polo shirt. The words, *Andrews Sporting Goods,* were stitched in white letters on the left side of his shirt, just above the chest area. His right leg was propped up on the coffee table and his left leg was dangling off the couch. His left foot was missing. A prosthetic foot with a Timberland boot on it was resting on the couch next to him.

"Good to see you, Danny. Grab yourself a beer, and while you're at it, grab me another one."

Daniel made his way through the living room and into the kitchen. When he opened the refrigerator door, he saw two white Chinese takeout containers, a half-empty bottle of orange juice, and eleven bottles of Corona. He took out two of the Coronas and opened them up with a bottle opener that was on the counter. He walked back into the living room and placed one of the beers in front of Keith before taking a seat on the couch. Keith was watching live coverage of troops being interviewed in Kuwait on CNN.

"They have been interviewing these guys since they crossed the border on Sunday and have been making a big deal about the last combat troops leaving Iraq, as if the war is suddenly over or we are actually leaving. I guess we won! It's pretty funny, if you ask me. The Hajis were killing each other long before we got there, and they will be killing each other long after we leave. Did anyone really think that we were going to change that? I guess it's hard for some people to accept reality. At least we got to have a little fun while we were there, right, Danny? All is well that ends well."

"I have said this before, but I really think that you need to seek some professional help."

"Relax, Danny. You are wound too tight. You always have been. You take life too seriously. Those idiot counselors at the VA are screwing with your head. I warned you about that."

"Yeah, well, it keeps my family off my back and they give me free drugs. Speaking of the VA, didn't you have your weekly physical therapy appointment today?"

"I skipped it. They replaced my smoking hot therapist, Angela, who also happened to be an aerobics instructor, with some crusty old Vietnam Vet. I don't mind getting my foot blown off, but I draw the line at some creepy old dude putting his hands all over me."

"I know how much it sucks going to the VA. Believe me, I do, but you still need to go to get the adjustments done on your prosthetic. You shouldn't just skip your appointments like that."

"Luckily for me, they were so concerned that I missed my normal appointment that they called to re-schedule me for Friday at 5:00 pm. I accepted the appointment, so you don't have to get your panties in a bunch worrying about me. The actual reason that I cancelled was because my brother had a crisis at the store. They sent the wrong shipment and he was freaking out because we wouldn't have enough inventory for the last-minute Christmas shoppers. He needed me to watch the store while he drove to Rochester to clear it up with the distributor. Talk about a guy who is wound too tight."

"How has business been?"

Keith shrugged his shoulders.

"Who knows? I don't really get involved. I can't imagine it's too good. People shop online or at chain stores now. It's much cheaper and much more convenient. Nobody buys sporting goods from Mom and Pop shops anymore. My brother and my old man have been killing themselves for years trying to keep up with the competition. They refuse to sell the place and give up. Like I said, it's hard for some people to accept reality."

"I'm sorry, man. I know the store has been in your family for a long time. Hopefully, they can turn things around."

"Not likely. What are you going to do? Easy come, easy go. Forget it. It's not worth worrying about. I'm a little more worried about you. In all honesty, you look like shit. And that's coming from a guy with one foot. I think you need to blow off some steam. Why don't we head over to Fantasies?"

"A strip club? It's 11:30 in the morning."

"What's your point? A fine piece of ass is a fine piece of ass. I don't see what the time of day has to do with it. You desperately need some tits in your face and I'm hungry. If we leave now, we can get there just as they are putting out the lunch buffet. Surprisingly, they make a hell of a chicken wing."

"I don't know, man. I'm not really in the mood."

"So, what else is new? Look, you are the one who insists that we get together. Every time we do, you are always moping around. It's really starting to bum me out. I can't take it anymore. It's either this or I go back to work. And considering that I want to deal with my brother even less than I want to deal with you right now, we are going. As I see it, you don't have a choice. I saved your life and lost a foot in the process. Chug your beer and mount up! We move out in five mics, soldier."

"You really are an asshole."

Fantasies Gentlemen's Cabaret was a strip club on the east side of Syracuse. Keith had been going there since he was sixteen years old. The first time that he went was after a baseball game in high school. A few of the guys on his team wanted to celebrate their win. The club served alcohol, and twenty-one was the minimum legal age to be let in, but the owner tended to be relaxed when it came to enforcing certain laws. Several of the regular patrons were Syracuse police officers. They looked the other way in exchange for free alcohol and lap dances. The owner only concerned himself with whether or not customers could pay.

Daniel and Keith were met at the front entrance by a six-foot, five-inch, muscular gentleman with a bald head and a dark goatee. He greeted Keith by name. Since returning home from the Army, Keith visited the club on a weekly basis. He was a familiar face to the staff.

The inside of the club was a large, wide-open space with two stages at opposite ends of the room. There was a bar lined with black leather stools on the far-right wall. Cocktail tables were set up throughout the middle of the floor and there was a VIP area with velvet covered couches and lounge chairs on the far-left wall. There were only a handful of customers in the club when they arrived. It was normally slow at that time of day.

Keith guided Daniel over to a table in the middle of the room. A young petite Asian waitress came over to the table to take their order. She was wearing a short black skirt, a black laced bra, and high heels. Daniel ordered a Sam Adams Boston Lager. Keith ordered a Corona and two shots of Crown Royale. She smiled at them and then walked over to the bar to put in their order. When she returned, Keith gave one of the shots to Daniel and held the other one up for a toast.

"Here's to you, Danny!"

They tapped their glasses together and downed their shots.

"Thanks. This is quite a place. I take it you come here often?"

"It's a way to pass the time."

One of the dancers saw Keith from across the room. She was a skinny blonde with blue eyes. She had a tattoo of a winged heart on her lower back and was wearing a dark red bra and a matching thong. She walked over and took a seat on Keith's lap.

"Hey, baby, how have you been? Who is your friend?"

"I've been good. This is my buddy, Danny. We are actually here today because he needs some cheering up."

"Danny, allow me to introduce the lovely Alexis."

Alexis Nesmith was born in Whitesboro, NY. She was raised by her grandmother, Ida. Her mother, Jennifer, had her when she was only sixteen years old. She never met her father. Jennifer had several boyfriends around the time that she got pregnant and they were all over the age of twenty-one. Jennifer never told Ida who the father was.

Ida wasn't sure if Jennifer even knew herself. It wasn't surprising that none of them came forward.

After Alexis was born, Jennifer lived with Ida for six months. One Friday afternoon, she left and never came back. Ida didn't bother looking for her. She knew that she didn't want to be found. Even if she did, she wasn't equipped to be a mother. Ida's main concern was for Alexis. She focused entirely on her. She created a loving and supporting environment for her. Growing up, Alexis was a good student and had many friends. She was a normal, happy little girl.

When she was ten years old, tragedy struck. Ida was driving home from work one night during a snowstorm and she could barely see the road. She made a left-hand turn directly into the path of an oncoming snow plow. She was killed instantly. Alexis was at a neighbor's house when the police arrived to tell her the news. Children and family services took her into their custody that night. She had never spent a night away from her grandmother before. That night, she had to sleep in a strange room all by herself with nobody to comfort her. She cried all night. Ida was her whole world, and in an instant, she was gone.

Alexis was placed into foster care. For the next five years, she bounced around from home to home. Some of her foster parents were better than others. Some of them genuinely cared about the children in the system and wanted to help them. Others were just using the system as a means of extra income. She experienced all types. The last family that she was placed with was the worst. They were a married couple and both alcoholics. Their house was a mess and they never bothered to make sure that she had food or clean clothes. They couldn't have cared less if she went to school or not as they barely acknowledged her. It was clear that they were only in it for the money. One night, they both came home drunk. The wife passed out on the couch and the husband came into Alexis' room while she was sleeping. She woke up to find him on top of her. She tried to fight him off, but he was too strong. He raped her and then passed out on the bedroom floor. She gathered up all of her clothes into a duffel bag, took what little money was in their wallets, and left.

She took a bus to Syracuse. For the next six months, she lived on the streets. She tried to avoid sleeping in shelters because she didn't want anyone to find out her age and put her back into the system. She relied on hand-outs for money. Occasionally, she would resort to prostitution. Some nights she would have enough money for a motel room, but most nights she slept outside in back alleys or under highway bridges. She decided that she couldn't keep living on the streets. She met two girls who danced at Fantasies and they told her that the owner was the type of guy that would hire her and not ask too many questions. She decided to go into the club one night and ask for a job. The owner knew right away that she was underage. He also knew that she would bring in a lot of money. He agreed to get her a fake ID and let her work there.

"It's nice to meet you, Danny. Why so sad? Is there anything that I can do to cheer you up? Maybe a private dance? Since you are a friend of Keith's, I could give you a special rate."

"I'm doing just fine. I appreciate the offer, but I'll pass."

Keith interjected.

"What do you mean you will pass? No, No. You're not getting out of this one. I'm paying. Believe me, it will be worth it. She has a special talent for making you forget all of your problems. Why don't you stop being a buzzkill and let the lady do her job? It's why we are here. You don't want to hurt her feelings, do you?"

"No, I don't want to hurt her feelings. It's just really not my thing. Why don't you two go have fun? I'll sit here and enjoy my beer."

"It's OK, hun. I get it. You are just not into blondes. I have a friend that you might like. I think she is a little more your style."

"No, really, I..."

Before Daniel could refuse, Alexis signaled to her friend who was sitting in the VIP area to come over to the table and join them. A young Hispanic woman with a slim athletic build began walking towards them. She was wearing a white lingerie-style bra with matching panties. She had dark brown eyes and long, dark brown hair pulled back into a ponytail. She had on just enough makeup to accentuate her natural features.

"This is..." Alexis said, trying to introduce her.

Daniel stood up and interrupted her.

"...Sonya."

Daniel couldn't believe it. Alexis' friend was his ex-girlfriend. They were together all throughout high school. He hadn't seen her since they broke up."

"Daniel?" Sonya said, equally as shocked.

Daniel first met Sonya Alvarez in the seventh grade. They were students at John F. Kennedy Junior High School. Daniel, Sonya, and Shawn were all in Shawn's mother's fourth-period math class. Sonya was the first girl that Daniel ever had a crush on. He was always too nervous to talk to her and Shawn used to make fun of him for it. One Saturday afternoon, Daniel and Shawn were in 315 comics when Sonya came in. Shawn told Daniel that it was his chance to talk to her, but Daniel was still too nervous. Shawn tried relentlessly to get him to do it, but he refused. Sonya overheard their conversation and began to laugh. She decided to go over and introduce herself. Shawn did most of the talking at first. Once they started discussing comic books, Daniel began to feel more at ease. He couldn't believe his luck. He never thought that he would meet a girl who was as into comic books as he was. The three of them spent the entire afternoon in the shop reading and discussing comics. After that, their duo became a trio.

Comic books were an escape for Sonya. Her home life was rough. She was born in Syracuse and her mother, Carolyn, was born and raised in Utica. Her father, Marco, was born and raised in Havana, Cuba. He left Cuba on a student visa to study engineering at Syracuse University at the age of twenty-five. He met Carolyn in a bar one night. She was only eighteen at the time, but she had a fake ID to get in. They began dating and after three months, she discovered that she was pregnant. Marco was a devout Catholic, so he insisted that they get married and move in together. Although they had only been together for a short time, they loved each other. Carolyn agreed to marry him. She was anxious to start a new life with her husband and move out of her mother's house.

She and her mother, Sandra, had a very tumultuous relationship. They did not get along. Sandra was extremely religious. Carolyn's father left the family when she was seven years old and they never heard from him again. She was a wild child and her mother never approved of her lifestyle. She disowned her when she found out that she had gotten pregnant out of wed-lock. They never reconciled and Sandra died three months before Sonya was born.

After Carolyn and Marco got married, they moved into a small one-bedroom apartment a few blocks away from the university. Marco worked as a waiter at a small family-owned restaurant to make ends meet. One night, he was driving home from working a double shift. It was almost midnight and as he was driving through an intersection, another car ran through a red light and crashed into his driver's side door at seventy-five miles per hour. The speed limit on that street was thirty miles per hour. Marco was killed instantly. Sonya was born the following month. Carolyn did not have a job and the apartment was leased in Marco's name. She had to move out shortly after Sonya was born. She moved back to Utica and was able to get into section eight housing. They lived in a section of East Utica known as Cornhill, which had the highest crime and poverty rates in the city.

Sonya and Carolyn were on their own. They didn't have any family in the area. Carolyn worked odd jobs, but the majority of her income came from welfare. She also suffered from bouts of depression and felt incredibly overwhelmed and alone. It wasn't easy raising Sonya on her own at such a young age with no money and no support system. She often turned to drugs and alcohol. She was in and out of rehab several times over the years.

Carolyn's other way of coping was by turning to men. She had a revolving door of boyfriends. Many of them had criminal records. They were involved in drug dealing and robbery among other crimes. The one thing that they all had in common was that they were just using her for sex. None of them cared about her or Sonya.

Sonya was removed from Carolyn's care at the age of fifteen. Carolyn had taken off with her latest boyfriend and left Sonya home alone for over a week. Despite living in a tough neighborhood and having an absentee mother, Sonya was a good student and she never missed a day of school. One day, she became overwhelmed with emotion and started crying in the middle of her English class. She ran out of the classroom and into the bathroom. Her teacher followed her. When she caught up to her, Sonya told her about her mother leaving. The food in her house ran out the night before and she didn't have any money to buy more.

Her teacher brought her into the principal's office and they contacted the office of children and family services. She was taken to the House of Good Shepherd, an organization that took in at-risk youth. Most of the children who were sent there were returned to their families or placed into foster care after a short stay. Sonya stayed until after she graduated high school. The office of children and family services would not allow her to return to her mother's home because of her ongoing drug use and neglect. She asked to not be placed into foster care. She enjoyed living at the House of Good Shepherd. It was a place of great comfort to her.

Daniel and Shawn were also a tremendous source of support for her. They were the closest friends that she ever had. She enjoyed getting lost in discussions about comics with them. Her favorite character was Elektra, the love interest of Daredevil. Elektra was a highly-trained assassin of Greek descent who wielded a pair of bladed Sai as her trademark weapon. The traits that she most admired about her were her inner strength and her unwavering resolve in the face of darkness. It was a source of great inspiration for her. She didn't want the darkness in her own life to consume her, or to define her.

Daniel and Sonya's relationship changed during their freshman year in high school. It evolved from a friendship into a romance. It was the first such relationship for the both of them and was the happiest time in her life. She thought that they would get married someday, but things changed when Daniel's mother was moved into assisted living and he had to move in with his aunt and uncle. Instead of leaning on her for support, he began to pull away from her. She could tell that he was feeling the weight of the world on his shoulders and wanted to help him, but he closed himself off from her. Right before graduation, he told her that he was going to enlist in the Army. They broke up the night before he left for basic training. That was the last time they spoke to one another.

"Oh my God, Daniel! Is it really you?"

Before he could answer, she hugged him as tightly as she could, not wanting to let him go. Daniel responded when she finally released him.

"Yes, it's me. I had no idea that you were…"

"…a stripper," she said before he could finish his sentence.

"Well…no. I will admit that is a bit of a surprise, but I didn't even know that you were living out here. It's been a while. I'm sorry that I haven't been in touch."

She held his hand in hers. He could feel her tremble. Tears began to well up in her eyes.

"It's OK. Shawn called me when you got hurt. I was so worried about you."

"He never mentioned that he talked to you."

"I asked him not to. I didn't want to make things any harder on you than they already were. I haven't actually seen him since I last saw you. Before you left, I asked him to promise to call me if anything ever happened to you. He was just being a good friend."

Daniel stared into her eyes. It was as if all of the time that they had spent apart suddenly melted away. He wanted to profess his love to her, but he just stood there silently, not knowing what to say. Like the first time that they met, she made the first move. She kissed him gently on the cheek.

"Do you want to get out of here?" she asked as she pulled back slightly.

He wanted nothing more in the world than to be alone with her at that very moment. He nodded his head with a resounding yes.

"Do you think that you can get a ride home?" Daniel asked Keith.

"No problem, Danny. I can call a cab. Go take care of business."

Keith turned his attention to Alexis.

"I'm sure I can find a way to entertain myself," he said with a big grin on his face.

"Get out of here, girl. I'll cover for you. This place is dead right now anyway," Alexis said to Sonya.

Daniel and Sonya turned and walked out of the club as if they were the only two people in the world.

Chapter 7

Sonya led Daniel by the hand through the front door of her apartment. His first impression of the place was that it was the complete antithesis of Keith's apartment. It was a luxury two-bedroom, two-bathroom unit which sat on a picturesque section of Onondaga Lake. It had a balcony off the living room with a full view of the lake and the courtyard below. The courtyard housed a swimming pool and tennis courts.

The interior was decorated with fresh flowers and candles. There were large framed photo-prints of Paris, Rome, and Venice on the walls. There was a cream-colored suede-leather sofa-sectional in the living room that faced a silver metal and glass entertainment center, which held a flat screen television, a Blu-ray DVD player, and a surround sound system. The kitchen had oak-wood espresso stained cabinets with stainless steel appliances and granite countertops. There was a dinette area attached to the kitchen. It had a pub-style table with four high-top leather chairs arranged around it. A bouquet of lilacs in a purple glass vase sat in the middle of the table. Their scent permeated the entire apartment.

"Do you want something to drink? I haven't had a chance to go shopping, so your choices are mineral water or diet ginger-ale," Sonya asked.

"Water is fine. Thanks."

Sonya grabbed two bottles of water from the refrigerator and took a seat on the sofa as Daniel continued to look around the apartment. He hadn't said much since they left the club. When they were dating, she could read him like a book. She always knew what he was thinking without him having to say anything. That was no longer the case. She couldn't tell what was going through his mind. He seemed different to her. She guessed that much of it had to do with his experiences in Iraq.

"So, what do you think of the place?" she asked in an attempt to get his attention.

"It's nice," he replied, still standing in the kitchen.

"If you think it is so nice, why don't you stay awhile? You can come in and sit next to me. I won't bite, unless you want me to."

"I'm sorry. This a great place. It's much nicer than my current dwelling," he said, realizing that he was creating an awkward silence

He finally took a seat next to her on the sofa.

"How long have you lived here?"

"I have been here for almost five years now. Alexis had the place first. She lived here with her boyfriend, but they ended up breaking up and he moved out. She needed a roommate to help cover the rent. She found me."

"Is that how you ended up working out here?"

"You mean working as a stripper?"

"No. I meant, well, yes, kind of. I don't know. I'm sorry. I didn't mean to pry. It's really none of my business. You don't owe me any explanations and you don't have to talk about anything that you don't want to."

She giggled at him.

"Wow. When did you get so uptight? Relax, sweetie. It's OK. I'm not embarrassed. Everybody has to pay the bills. This is just how I choose to pay mine for now. I don't mind talking about it, and it won't be forever."

"I'm sorry. I don't know where my head is at. I woke up this morning expecting to hang out with Keith and drink a few beers. The next thing I know, I'm here with you."

"Is that a good thing?"

"Are you kidding me? Of course, it is. I've been wanting to call you for a long time. I just didn't know what to say. I didn't know if you would be mad at me. A lot has happened since we last saw each other and I didn't want to put any of that on you. I didn't think it was fair, given the fact that I left and never bothered to see how you were doing. I have missed you though, more than you could ever know."

Taking him by surprise, Sonya leaned in and began kissing him.

"Does this mean that you are not mad at me?" he asked, momentarily pulling back.

"I wasn't, until you stopped kissing me. Were you this clueless when we were together?"

He laughed out loud. It was the first time since they had been reunited that he truly felt comfortable with her. It was a familiar feeling that he thought he would never experience again. It was also the first time that he felt real joy in a long time.

"Do you not remember how long it took me to talk to you? You know how bad I am at this. Yet, you still agreed to date me. I think that says more about you than it does about me."

"I have to admit that you have a point. You are hopeless, but I did fall hopelessly in love with you. I guess we are both losers. Speaking of losers, how has Shawn been? We really didn't get a chance to catch up when he called to tell me about you."

"He ended up buying 315. Who would have thought it? Other than that, he's exactly the same. It seems like everyone I know has changed in some way, but he is still the same pain in my ass. Not only that, he is also now my boss and my landlord. I must have done something to piss somebody off."

"Good for him. It's good to see that some things never change. We should all hang out soon, just like the old days."

She abruptly stood up and kissed him on the forehead.

"I'm going to change. Make yourself comfortable. I'll be right back."

Daniel walked out onto the balcony and gazed out at the lake. He felt the chill of the December air as it blew off of the icy water. He had always preferred cold weather to warm weather. Extreme heat was maddening to him. There were some days in Iraq that felt like pure torture. He remembered coming inside after being out on a mission, feeling like his whole body had just been dropped in a skillet and fried up like an egg.

The wintery landscape was serene. It felt like home to him, but it was more than just the scenery. It was Sonya. Being with her truly felt like home. He tried to put her out of his mind for so long, but to no avail. All of his feelings for her came rushing back like a tsunami, the instant that he saw her. He told himself that he would hang onto her this time, no matter what. He only hoped that she felt the same way about him. He knew that he couldn't bear to lose her a second time.

At the moment of that thought, he felt her arms wrap around his waist. He turned around to find that she had changed into a white silk robe. He kissed her and then pulled her into a tight embrace. When he released her, she laid a soft kiss on his lips while staring deeply into his eyes.

She began to shiver. Her outfit was not exactly conducive to the weather. He took her by the hand and led her back inside. He grabbed a fleece blanket from the sofa and wrapped it around her. They sat down on the sofa together and nestled up against one another.

A single tear slid down her cheek.

"I've thought about this moment for so long. I almost gave up hope that it would ever happen. I began to believe that we would never be together again," she said.

"I know. I thought the same thing. I didn't think that I would ever find my way back to you. I have felt incomplete without you. I was so stupid to ever let you go. I don't want to make that same mistake again. I want to be with you now and forever."

Her eyes welled up as her single tear became many.

"I want that too, but before we can be together, I need to tell you some things. A lot has happened in my life too since we broke up. I've done things that I'm not proud of. I never thought that I would have ended up where I am now. I always thought I would be able to overcome the life that I was born into, but I wasn't strong enough. At some point, I gave up fighting and just gave in. Seeing you again feels like a second chance. I want nothing more than to be with you, but I have to be honest with you, even if it changes the way that you feel about me. It's the only way that we can truly move forward."

"I want you to tell me everything. I also want you to know that there isn't anything that you could tell me that will change the way I feel about you. I've been to some of the worst places on Earth. I've witnessed horrible things, things that I could never have imagined. I've seen people succumb to the darkness inside of them. I've also seen people fight with everything that they had to escape that darkness. When people's backs are up against the wall, they make choices to survive, choices that they wouldn't have made otherwise. It's nothing to be ashamed of. I'm with you now. I'm not going anywhere," he said as he wiped away her tears.

"OK. Here goes," she said as she took a deep breath.

"I stayed on as a staff member at the House of Good Shepherd for about a year after you left. They let me live there for a while. It was only a temporary arrangement. Eventually, I managed to save up enough money to get a small apartment downtown. I had to work several jobs to make ends meet. I was a cashier at a Nice N Easy. I was a waitress at the Spaghetti Kettle. I even worked for a landscaper during the spring and summer. Despite all of the hours that I had to devote to work, I managed to find a few extra to take some classes at Mohawk Valley Community College. I went part-time and was working towards getting a nursing degree. That was pretty much my life for five years. Work, go to school, more work.

When I turned twenty-one, I got a job bartending at Rip Tide's. The tips were slightly better than waitressing, but not by much. I worked mostly nights, so I cut back on my classes to just one per semester. The bills kept adding up. What was worse than that, I felt like I wasn't getting anywhere. Whoever said that hard work pays off was full of shit. For me, hard work just led to more hard work. I decided to quit school. At the rate I was going, I would have gotten a social security check before I got a degree. I started working full-time at the bar. That became my life. I was hopeless, going nowhere, and listening to a bunch of drunks whine on about how hard their lives were.

One night, Alexis came into the bar. She was in town for the weekend. Occasionally, she would come to Utica to dance at Peepers. She didn't make as much money there as she did at Fantasies, but her drug dealer ex-boyfriend lived in town. He would give her a discount if she gave him a blow job first. He was a real classy guy.

Anyway, she was having a few drinks at the bar and told me that she didn't have the money to pay her tab. She said that she forgot to go to the ATM and didn't realize that she didn't have any cash left in her wallet. This was after five rounds, mind you. I knew instantly that she was bullshitting me, but I didn't care. The owner had been shortchanging me on tips, so I figured that it would be a good way to get back at him. She offered to give me some ecstasy pills in exchange for the drinks. I told her that I wasn't interested, but that I would let her skate on the check as long as she promised to not come in empty-handed again. She thanked me and asked me if I wanted to at least smoke a joint with her before she left. It had been a long night and I needed a break, so I took her up on her offer.

We smoked up and got to know one another outside behind the bar. I could tell that she was the type of chick that worked every angle to get by. I actually admired that about her. She seemed to be doing a lot better than I was. Despite having no cash, she had designer clothes, a Coach handbag, and a BMW. She told me that she was a dancer at Fantasies in Syracuse and asked me if I had ever considered dancing. She said that I had the perfect body for it. I laughed at her at first. She told me that it was no joke. She pulled out a roll of hundred-dollar bills from her bag. I asked her why she lied to me about not having the money to pay her check. She said that she heard me arguing with the owner about my tips. She put one of the bills in her mouth, got down onto her knees, and slipped it into the waistband of my panties. It freaked me out a little bit. She stood up and told me to never let a man keep me down. She gave me a card from the club with her number on it and told me to give her a call if I was interested. She also said that she had a spare bedroom in her apartment and was looking for a roommate. Before I could say anything, she kissed me on the mouth. It caught me completely off guard and I just stood there, not knowing what to say. She thanked me for the drinks and walked away."

"You wanted more out of life. There is nothing wrong with that. Would you have been happier killing yourself for shitty tips at some bar? Nobody has the right to judge you for the choice that you made, not even me."

"Thank you for saying that, but there is still more that I need to tell you. That was only the beginning. I took Alexis up on her offer, obviously. It was hard at first, taking your clothes off for strangers, but I got used to it. Sometimes I think I got too used to it. Alexis was a good friend to me. She has always stood by me. I will always be grateful to her for that, but there is a downside to being in her world. She is a true party girl and never turns away from temptation. There were a lot of pitfalls along the way. I tried to avoid most of them at first. I just danced. I treated it like any other job. I didn't want to be taken over by drugs and alcohol like my mother was. It's not like I never used them, but I always kept things in check. I never relied on them and I never did hard drugs. One night, Alexis asked me if I wanted to do a private gig with her at a hotel in New York City. A few of the other girls from the club went along too. It was a bachelor party. The guys were all stockbrokers at the same firm. I thought that it was just dancing, but it quickly became clear that they wanted more. I asked Alexis if she knew what they were expecting when she booked it. She said yes, but that I didn't have to do anything that I didn't want to do. Still, she made it clear that the more I was willing to do, the more money I would make. It was my choice. The guys were cool. They weren't rough with us and didn't try to force us to do anything that we were uncomfortable with. One of the guys offered me five thousand dollars to fuck him. I didn't know what to do. I was really nervous. Alexis gave me an ecstasy pill. She said that it would calm my nerves and even make the experience enjoyable. I decided to take it. It kicked in pretty fast. I had never felt anything like it. I ended up fucking the guy.

I felt ashamed of myself the next day. I told myself that it was a one-time thing, but I was lying to myself. I started partying with Alexis more and more. As a consequence of that, I started drinking and getting high on a regular basis. We did more gigs like the one in New York from time to time. The drugs were a quick way to get rid of any shame or apprehension that I had about doing them. I tried my entire life to avoid being my mother, and it turned out that all of my efforts had been in vain. One day, I woke up and realized that I was her. The thing that bothered me the most was that I didn't care."

Sonya began to cry again. She turned away from Daniel, trying to hide her tears. He wiped the tears away from her cheeks once more and kissed her on the top of her head.

"It's OK. I'm still here. The past doesn't matter. All that matters is that we are here together right now. You are not your mother. You are the girl that I love, that I have always loved. You are a beautiful person, inside and out. Just because you might have lost sight of that for a little while, doesn't make it any less true."

"I want you to know that I'm sober now. I've been dancing at the club, but I stopped doing private gigs. I've been trying to get my life back on track. A few months ago, I enrolled at Onondaga Community College and I've been taking courses again to get my nursing degree.

I'm hoping to transfer into the RN program at Syracuse University next year."

"That's awesome. I'm so proud of you. I know you can do it. You have always been strong."

"I want to believe that. I'm trying to believe that, but I didn't just wake up one day and make those choices on my own. There is one more thing that I have to tell you. About nine months ago, I was leaving the club around 1:00 am. I was drunk and high out of my mind and I was walking to my car to drive myself home. I think it's fair to say that my judgment wasn't the best. I was looking for my keys in my purse. I couldn't even see straight, so it took me a few minutes to find them. When I finally did, I dropped them on the ground and they fell underneath my car. One of the customers from the club saw me struggling. He came over to help me, or so I thought. He asked me if I wanted to go get a drink with him. I told him that I didn't date customers and I was going home. He grabbed me and forced me to the ground. He got on top of me and pulled down his pants. Can you believe that? That asshole was going to rape me right there in the middle of the parking lot. I struggled and screamed. He got angry and punched me in the face. He almost knocked me out. Luckily, another customer who was coming out of the club heard me scream. He was an off-duty police officer and he pulled the guy off of me and handcuffed him on the ground. Between being punched, high, and drunk, I didn't even know what was going on. The next thing I remember was waking up in the hospital. The entire right side of my face was bruised and my eye was swollen shut. I felt like I had been hit by a truck.

111

The police officer who helped me came by the next day to check on me. I thanked him for what he had done. He was actually a detective and friends with the assistant district attorney who'd been assigned my case. He told me that the guy who attacked me was being charged with attempted rape, assault, and battery. He also told me that my blood tested positive for marijuana and cocaine. He managed to convince his friend not to charge me for having the drugs in my system. I was grateful to him and then he pulled out my stash. I had coke, weed, and ecstasy on me when I was attacked. I completely forgot about it. He told me that it fell out of my purse and it was enough to send me to jail for at least five years. He said that he hadn't turned it over to the DA's office, but that he would unless I agreed to go into rehab as soon as I was discharged from the hospital. He arranged a bed for me and said that he would drive me there himself. He also made it clear that it was a one-time offer. If I said no, he would call the ADA and tell him about the drugs. I didn't really have much choice, so I agreed. The first few days were the worst. It's when you detox. I hadn't realized how dependent my body had become on drugs and alcohol. It was unbelievably painful. I felt like I wanted to die. Luckily, I was in a good facility. The staff there were very kind and caring. They helped me through it and then it got better, little by little. By the end, I was sober and wanted to stay that way. They recommended that I quit dancing, but I couldn't. I still needed the money to support myself and to get through school. It hasn't been easy to stay clean, especially working at the club, but I've been doing it. I'll keep doing it."

Daniel was speechless. The only coherent thought that he could form in his mind was that he was responsible for what had happened to her. If he hadn't abandoned her, none of it would have occurred. He turned away from her and dropped his head towards the ground. He couldn't bear to look her in the eye.

Sonya could finally sense what he was feeling inside. Guilt was the last thing that she wanted him to feel. Without saying another word, she took his chin in her hand, turned his face towards hers, and kissed his lips. As he looked up at her, she stood up, untied her robe, and let it fall to the ground. The sight of her naked body made his heart skip a beat. She was beautiful. She lifted off his shirt and then straddled him. He began kissing her breasts and her neck. She wrapped her arms around his neck and pulled his head back by his hair. She pulled him in for a kiss and slipped her tongue into his mouth. He undid his belt buckle as they continued to kiss. She stood back up, pulled down his jeans, and quickly re-mounted him. He grabbed her by her buttocks as she slipped him inside of her.

"Make love to me, Daniel!" she cried out in a moment of pure ecstasy.

Chapter 8

Daniel turned his Jeep onto Sherman Drive in East Utica. The neighborhood consisted largely of working-class families. It was less than a mile from Thomas R. Proctor Senior High School, where Daniel attended. It was also the same neighborhood where he grew up.

He parked his car in front of his Aunt Deanna and Uncle Vincent's house. It was a single level ranch style home, originally owned by his grandparents. Vincent purchased the house from his parents when they retired and moved into senior living apartments. Growing up, Daniel spent every Sunday over there for family dinners. Those were occasions of joy and celebration. The occasion for which he was there on that night was anything but joyful and celebratory. He was there to discuss the arrangements that needed to be made for the final months of his mother's life.

He turned off the engine and sat in silence for a few minutes. He glanced over at the house across the street. It was his former home. His parents purchased it when they got married. Vincent, Deanna, and his grandparents gave them the money for the down payment as their wedding present. Owning his own home was an incredible source of pride for his father, Donald. Donald's mother died during childbirth and he never knew who his father was. He grew up in a Catholic orphanage and didn't have anything that he could truly call his own until he bought that house. He was grateful that he was able to give Daniel all of the things that he never had growing up. As much as he missed his father, Daniel was grateful that Donald wasn't around to see it be sold off to pay for his mother's care. It would have broken his heart. Daniel felt a profound sense of loss, second only to losing his father when the house was sold. He visited Deanna and Vincent on occasion, but he avoided returning to the neighborhood as much as he could. It was just too difficult to be reminded of all that he had lost in his life.

As he was opening the door to get out of his car, his phone vibrated. He pulled it out of his jacket pocket and saw a text message from Sonya.

It read, "Hey Cutie. I had a great time this afternoon. Alexis will be driving to Utica tomorrow to dance and see her "special guy." She said that she could drop me off at your place, if you are going to be around."

He texted back, "Definitely! I'll be at 315. Have her drop you off there."

"Ok, see you then! Get some rest tonight because tomorrow I'm going to fuck you all night. In the meantime, here is a little something to keep you thinking about me. Love you!!!"

Her final text was a picture of her laying on her bed topless, wearing a thong.

After seeing that, he didn't know how he was going to be able to wait until the next day to see her. He couldn't help but be excited about the prospect of being with her again. Unfortunately, the grim reality of the reason for his visit to his family's home quickly creeped back into his mind. He knew that he couldn't avoid it any longer. He took a deep breath, got out his car, and walked to the front door.

He was greeted at the door by his Aunt Deanna. As he walked in, the familiar aroma of homemade Italian cooking immediately overtook him. Deanna was a full-blooded Italian. She started learning to cook at the age of five from her mother and grandmother. Most of her recipes had been passed down through her family for generations. It was true old-world Italian style cooking. Deanna's cooking was the one thing that Daniel always looked forward to when he visited. He even had dreams about her lasagna when he was in Iraq.

Deanna greeted him with a hug and a kiss on the cheek, as she always did.

"Hi, sweetheart. It's good to see you. Come in. Everyone is in the living room."

Daniel hugged her back.

"Hi, Aunt Deanna. It's good to see you too."

She took his coat and looked him up and down.

"You look so skinny. Have you been eating?" she asked with obvious concern in her voice.

Daniel hadn't lost any weight since the last time that he saw her. She asked him the same question every time she saw him. He was convinced that she would still be worried that he wasn't eating enough even if he showed up two hundred pounds heavier. The irrational fear that a loved one wasn't getting enough food was part of the genetic make-up of Italian mothers and grandmothers.

"The other day, I tried to make some Spaghetti O's at the shop, but I burned them. Shawn and I have been living on Slim-Jims and Fritos ever since," he joked.

She shook her head in a disapproving manner.

"The two of you are going to give me a heart attack. I don't know how you are still alive. I'll pack up some leftovers for the both of you before you leave. God knows you won't get a decent meal otherwise. Go sit down with everyone. Dinner will be ready shortly."

Daniel walked into the living room. His Uncle Vincent was sitting in his recliner enjoying a cocktail. His cousin, Nick, was sitting on the couch with his wife, Karen. Vincent stood up and greeted him with a hug.

"It's good to see you, Danny-boy. How have you been?"

"Good to see you too, Uncle Vincent. I'm doing OK."

Vincent was the Utica City Police Department's Chief of Police. He joined the force after he returned home from Vietnam. He was drafted in 1970 and served as a rifleman in the 25th Infantry Division. He and Daniel shared a unique bond. He too had been seriously injured and almost lost his life in combat. During his last month in country, Vincent's platoon was ambushed by the Vietcong during a night-time patrol. The enemy force outnumbered them three to one. When it was over, fifteen men lay dead and another twenty were wounded, including Vincent. His first cousin, Raymond, was in his platoon and among the dead.

When the platoon's gunner was killed, Vincent picked up the M-60 machine gun. He dug into a fighting position and held off the enemy throughout the entire battle. It was because of him that the platoon's line was not penetrated. He bought them enough time to fall back and evacuate the area. During the course of the battle, he was shot several times in the shoulder, leg, and lower abdomen. Despite being wounded, he never abandoned his position. He continued to fire on the enemy until he passed out from a severe loss of blood. Two members of his squad heard the gunfire from his M-60 abruptly stop. They rushed to his position and found him unconscious, laying on top of his weapon. They carried him back to the casualty collection point. He was helicoptered out just in time. The doctors later told him that if it had not been pulled out when he was, he would have died on the battlefield. He was awarded the bronze star for valor for his actions that night.

Despite having similar near-death experiences, Daniel and Vincent never discussed the full details of their experiences with one another. Vincent briefly brought up the subject when Daniel first returned home. He wanted to let him know that he understood what he went through and that he would be there for him if he needed him. Daniel was grateful, but he didn't want to talk about his time in combat any more than Vincent did. That was the last time that they ever discussed war together. They both felt that reliving its horrible realities was counterproductive to moving forward in life. It became an unspoken understanding between them.

"Do you want a drink? A buddy of mine decided to quit drinking. He gave me a twenty-year-old bottle of scotch that he had been saving for a special occasion. The only special thing that I need to drink twenty-year-old scotch is a clean glass. What do you say?" Vincent asked.

"Sounds good. Make it a double," Daniel replied.

"Ha! That's my boy! Nick, fix your cousin a drink."

Nick Morello was Vincent and Deanna's eldest son. His younger brother, Michael, was a sophomore at Ringling College of Art and Design in Sarasota, Florida. He was studying graphic design and illustration. Nick decided to follow in his father's footsteps. He was a detective in the Utica City Police Department.

Being a police officer was Nick's second career choice. Growing up, he wanted to play professional baseball. He grew up as a diehard New York Yankees fan. His favorite player was Don Mattingly. He even became a first-baseman because of him. The happiest day of his life was when the Yankees beat the Braves in game six to win the 1996 World Series, after having lost the first two games at home. The Yankees went on to win more championships after that, but the 1996 team always held a special place in his heart. It was the first Yankees team to win the World Series in his lifetime.

Nick dedicated himself to the game. His athletic talent was apparent from the age of five when he first started playing T-ball. His work ethic and determination were second to none. He was a switch hitter who could hit for both power and average. He also had exceptional defensive skills in the field. In high school, scouts from several major-league teams were interested in signing him, including his beloved New York Yankees. It seemed that he was on his way to realizing his dream of becoming a big-leaguer.

Unfortunately, it wasn't to be. He was badly injured during a game in his senior year of high school. His team made it to the state championships and he was on second base with the game tied in the seventh inning. The batter at the plate looped a single into left field. Trying to give his team the lead, he hustled around third and headed for home. The throw from left field beat him to the plate. He ran into the catcher at full speed, hoping to knock the ball out of his glove. Instead, he knocked his right shoulder out of its socket and shattered his collarbone. The catcher managed to hold onto the ball and Nick was called out at the plate.

He was taken to the hospital and his team lost in extra innings. It turned out to be the last game that he ever played. He had three surgeries on his shoulder over the next four years and went through extensive physical rehabilitation, but his shoulder never returned to full strength. The offers from pro-teams never materialized.

Losing baseball left a huge void in his life. He never pictured himself doing anything else. Luckily for him, his parents wouldn't allow him to sit around and feel sorry for himself. They gave him the option to get a job, go to college, or move out. He decided to enroll at Utica College.

College gave him the time that he needed to find a new direction in life. He felt the need to channel his energy and enthusiasm into another pursuit. He couldn't see himself sitting behind a desk and working in some cramped office for the rest of his life. He wanted a job that was as physically and mentally challenging as baseball had been. Despite being injured, he kept himself in top physical shape. During his sophomore year, he decided to pursue a career as a police officer like his father. He became a criminal justice major and entered the police academy when he graduated.

Being the Chief's son cast a shadow of skepticism over him at first. People weren't sure if he would be up to the job, or if he expected a free ride because of who his father was. Those thoughts quickly dissipated. It became clear that he was extremely qualified and competent as a police officer. He was a natural. He graduated first in his academy class and progressed quickly up through the ranks, making detective after just five years on the job. Nothing was handed to him. He worked hard and forged his own reputation within the department.

Nick handed Daniel a glass of scotch.

"Here you go, man. How is life down at the comic book shop?"

"Not too bad. Same old, same old. That reminds me, Mikey ordered an *Aquaman* special anniversary edition a couple of weeks ago. It came in the other day. I meant to bring it with me, but it slipped my mind. Is he home?"

"No. He went out to Vegas with a few of his friends from school. Actually, I think it was for some big comic book convention. You would probably know more about it than me."

"That's right. Comic-con. He told me about it. I guess that also slipped my mind."

"I'm sure he'll come pick it up when he gets back. He practically lives down there with you guys when he is home from school."

Nick paused to take a sip of his own glass of scotch.

"How are things otherwise? Any ladies in your life these days?"

"Maybe. I sort of ran into an ex-girlfriend this afternoon," Daniel replied with hesitancy in his voice.

"Wow. Who? Do I know her?"

"Yeah, it was Sonya."

"Sonya Alvarez? I haven't heard that name in a while. You guys were quite the item in high school. In fact, I can't ever remember seeing the two of you apart back then. Where did you run into her? Is she still living in Utica?"

"No, she lives in Syracuse now. I went out there to visit my buddy, Keith. We went out for a few beers and we just ran into her."

"That's great, man. What has she been up to?"

"She is just working at a bar. There is not too much to report."

Nick's detective intuition kicked in. He could tell that Daniel was being intentionally vague and holding something back. He continued to probe him for information.

"Really? You haven't seen her in ten years and you don't have anything to report? Do you plan on seeing her again?"

As Daniel was about to answer, Karen jumped in the conversation to rescue him.

"Nicholas! Can you lay off? He's not a murder suspect. He's your cousin. Maybe he doesn't want to discuss the intimate details of his personal life in front of the whole family."

"I'm sorry, you will have to excuse Columbo over here. We haven't found his cop off switch yet," she said to Daniel.

Karen Morello, formerly Karen Alberico, and Nick were high school sweethearts. They started dating during their sophomore year. Karen was also an accomplished athlete in high school. She ran track and finished second in the one-hundred-meter individual medley at the state championships in her senior year. After high school, she attended Utica College with Nick. She was accepted into the registered nurse program. Both of her parents were in healthcare. Her father, John, was a pediatrician and her mother, Sarah, was a nurse practitioner. After graduation, she began working as an emergency room nurse at St. Elizabeth's Medical Center in Utica. She and Nick got married shortly after he graduated from the police academy.

Karen was particularly sensitive to Daniel's situation with his mother. When she was twelve years old, her mother was diagnosed with breast cancer. She died two years later. Karen helped care for her until she passed away. It was incredibly painful to watch her deteriorate little by little each day. When she finally succumbed to her illness, Karen felt lost and alone. After Sarah died, Karen decided that she wanted to become a nurse to honor her memory. She wanted to be able to bring comfort to those who were suffering.

Jacklyn was one of those people. Her MS began progressing rapidly, not long after Karen began dating Nick. She could tell how stressful the situation was on the entire family. She volunteered to help out. She brought her groceries, did housework, and drove her to doctor's appointments. She also spent time just sitting and talking with her. When Sarah was sick, it meant so much to her to just feel normal for a little while. The same was true for Jacklyn. Karen and Jacklyn would discuss the mundane things in life like shopping or who was on Oprah that day. For Jacklyn, it was hard not to be reminded on a daily basis that she was suffering from a degenerative illness. Being able to forget that for a few hours felt better than anything that her doctor could prescribe. She always looked forward to seeing Karen, even on her most painful days.

Being such a help immediately endeared Karen to the whole family. Deanna warned Nick that he better not let her go. She told him that if he screwed things up with her, she would never forgive him. He could never tell if she was kidding or not, but he felt the same way about her. She was his first and only love. They stayed together through the good times and bad.

Daniel was appreciative for all that she had done and continued to do for his mother. Karen felt like the sister that he never had. As such, she also gave him advice on women from time to time, a subject that he was not a foremost expert on. He appreciated her guidance in that area as well.

"It's OK. Seeing her today was rather unexpected, but it was a pleasant surprise. She's actually coming into town tomorrow, so maybe I'll have more to report the next time that I see you guys," Daniel said.

"That's fantastic, Daniel. I'm happy for you. Sonya was a real sweet girl. You guys were good together. I hope things work out. You deserve some happiness," Karen said.

"Yeah, bud, I'm happy for you too. Sorry for the third degree. I guess it's hard to put the badge down sometimes," Nick added.

"Try living with him," Karen joked.

They all shared a laugh as Deanna came into the living room to announce that dinner would be ready in another ten minutes. Vincent refilled his glass of scotch and the three of them took a seat on the couch.

"I don't want to put a damper on the good mood, but we do have some things that we need to discuss," Vincent said when he finished pouring.

"Dr. Spencer told me that he talked to you about your mother yesterday," he said to Daniel.

Daniel's cheeks went flush and the muscles in his stomach tightened as the reason for his visit once again dawned on him.

"Yeah, he filled me in."

Vincent took a healthy sip of his scotch before he continued.

"Look, I know this isn't easy. She's my baby sister and she isn't doing well. I know that none of us want to lose her, but we need to think about what is best for her at this point. As her health care proxy,

I have the final say, but I want you to know that we aren't going to make any decisions without you. She is your mother and you have every right to be involved. We are going to make this decision as a family."

Daniel nodded silently. He didn't know how to respond.

Karen put her hand on Daniel's shoulder.

"I talked to my Dad. One of his friends from medical school runs a hospice facility out in Rome. They have a great reputation. She would have her own room and there are no limits on visiting hours. It's a very family-centric facility. One of their main goals is to provide their patients and their loved ones with as much time as possible to spend with one another. He took me there last week. I talked with the staff and met some of the patients. It's a nice place. I think she would like it there. If you want, I can take you there so you can see it for yourself."

"We can all go. Like Dad said, we will do this as a family. Whatever it takes," Nick said.

Vincent could tell that Daniel wasn't taking it well. He still wasn't saying anything.

"Talk to me, Danny-boy. What do you think? Do you want to go see this place?"

Daniel thought that he was prepared to deal with the situation, but discussing it with his family out loud made it all too real. He began to sweat and the tightness in his stomach turned to nausea. He stood up from the couch in an attempt to stop himself from vomiting all over the living room.

"I'm sorry. I have to go. I'm not really feeling that well right now. I know we have things that we need to figure out. I'll call you soon. I promise."

Daniel abruptly walked out of the living room. He opened the closet door in the foyer and took out his coat. Deanna saw him getting ready to leave from the kitchen.

"Daniel, sweetheart, is everything OK? Are you leaving?"

"Yeah, I'm sorry to head out like this. I know that you went to a lot of trouble with dinner. I'm just not feeling well. It's my stomach. I think I need to go home and get some rest," he replied, trying to avoid being talked out of leaving

"Ok, do you want to take some food to go? You might be hungry later. I could make you some tea. That might settle your stomach."

Vincent joined them in the foyer.

"If you are not feeling well, you can lay down upstairs in Mikey's room. We don't have to talk about anything else tonight if you don't want to. You can just rest," he said.

"That's a good idea. You could stay the night. You could use a good night's sleep. I'll make your favorite in the morning, French toast. What do you say?" Deanna asked.

"Thanks, but I'll be OK. I'll give you a call tomorrow. I promise."

He kissed Deanna on the cheek and walked out the door.

He got into his car and sped off. As he was driving past the high school, his nausea grew substantially worse. He pulled into the parking lot. It was after school hours, so it was deserted. He put the vehicle into park, jumped out the door, and vomited on the pavement. He fell onto his knees and began sobbing uncontrollably. All of the emotions that he had been bottling up for so long came rushing to the surface at once, along with the contents of his stomach.

He continued crying for several minutes before he looked up. When he did, he saw a woman in the distance staring at him. She was standing underneath a streetlight. His vision was blurred by his tears, so he couldn't make out her face at first. As he wiped them away, he saw Aashirya staring directly at him. Instead of pursuing her this time, he closed his eyes and counted to ten. When he opened them, she was gone. He got back into his car and pulled out a second bottle of Risperdal, which he kept in his glove compartment. Without water, he swallowed four pills, double the prescribed dose.

Chapter 9

In an attempt to drown his sorrows, Daniel sat alone atop a bar stool in Griffins Pub sipping on a frosty Labatt Blue draft. A few minutes later, Shawn meandered in the door and took a seat on the stool next to him.

"Did you close up early tonight?" Daniel asked as he took another sip of his beer

"Yeah, it was a slow night and it's the holiday season. I thought, why not treat myself to a few adult beverages? I deserve to spoil myself every once in a while. It was either this or a hot stone massage. I'm surprised to see you here. Weren't you supposed to be having dinner at your aunt and uncle's house tonight?"

"I went there, but I wasn't feeling well, so I left early."

"I see that you have already taken your medicine. I assume that you are feeling better now," Shawn commented as he stared down at two empty shot glasses turned upside down on the bar in front of Daniel.

"Not quite, I'll probably need a few more before I'm one hundred percent."

"Then it looks like I got here just in time to join you. It's funny how things work out sometimes, isn't it?"

"I must say, it is an amazing coincidence that we both ended up here at the same time, yet neither one of us was planning on being here tonight. So, who called you, my aunt or my uncle?"

"It was Karen actually. However, I did hear them in the background telling her to make sure that she didn't let on that they were in on it."

"Well, I have to say, the entire group of you are quite an outfit. You should really think about applying to the CIA's black ops program," Daniel said with a chuckle.

"I'll keep that in mind. I'm sorry. I know how much you hate it when everyone worries about you. I know you need your space."

"So, to give me my space, you track me down and take the seat right next to me?"

"I said I know you need your space. I didn't say that I would actually give it to you."

"It's OK, man. I'm not mad. I know everybody means well. I've come to accept the reality of your overbearing personalities. Besides, it beats drinking alone. Since you are here, why don't you let me buy you a round?"

Shawn was surprised at how understanding Daniel was being.

"Absolutely! I thought I was going to have to buy the drinks tonight."

"I said round, as in one. I'll be charging the remaining rounds of the evening to your tab, and I plan on having several."

"Fair enough. Let's get shitfaced! Since we will be here for a while, why don't I grab a table while you order the drinks?"

Shawn made his way to the back of the room and sat down at an empty table. Daniel chugged what was left of his beer and then ordered two more shots of Jack Daniels and a pitcher of Labatt Blue. The bartender poured the shots and told him that she would bring the pitcher over to the table. He walked the shots and a basket of popcorn from the bar over to the table. He placed a shot in front of Shawn and took a seat. Shawn held up his glass for a toast. Daniel responded by lifting his glass. They toasted and quickly downed their shots. The bartender brought the pitcher of beer over to the table along with two empty glasses. She filled each glass and then returned to her station behind the bar.

"Despite how we ended up here tonight, I'm glad that we are here together. I miss just hanging out with you and having a good time," Shawn said.

"Me too, man. I know I haven't been a barrel of laughs since I came back from Iraq. I feel like I have this dark cloud constantly hanging over me. I try to get out from under it, but no matter how hard I try, I can't shake it. I've also come to realize that because of it, I can be a real asshole sometimes."

"Don't beat yourself up. It's understandable. The important thing is that I get to enjoy a few drinks with my best friend tonight. Maybe more than a few by the time the night is over. Tonight, life is good. Tomorrow might be a different story, but we'll deal with tomorrow when it comes."

Daniel smiled and held up his beer glass for another toast.

"Sounds good to me. Cheers!"

"Cheers!"

"Speaking of friends, Karen mentioned that you happened to run into an old friend in Syracuse today," Shawn said inquisitively.

"She would be correct."

"How is she doing? I assume she mentioned that I called her after your attack in Iraq?"

"She seems to be doing OK, and yes, she did mention that little tidbit of information."

"I'm also assuming that you aren't angry at me, given all of the goodwill that has just transpired here in the last few minutes. Before you answer, keep in mind, I am the one picking up the tab for the rest of the evening."

"Relax. I understand why you didn't tell me. It was my fault anyway. I took off and cut off all communications with her. That wasn't right after all of our time together. Just because I wasn't her boyfriend anymore, didn't mean that I couldn't be her friend. You guys were still friends, regardless of the situation between us. You were right to call her. You did what I should have done myself."

"I don't know how good of a friend I was. We lost track of each other after you left. I could tell how hurt she was when you two broke up. I got the impression that I would be a reminder of that. I didn't want to make things any harder on her, so I kept my distance. I figured that when she was ready, she would come to me, but she never did. The last time that I saw her was the night you left for basic training. She made me promise to call her if anything ever happened to you. I meant to call her a hundred times to see how she was doing, but I always found an excuse not to. Every time I tried to pick up the phone,

I felt guilty for not doing it sooner, and then I talked myself out of it. I knew that she was on her own. I thought that she would be mad at me for abandoning her."

"She's not mad at you. She's not even mad at me, even though she has every right to be. She just missed us. I missed her too. I didn't know how much until I saw her today. When I saw her, I couldn't remember what made me think that it would be a good idea to break up with her. At the time, I told myself that it would make things easier on her, given how complicated things in my life were becoming. I was lying to myself. I really did it to make things easier on me. I was scared and I wanted to run away from my life. She was a big part of that life. It would be pretty hard to run away if she remained a part of it. I took the cowards way out. Instead of facing adversity, I ran from it. Ironically, the place I ran to wasn't exactly without adversity."

"You aren't the only person in the world to have regrets in life. You aren't a bad person. Everyone gets scared once in a while. You can't judge yourself for how you reacted back then. The important thing is what you do now, and what you do moving forward. It seems to me that both of you have a second chance. You should take it. Are you going to see her again?"

"Actually, yes. Her roommate is coming into town for work tomorrow. She is going to drop her off at the shop."

"That's awesome! We can all hang out like the old days. Maybe she can introduce me to this roommate of hers. It's no secret that things with the ladies have been a little slow for me lately. Is she single? What kind of work is she coming into town to do?"

Daniel almost choked on his beer as Shawn asked him the question. He decided to have a little fun with him.

"They are both in the entertainment industry."

"Entertainment industry? What, like singing, dancing, acting?" Shawn asked confused.

"Mostly dancing, some acting I would assume," Daniel replied, continuing to tease him.

"Is she going to be performing somewhere in town? The Nutcracker is playing at the Stanley Theater right now. Is she part of that?"

"Not exactly, but she will be performing downtown."

"Where? I don't know of any other theaters downtown."

"It's not exactly a theater in the traditional sense, but they do put on a show. She'll be appearing at Peepers."

"Peepers? But that is a...Oooh. And that would mean that Sonya is also a...Oooh."

Daniel burst out laughing.

"For a minute there, I thought I was going to have to draw you a picture."

"Sonya is a stripper? How long? Why?" Shawn whispered as he finally put all of the pieces of the puzzle together in his head.

"First of all, you don't have to whisper. It's not top-secret intelligence. To answer your questions, she has been doing it for the last five years. She was struggling to make ends meet and the opportunity presented itself. She was tired of working hard with nothing to show for it. Who could blame her?"

"Hey, I'm cool with it. I understand being broke. If somebody was willing to pay me to take my clothes off, I wouldn't turn them down. Although, in my case, I think it would be more likely that somebody would pay me to keep my clothes on. What do you think about it?"

"Speaking for myself, I definitely want you to keep your clothes on. As far as Sonya is concerned, I was surprised at first, but it doesn't bother me. After all this time, the only thing that matters to me is her. You were right about that second chance. I have it, and I'm not going to screw it up this time. I don't care what is in my way. Nothing is going to stop us from being together, not my own fear and certainly not what she chooses to do for a living. I love her. I always have. Everything else is secondary as far as I'm concerned."

"I'm happy for you. I'm happy for both of you. I have a good feeling about this. It's going to work out. You'll see."

"Thanks. I appreciate that, but like you said, we can deal with tomorrow when it comes. Tonight, we have some hard drinking to do. First things first though, I need to take a leak."

Daniel stood up and stumbled a bit. He felt lightheaded. He was significantly buzzed from the drinks that he already drank. He was also hot because he hadn't taken his jacket off yet. He took it off and threw it towards his chair, but it landed on the floor. Shawn told him not to worry about it and that he would pick it up. Daniel thanked him and walked towards the bathroom.

When Shawn picked up the jacket, he felt something fall out of the pocket onto the floor. When he looked down, he saw an orange prescription bottle. He picked it up and read the label. It was Daniel's Risperdal, which had been prescribed by the VA. He noticed that there was a warning on the label that said it should not be taken with alcohol. He didn't know what the prescription was for, but the warning concerned him, given the fact that Daniel had already consumed a significant amount of alcohol.

He pulled out his iPhone and Googled Risperdal. He clicked on a link to Drugs.com, which provided detailed information about the drug.

It read, "Risperdal (risperidone) is an antipsychotic medicine. It works by changing the effects of chemicals in the brain."

Shawn wasn't sure what to make of it. He assumed that Daniel was taking some type of medication, but an antipsychotic was a bit of a shock. He feared that his struggles were even worse than he thought. Daniel came back from the bathroom while he was still reading about the drug. When he arrived at the table, he saw Shawn holding the bottle and staring at his phone.

"It looks like you found my crazy pills."

Shawn's head jerked up. He was caught.

"I'm sorry. I wasn't snooping. I swear. It fell out of your jacket. I picked it up and I saw the warning about mixing it with alcohol. It worried me a little bit, especially since I have been encouraging you to drink. Should you really be drinking while you are taking this?"

"No, probably not. Don't worry about it," Daniel replied without any concern in his voice.

Shawn handed the bottle back to him. Daniel put it back into his jacket pocket and sat down. He refilled his glass with beer and signaled to the bartender to bring them another pitcher. Shawn sat silently across from him, not sure what to say.

"Is there anything that you want to ask me?" Daniel asked, breaking the silence.

"I don't know. Are you OK? This is some pretty serious stuff."

"Relax. I'm fine. My psychiatrist prescribed it for me about six months ago. It helps keep my mind straight. Sometimes things get a little scrambled up there. She thinks that it might be the result of extreme stress. It's not a big deal."

"What do you mean scrambled?"

Daniel hadn't discussed his hallucinations with anyone except for his psychiatrist. In a way, he felt relieved. Hiding it had become exhausting. He felt the need to release some of that burden and there was nobody that he trusted more than Shawn.

"It means that sometimes I see things that aren't really there."

"Things? What kind of things?"

"People would be a more accurate description, dead people to be exact. The first time it happened was when I was twelve years old. It was the night that my Dad died. I woke up in the middle of the night and he was in my room staring at me. It seemed strange. He never did anything like that before. I had a conversation with him. It wasn't about anything important. He asked me whether or not we stuck to our curfew that night. It only lasted a few minutes. When it was over, he told me that he loved me and then he walked out of the room.

When I woke up the next morning, I heard my mother crying. I ran downstairs and saw her with my Uncle Vincent in the living room. She told me that my Dad had died. I ran around the house looking for him. She stopped me and told me that he died at work. One of the other custodians found him passed out on the floor. He had a heart attack and never regained consciousness. The EMT's couldn't do anything for him when they arrived. He was already dead. He had never come home that night.

I convinced myself that it was just a dream. It felt real, but how could it have been? He was never in the house. I never told anyone about it. I didn't want anyone to think that I was crazy. As time went on, it became easier to accept that it was a dream.

The next time it happened was the day that my team was attacked in Iraq. We were in a city called Al Diwaniyah. Our mission was to help the city rebuild a school that was destroyed during an insurgent attack. We recruited people from the local population to help with the rebuilding. One of the volunteers was a nineteen-year-old girl named Nella Kassab. She was found strangled to death the day before we left the city.

The IED went off under our Humvee at the same spot that Nella's body was found. Somehow, I remained conscious after the blast. I managed to get out of the Humvee, which was now on fire and on its side, and pulled Keith out. I dragged him away from the vehicle until I was sure that we were safely out of range of a second explosion. I went back to look for our other teammate, Aashirya. She had been in the gun turret, which was the most vulnerable position in the vehicle. When I found her, both of her legs were gone and the rest of her body was badly burned. After the Humvee exploded for a second time, I looked up and saw two people in the distance. I ran towards them, yelling for help. I got to within ten feet of them when the woman turned around. It was Nella. Before I could say anything, I got very dizzy and fell to my knees. The last thing that I remember before I passed out was a bright flash of light. When I woke up, I was in the hospital and I was pretty doped up. As I had with my father, I told myself that it was a dream. Also, just like the first experience, it felt extremely real."

"That doesn't sound crazy to me. You had a dream about your Dad. That's not unusual. The fact that it was on the same night that he died could be nothing more than a coincidence. As far as the girl in Iraq, it was a traumatic event. You had just been blown up. It might have been a dream or a hallucination, but under those circumstances, either one would be considered completely reasonable. It doesn't mean that you are insane."

"I appreciate your confidence in my sanity. My psychiatrist at the VA was of the same mindset for a while. However, as time went on, those memories began to feel more real, not less. She said that there is a possibility that I might have an underlying psychotic disorder. The other possibility is that I'm suffering from a severe form of post-traumatic stress disorder. The trauma that I have experienced could be making certain things seem real, even though they are only figments of my imagination. She said that my mind could be creating an alternate reality because my actual reality is too painful to deal with. At this point, there are more questions than answers. She felt that medication was the most optimal form of treatment for now. She's hoping that it will take the edge off and let my mind heal from all of the trauma that it has experienced."

"That makes sense. Has it worked?"

"It seemed like it was, until last night. I went outside to have a cigarette before I locked up. It was a nice night. There was a line of people waiting to be let into the café's open mic night. There was a woman at the back of the line who was looking over at me. She seemed familiar, but I couldn't see her face at first. It was too dark. When she reached the front of the line, I was able to get a better look at her because of the light shining out from inside the café. It was Aashirya."

"Wait, the girl on your team who was killed? Are you sure?"

"At the time, yes. Although, that experience was different from the first two. I wasn't asleep. I wasn't under any immediate stress or threat. I was just standing outside in front of the comic book shop. After she stepped inside, I ran across the street and into the café. When I got inside, the place was packed. It took me a few minutes to find her in the crowd. When I finally spotted her, I ran up to her. When she turned around, it wasn't her. It was a young Indian woman, but it wasn't Aashirya."

"Maybe it just looked like her. You said that it was dark and you only saw her from across the street."

"Maybe, but I saw her earlier tonight too. I told you that I left my aunt and uncle's house early. That was true. We started talking about my mom and I began to feel nauseous. I made an excuse and I got out of there. I drove off and made it as far as the high school parking lot. I jumped out of the car and puked my guts out. I guess everything just hit me at once. When I looked up, I saw her standing underneath a street light. She was staring right at me. I told myself that it wasn't real. I closed my eyes and counted to ten. When I opened them, she was gone."

"I don't know how to explain it, but that doesn't mean that there isn't a logical explanation for all of this," Shawn said in an attempt to convince not only Daniel, but himself.

"I agree. The logical explanation is that I am losing my mind. If I don't figure out how to stop it soon, I'm going to be spending my days wearing a straight-jacket and eating green Jell-O. My father worked at a nuthouse, and I'll be living in one."

"Like I said, it could just be some woman who looked like her. There is a very attractive Indian woman standing at the bar right now. In dimmer light, I'm sure she could be mistaken for this woman Aashirya."

Daniel turned around to look at the woman Shawn was referring to. He felt the hairs on the back of his neck stand up when he caught a glimpse of her. He whipped his head back around towards Shawn.

"Are you telling me that you can see that woman?"

"Yes, of course I can see her. In fact, I think that she is looking at us. Maybe we were being too loud."

"What is she wearing?"

"A white overcoat. Why, what are you getting at? Do you really think that she is Aashirya? You told me yourself that her legs were blown off. Unless I'm mistaken, that woman has two very healthy legs."

Daniel leaped up out of his seat. As he raced towards the front of the bar, the woman in the white coat walked out the front door. Four people walking towards him blocked his path. Without thinking, he shoved his way right through them.

When he finally made it outside, the woman was nowhere to be found. He looked around in every direction, but she was gone. Shawn was right behind him. He helped him look for her, but he couldn't find her either.

"That was her. That was definitely her. You saw her. It wasn't just me this time," Daniel said, out of breath.

"I saw a woman. I've never met Aashirya. I don't know if it was her or not. I don't see how it's possible. You said yourself that she was killed in Iraq more than three years ago. The woman that we saw could be a relative or someone who closely resembles her," Shawn said, trying to calm him down.

"No! I know what I saw. It was her," Daniel said adamantly.

Not wanting to upset Daniel any further, Shawn backed down.

"Ok, I believe you, but we can't prove that right now. She is nowhere to be found. Why don't you go home and get some rest? We can look for her in the morning. You have seen her twice in two days on the same block. Maybe she lives around here. It will be much easier to sort all of this out during daylight hours when we are sober. I promise, I will help you get to the bottom of this, just not tonight. It's been a long day. I'll go pay the tab and you head home."

Daniel was exhausted. As much as he wanted answers, he conceded. He nodded to Shawn in agreement and walked up the street. His apartment above 315 was just one block away.

When he arrived at the building, he entered through the back door. He tripped up the first few stairs, still feeling the effects of the alcohol. When he opened the door to his apartment, he flicked on the light. He nearly jumped out of his shoes when he saw a person in his living room waiting for him. Sitting in his recliner with her eyes fixed directly on him was Aashirya. She stood up and walked towards him slowly.

"Hello, Daniel. It's good to see you again. It's been a while."

Chapter 10

Daniel stood paralyzed in the doorway as his mind raced, trying to come up with a rational explanation for what he was seeing. The woman standing before him appeared to be his deceased friend, but that seemed impossible. The last time he saw her, she was burned to the point of being almost unrecognizable. Her legs were blown clean off. This woman was perfectly healthy and without a scratch on her. His first coherent thought was that he was hallucinating again. He closed his eyes, as he had earlier that night, and counted to ten. This time, when he opened his eyes, she was still standing in front of him. His hands began shaking as he reached into his jacket pocket for his Risperdal. When he tried to open the bottle, it slipped out of his hands and fell onto the floor. It landed right in front of Aashirya's feet. She picked it up and walked towards him to hand it to him. He began backing away from her. As he was about to turn and run out of his apartment, she spoke once again.

"Daniel, there is nothing to be afraid of. I'm here to help you. I've been watching you for some time now."

He closed his eyes again and started talking to himself.

"This is not real. You are not real. You are dead. I saw you die. I visited your grave in Boston. I'm losing my mind."

She reached over and grabbed him by the shoulders.

"Daniel, you need to calm down. You are not losing your mind. I am real. However, you are correct about one thing. I did die. There are some very important things that I need to tell you. I will explain everything, but I need you to trust me. I need you to trust yourself. Please, come sit down on the couch. I will get you a glass of water and then we can talk."

Not knowing what else to do, he agreed to her request. He slowly walked over to the couch and took a seat. She closed the front door and walked into the kitchen. He watched her take a glass out of one of his cabinets and fill it with water. He continued to believe that he was hallucinating. She walked back into the living room and handed him the glass. She then placed his bottle of Risperdal on the coffee table in front of him. He stared down at it as he drank the water.

"You don't need those. You never did," she said as she sat down next to him.

"I'm not so sure of that, given the fact that I'm having a conversation with a ghost in my apartment. A ghost who just poured me a glass of water," he joked with a quiver in his voice.

"Oh, Daniel. I must admit, I have missed your sense of humor," she said giggling.

"I guess it's good that I still have it, seeing as my sanity is long gone."

"Daniel, you are not insane, and I am not a ghost. Seeing me now makes you no more insane than seeing your father when he died, or Nella when she died," she said as she placed her hand on his knee.

"How did you know about that? Who are you? What is going on here?"

"I know everything about you. In life, I was your friend. In death, I will be your guide."

"Guide? Guide for what? This doesn't make any sense. If you are dead and you are not a ghost, how are you even here right now?"

"I am here because I was chosen to be. You have also been chosen."

"This is nuts. I don't know who you are or how you know these things about me, but this is over. You need to leave or I'm calling the police."

"I know that this might be hard to accept, but you must not doubt what your senses are telling you. I am not trying to deceive you. When I first joined the team, you went out of your way to mentor me and guide me in the right direction. I'm here to do the same for you now. I understand that this must seem confusing and overwhelming. I promise that I will explain everything. I just need you to give me that chance and keep an open mind. Can you do that?"

Daniel looked into her eyes. It made him recall the moment that he watched her dying in the desert, years earlier. He remembered looking into her eyes as she was gasping for air and clinging to life. He couldn't explain how, but he knew that he was looking into the same eyes. The woman in his apartment was Aashirya. Of that he was sure, but that was all he was sure of. He took another sip of water and stared back down at his bottle of Risperdal. He had a brief thought of swallowing all of the pills in the bottle in the hope that it might snap him back into reality. He could chalk everything up to another extremely bizarre and realistic dream. Only this time, he knew that he wasn't dreaming.

Daniel questioned his sanity in one form or another since he was twelve years old. He had been searching for answers ever since the night that he saw his father in his room. He entered therapy reluctantly at his family's request. When he first began, he believed there was a possibility that his questions might be answered. As time went on, he knew that he was looking in the wrong place. He only continued with therapy to keep his family's minds at ease. Now, he thought perhaps this was the opportunity he had been waiting for, the opportunity to finally learn the truth about himself. He silently nodded his head, indicating that he was willing to listen, and Aashirya began.

"What you must first understand is that life and death are not necessarily what you think they are. They are not simply one beginning and one end. Our existence is cyclical. Life and death are two separate but equal plains of existence. Our souls cross between these plains at designated times. When a person comes to the end of one life, their soul is released and then they cross into death. Just before they cross over, all of their memories and experiences from that life are erased. Their soul remains in death until it is time to begin a new life, unencumbered by their previous one.

A very delicate balance must be maintained between the number of souls that exist in life and those that exist in death. Even the slightest imbalance could place all of existence into jeopardy. One soul is chosen to act as the gatekeeper between the plains and maintain the balance. This individual is given the title of the Reaper. The Reaper chooses others to assist in this task.

Shepherds are chosen at the time of their birth. When a person's designated time of death comes, a Shepherd is tasked with releasing their soul from their body and guiding them to the gateway, where they are met by the Reaper. The Reaper extinguishes their memories and then they cross into death. Acolytes are chosen at the time of their death. They are tasked with relaying the Reaper's orders and guiding the Shepherds in their responsibilities.

At the time of my death, I was chosen to serve as an Acolyte. I have been sent here to guide you, Daniel. You were also chosen. At the time of your birth, you were chosen to serve as a Shepherd."

Daniel jumped up off the sofa and backed away from Aashirya.

"Do you expect me to believe all of this?"

"I think that you have always believed it on some level. You have known for some time that you were different. You tried to convince yourself that you were hallucinating because it was the easiest explanation, but you never truly believed it. I know what you felt when you looked into my eyes. You knew it was me. Your friend, Shawn, saw me at the bar earlier. I am real. I am just as real as you are. You know that you can trust me. You are very special, in more ways than you can imagine."

Her words made him recall a memory.

"That's the last thing that my father said to me before he walked out of my room that night. Did he know about this, about me being chosen to be this Shepherd?"

148

"He was told about it when he died. Before a person meets the Reaper at the gateway, they are given the opportunity to see one person from their life before that life is erased and left behind. They can choose to see anyone they want. Your father chose you. In most cases, the person being visited is unaware of the person visiting them. Only those who have been chosen or possess the knowledge of the true nature of existence would be aware of what was happening. That is why you saw your father in your bedroom and Nella in the desert."

As Daniel started to accept that what was being told to him was the truth, he began to feel overwhelmed by the enormity of the responsibility.

"What if I don't want this? What if I say no?"

"You are not the first person to be frightened by the prospect of being one of the chosen. I felt the same way that you are feeling right now. In addition to that, I also had to come to terms with the fact that I had been killed and my life was over. It wasn't easy.

This is a tremendous responsibility, which has far-reaching consequences. It will take some time to get used to the idea. I will tell you the same thing that was told to me. You were chosen for a very specific reason. It was not a choice that was made lightly or randomly. There is a strength within you, a strength that few possess. I believe in you. I always have. I know that you will do what is right, and I will stand by you as you take this journey."

Daniel turned away from her and walked into the kitchen. He pulled out a pack of cigarettes and a lighter from one of the drawers. He lit one and took an extended drag before exhaling a large plume of smoke into the air. He walked back into the living room and took a seat in his recliner. He threw the cigarettes and the lighter on the coffee table, and then looked up at Aashirya.

"The irony here is that you tried to get me to quit smoking for so long. Last week, I was seriously considering quitting, and then this week you started showing up. Now, I don't think I'll ever quit. On the bright side, now that I know we have these multiple lives to live, I don't feel guilty anymore."

In response, Aashirya pulled a cigarette out of the pack, picked up the lighter, and lit it. To Daniel, watching her smoke was only slightly less shocking than seeing her return from the dead.

"I will admit that eternity has its advantages," she said with a big smile on her face.

"I think I might like the new you. So, why don't you tell me a little more about our new mission, Sergeant. When do we start?"

"The time will come soon. I cannot tell you the exact time that you will be called upon. Every shepherd is assigned a flock or a group of souls. Only the Reaper knows the identities of these souls, as well as their designated times of death. This is by design. It prevents any possible disturbances to the balance. When the designated time comes for one of them, you will be contacted. You will receive a message that contains the location where they lie in wait for you, and nothing more. You must proceed to that location and then release their soul from their body."

"How do I do that?"

"All souls were created from the same naturally occurring light-energy. It forms the basis of our consciousness and exists within all of us. Accessing this energy within yourself will give you the ability to release a person's soul from their body.

When you arrive at the location, you will notice a dull greyish glow emanating from the person's body. That indicates that their designated time of death has come. You must first make physical contact with them by placing your hand in the middle of their chest. Next, you must concentrate and channel the light-energy within yourself until you feel it surge throughout your entire body. This will allow you to make an internal connection with the other person's light energy. It will feel as if you have their consciousness within your own mind. Once you have made this connection, you must keep a firm grip on it. At first, it will feel as if the person is pulling away from you. This is merely an instinctive reaction and won't last long. Once that feeling ceases, let go, and the person's soul will be released."

"What happens after I release their soul?"

"As with your father, everyone is permitted to see one person from their life, if they choose, before they cross over. You will explain this to them. Instruct them to close their eyes and think only of the person that they wish to see. When they open their eyes, they will find themselves before that person, wherever they might be. They will have a few minutes to say goodbye. When their time is up, they will find themselves back with you. A light will then appear. This is the gateway between the plains. You must guide them towards it, but they must make the decision to walk into it themselves. Once they reach the gateway, they will find the Reaper waiting for them. Their memories from their life will be erased. Finally, they will cross into death."

"Does that mean that I have been given some special power to do this?"

"It is not so much of a power as it is an awareness and understanding of the true nature of existence. This knowledge is what will give you the power to carry out your duties. It's simply a matter of believing and having faith in yourself. As I've told you before, you were chosen for a reason. This knowledge can only be shared with a select few individuals. You are one of the few that can be trusted with it. If the wrong person were to obtain this knowledge, they could use it to further their own ends. The consequences could be disastrous. You are part of an elite group, charged with the greatest of responsibilities."

"No pressure, right?"

"As I said, it will take some time to get used to all of this. I have faith in you. I know that you are up to the challenge."

Daniel sat silently for a few minutes, trying to take it all in. Aashirya got back up and walked into the kitchen. She opened the refrigerator and took out two cans of Bud Light. She walked back into the living room and handed one to Daniel.

"It looks like we finally got to have that real beer together. I'm sorry that it took me so long to make it down here. I got a little hung up. Actually, I got a little blown up," she joked.

"It's OK. I understand. I did make it to Boston though. I met your parents and Monica. I was still in the hospital in Germany when they held your funeral, but I went to visit the first chance that I got. I felt so guilty. I blamed myself. Things never should have happened the way that they did. I shouldn't have stopped when that man and his son crossed in front of us. I should have driven around them. I got complacent. I'm so sorry."

"It's not your fault. It was my time. I hope you understand that now. You are not to blame. I had a greater purpose ahead of me. That day was one short leg of a much longer journey."

"Do you miss it? Your life, I mean?"

"Yes, I do. When I died, the memories from my life remained with me. That was part of my sacrifice for the greater good. There are times that I envy those who cross into death, completely free from the constraints of their former lives. It's painful to be disconnected from the people that you love, knowing that you can never reconnect with them. Still, I feel lucky. I get to hold onto all of the good memories too, like when my parents and I went to Nantucket for vacation each summer, or the first time that Monica and I kissed. It is important that I remain connected to life, even in death. Without those memories, I wouldn't be able to perform the duties that I have been tasked with. They give me purpose."

"If it helps, your family was very proud of you. They miss you terribly, but they understand that you died doing something that you believed in. I was nervous about how they would react to seeing me, but they welcomed me with open arms. I told them how dedicated you were to the mission and how passionate you were about it. I tried to give them a sense of how you lived over there, not just how you died. We talked for hours. They showed me all of the pictures that they had of you growing up. They even showed me your report cards. I'd never seen so many A's in my life."

Aashirya smiled at the thought of her parents bragging about all of her accomplishments. They did it all the time when she was growing up. It used to embarrass her, but now she would give anything to witness it one more time.

"I also got a chance to speak with Monica. She loved you very much. When the Army sent your belongings home to your parents, they found the engagement ring that you bought for her. They gave it to her. Not only that, they purchased wedding bands for the both of you. They held a private ceremony so that the two of you could be married before they buried you. They insisted that your headstone read, *Beloved Wife and Daughter*."

"Thank you for telling me that. It means a lot. I was very lucky to have all of them in my life," Aashirya said as tears slid down her cheeks.

"Have you ever thought about going to see them and telling them about all of this?"

"No. It's not permitted. My life ended. I cannot go back. They have their own lives to live now without me and they each have to go their own way. If I returned to their lives, it could cause a disturbance in the balance. As I said, only the chosen are permitted to know about the true nature of existence. As difficult as it might seem, you must keep all of this hidden from the people that you love as well. It's for their own protection."

"What will happen if the balance is disturbed?"

"A small imbalance could lead to a greater one. If not undone, at a certain point, all existence would cease."

"Oh, so no big deal then."

"Daniel, this is very serious. You must heed my warning. You must not tell anyone about this, not even Sonya."

"You know about her?"

"I told you that I have been watching you. I had to so that I could gauge your state of mind before I approached you. I know that your feelings for her are strong. Keeping things from her will be difficult, but you must remain focused on what is at stake."

"I have the luxury of no longer being in the lives of the people that I love. You do not. This will be your sacrifice for the greater good. You were a soldier once, so you understand what is required to complete a mission. You will always have a responsibility to the people around you, but your first priority must always be to the mission. This mission must even be placed above the needs of those that you love the most. You must always remember that."

"I understand. I will do what is necessary. I promise."

"I know you will. Before I leave, there is one more thing that I must warn you about. When a person reaches their designated time of death, it is often hard for them to accept it. The thought that their life has come to an end is too much to bear. They will plead with you to return them to their body and their life. They will give you all kinds of reasons as to why you should grant their request. They will tell you that their children need them, or their spouse needs them, or that they still have so much to do. You will no doubt empathize with them and be tempted to do what they ask. While you also have the power to return their soul to their body, you must remain vigilant. You must remind yourself that there are greater concerns than that of a single life. Every person has a greater purpose than the life that they are leaving behind."

Aashirya turned and walked towards the door.

"Wait, how will I find you if I need you?"

"I will be close by. For now, you have everything that you need within yourself. Goodbye, Daniel."

"Goodbye. It was good to see you again. If you have any free time, feel free to drop in for another beer."

She smiled and walked out the door. Daniel was left in the middle of his apartment alone with his thoughts. He looked over at the coffee table, where his bottle of Risperdal was still sitting. He picked it up and went into the bathroom. There was a small plastic cup on the back edge of the sink. He turned the water on and filled it up. He opened up the bottle and stared down at the pills inside of it. He poured several of them into his hand. With the other hand, he picked up the cup of water. He paused and closed his eyes for a few seconds. When he opened them, he looked at his reflection in the mirror. The image of himself seemed clearer than it had in a very long time. He felt that he was finally in control of his own senses. He poured the water from the cup back into the sink. He then lifted up the toilet lid, turned his palm upside down, and let the pills fall into the water. He poured the remaining pills from the bottle into the toilet as well. Finally, he flushed the toilet and watched as all of the pills disappeared down the drain. When the last pill vanished, so too did his long-held belief that he was losing his mind.

Chapter 11

While it was the peak of the holiday shopping season, one would be unaware of that fact if they were shopping at 315 Comics. There were only a handful of customers in the shop. Shawn sat perched on a stool behind the sales counter enjoying a bag of potato chips and reading one of his favorite graphic novels, Watchmen. Watchmen was a twelve-issue limited series of comic books that was published by DC Comics in the eighties and then republished as a complete graphic novel later on. It chronicled the lives of former costumed heroes who struggled with their individual human weaknesses in a world that once looked to them to save it from itself, only to have it turn on them. He had read it dozens of times. It was a complex story with many layers. He seemed to discover a new aspect of the story each time he read it. It also helped pass the time when business was slow.

The front door chimed and a young woman entered the shop. Shawn was too engrossed in his comic to even look up.

"Excuse me. I was wondering if you could help me. Do you have the latest copy of Elektra?" the woman asked.

When he finally lifted his head to acknowledge her, he discovered that the voice belonged to his old friend. He nearly fell off his stool.

"Sonya? Is that really you?"

"As far as I know. How have you been, Shawn?"

"I can't believe it's you. It's been so long," he said as he rushed around the counter to give her a hug.

"It's been too long. I'm doing good. I can't believe that you own this place. I can't remember the last time that I was in here. It looks exactly the same."

"It's held up pretty well over the years. Still, it needs a few minor repairs and could use a fresh coat of paint. Unfortunately, I've had a little cash flow problem lately. People these days seem to be reading more and more comics online. It really cuts into business."

"You shouldn't change a thing. It's amazing. I missed this place. I couldn't even begin to guess how many hours that we all spent in here when we were kids. It really takes me back. How did you convince Bob to sell it to you?"

"I didn't. His wife did. Apparently, she had enough of upstate New York winters. They bought a house on the South Carolina coast. She told him that it was her or the comic book shop."

"Wow, and he chose her?"

"It surprised me too. She told him that she was taking the dog, so he gave in."

"I never thought I would see the day when Bob wasn't behind that counter. I'm glad that he sold it to you. I wish I had known. I would have come to visit. I'm sorry about that, I should have been a better friend."

"No, it's me who should apologize. I knew how rough it was on you when Daniel left. I should have called you to see how you were doing."

"You know what? Life is too short to be apologizing for every little thing. Why don't we agree that we are both assholes and move on?"

"Sounds good to me. Do you want something to drink? I have Coke, water, and a few beers in the fridge. Just a warning though, the beers might be a little skunky."

"Skunky beer sounds tempting, but I'll take a water."

Shawn took out a bottle of water from the mini-fridge behind the counter and handed it to her. He then told her to stay where she was as he ran into the back room. He returned a few seconds later with a stack of comic books in hand. He placed them on the counter in front of her.

"What's all this?"

"You asked me about Elektra comics, didn't you? Daniel told me that you were coming here today. I went through the shelves and pulled as many issues as I could find. You might have already read some of them, but they are always good for another read. They are all yours."

"Thank you so much. This means a lot. I can't believe you remembered," she said kissing him on the cheek.

"Are you kidding me? Of course, I remembered. Have you been keeping up with the latest issues?"

"No. I hate to admit it, but I haven't read any comics in quite some time. I'm ashamed of myself. I'm almost as bad as those traitors who read them online."

"Don't be so hard on yourself, and never compare yourself to online readers. They are going to bring down the whole industry. Now that you are here, you can make up for lost time. You can read as many issues as you want. If there are any new issues or series that you want, I can create an order list for you."

"You are the best, Shawn. I wish there was something that I could do for you."

"You being here is more than enough. However, if it's that important to you, you could always introduce me to your roommate. Daniel told me that she was in the "entertainment" industry."

"So, that's what Daniel told you, is it?"

"Yeah, you know, he mentioned that the two of you were kind of…"

"…kind of strippers," she said, finishing his sentence.

"I think the term he used was dancers, if I remember correctly. I don't have the greatest of memories. You know me," he said as his cheeks turned beet red.

"Yeah, I know you. Relax, I'm just messing with you. If you want, I'll introduce you to Alexis when she comes here to pick me up tomorrow. I'm warning you though, she is a bit of a handful. I'm not sure she is your type."

"My type? She is a girl, right?"

"Yes, she is most definitely a girl."

"Perfect. That is my type. I'm sure that we will get along famously. I'm assuming that her type is nerdy black guys who own their own comic book shops?"

"The guy part is her type, or girl for that matter. Beyond that, she goes for anyone with money."

"I see. I do have a savings bond that my grandmother gave me when I graduated high school. In a few more years, I will have seventy-five whole dollars. Do you think that she would be willing to wait that long?"

"With your charm, I don't see how she could resist. I'm finding it hard myself."

"I hate to disappoint you, but you are my best friend's girl. I could never take you away from him. I'm sorry. I hope you understand."

"I will do my best to get over it. I'll just have to live with the thought of what could have been and settle for my second choice. Speaking of which, where is he?"

"I assume he's upstairs in his apartment. He was supposed to be down for work a few hours ago, but I didn't want to bother him. I was hoping that he was getting some sleep. Last night was a little rough."

"Rough? What happened?"

"Oh. Nothing. You know, we just had a few too many. That's all. It happens. He probably needed to sleep it off," he replied, realizing that he might have said too much.

"I see. You seem fine. Why aren't you in bed or hunched over a toilet right now?"

"What I meant was, he had a few too many. I just had a couple. Also, I handle my liquor much better than he does."

"Right, like the time when we were drinking in your parent's basement while they were away for the weekend. I seem to remember you drinking two and a half Mike's Hard Lemonades and throwing up. That was before you passed out at 7:30 pm, if I recall correctly. I also remember helping Daniel carry you upstairs, where we put you into bed and tucked you into your Justice League sheets."

"If I didn't know any better, I would think that you were insulting me."

"Come on, Shawn. What's going on with Daniel?"

"I don't know if I should say anything. I'd feel like I would be betraying his confidence. I'm sure he will tell you when he is ready."

"Yes, I'm sure he will tell me all about his feelings. You men are so open and honest when it comes to that kind of thing. Look, you are not betraying his confidence. We all go back a long way. If one of us is in trouble, we should all know about it. I'm sure he will tell me eventually if I drag it out of him, but I want to know now. Please, it's important to me. I need to know if he is in trouble."

"OK, I will tell you. Just promise me that you won't say anything. He can't know that I told you. You will have to let him come to you in his own way."

"I promise. Now, out with it."

"It's not just one thing. It seems to be more of a combination of things. He has been going through a lot lately. Everything seems to be adding up and hitting him at once. I think it goes all the way back to when his father died. He's never really gotten over it. It left a huge hole inside of him. I remember when it happened. He never really talked about it. I don't remember seeing him cry, not even at the funeral. He just bottled it up and kept moving forward. The same thing happened when his mother was diagnosed with Multiple Sclerosis. He never showed any emotions about it. He wanted to be strong for her, just as he had been when they lost his father. He felt that it was his responsibility to take care of her. You remember how he was when they had to move her into assisted living. He didn't talk about it with either of us. He finally admitted to me last night that he left to join the Army because he was scared. He couldn't deal with everything that was happening in his life and he needed to escape. That's why he broke up with you. He also said that he regretted that decision and that he doesn't want to lose you again."

"He told me that too. I feel the same way about him."

"I'm happy about that. He is going to need you now more than ever. His mother is dying. Her doctor said that she only has six to nine months left. Her health has been steadily declining for some time now. I can see the pain in his eyes every time he looks at her. I know about it because I feel it myself. I've known Mrs. Jefferies my entire life. She's like a second mother to me. If I feel this way, I can only imagine what Daniel is going through."

"Oh my God. I didn't know. I mean, I knew she was sick, but I didn't know that it had gotten to that point. We didn't really get into it yesterday. It's understandable that he wouldn't want to talk about it. We haven't seen each other for so long. He must be devastated. It's only natural."

"Yeah, it's pretty bad. Unfortunately, it's not the only thing that he is dealing with right now."

"What do you mean?"

"I don't know exactly, but it might have something to do with his time in Iraq. He told me that he has been seeing things?"

"Seeing things? Like what?"

"People. He has been seeing dead people."

"You mean, like ghosts?"

"I'm not sure. I don't think he is either. He said the first time that he had an experience was the night his father died. I was at his house that night for our normal Friday night comic book debate. As usual, Mrs. Jefferies had to break it up because we broke our curfew. I went home. After I left, he said that he went up to bed and woke up in the middle of the night to find his father in his room staring down at him. He said they spoke for a few minutes and then Mr. Jefferies left. When he woke up in the morning, he went downstairs and found Mrs. Jefferies crying in the living room. His uncle was also there. When they told him that Mr. Jefferies died, he started looking around the house for him, thinking that he was still there. When they told him that he died at work, he didn't know what to think. He was convinced that he had been in his room just a few hours earlier. As time went on, he came to believe that it was just a very realistic dream. What else could it have been?"

"That makes sense. Everyone has woken up from a dream that they thought was real at one time or another. The fact that his father died that same night could just be a coincidence."

"That's the point that I made, but he also had a similar experience in Iraq. The day before his team was ambushed, they were called out to the edge of the city by the police chief. A young local woman was found strangled to death. According to him, there wasn't anything that they could do to help with the investigation because they had been ordered back to their headquarters. The next day, when they were on their way out of town, the IED went off underneath their vehicle. Daniel managed to get out of the vehicle and pull out his team leader, Keith. He went back to look for the third member of their team, a woman named Aashirya. He found her badly injured and close to death. He saw two people in the distance. He said that he ran towards them for help. When he caught up with them, they stopped. One of them turned around. He claims that the person who turned around was the same woman who was found murdered the day before. Before he could speak, he got dizzy and passed out. He didn't tell anyone about either experience until a few months ago. At the urging of his family and myself, he agreed to start seeing a psychiatrist at the VA. We obviously didn't know anything about these experiences, but it was very clear to all of us that he was struggling with something."

"What did his psychiatrist say?"

"From what he told me, she is not completely sure what is causing all of this. She told him that it could be any number of things. It's been so long since the night he saw his father, I don't know if it's possible for her to determine if it was a dream, a hallucination, or something else entirely. As far as seeing the murdered woman in Iraq, it could have been the result of physical trauma or extreme stress. While she is trying to figure it out, she prescribed him a drug called Risperdal. Among other effects, it is supposed to control hallucinations."

"Is the prescription helping? Has he had any further experiences?"

"He said that he has been seeing Aashirya, the woman on his team that was killed that day."

"Where has he seen her?"

"He said that he has seen her in three different locations around the city. Two nights ago, he was having a cigarette out front before locking up the shop for the night. He saw her walking into the café across the street. Last night, he was driving home from his aunt and uncle's house when he started to feel nauseous. He pulled into the high school parking lot to throw up. When he looked up, he saw her standing underneath a street light staring at him. He saw her for the third time later on in the night when we were both at Griffins. I saw a young Indian woman staring in our direction, but I couldn't tell you if it was her or not. I've never met her."

"Did you speak to her?"

"No. She walked out of the bar before we could talk to her. Daniel ran after her and I followed him. When we got outside, she was gone. We looked all over. There was no sign of her. Maybe I'm hallucinating too."

"What if it was just someone who looked like her? It could be a relative. It's possible. You saw someone, which means that he wasn't imagining it. Maybe we should try to find her? If we did, it might put his mind at ease."

"That's what my initial thought was too, but now I think it might be a good idea to just let it go."

"Let what go?" a voice said, interrupting their conversation.

Shawn and Sonya turned around to see Daniel walking in from the back room. His clothes were wrinkled and his hair was unkempt. He had the appearance of a man who slept in his clothes and just rolled out of bed."

"Is there any coffee?" he asked.

"I made some this morning, but it's probably cold by now," Shawn replied, hoping to avoid answering his first question.

"What time is it?"

"It's four o'clock in the afternoon."

Sonya jumped in the conversation, also trying to avoid the subject of their discussion.

"Shawn was just telling me that you two tied one on last night. It looks like you might have overdone it a bit. Are you feeling OK?"

"Yeah, I'm good. Just a few too many. I guess I'm not as young as I used to be. I must have passed out and lost track of time."

There was a coffee maker with a half-filled pot behind the counter. Its power went off hours earlier. Shawn picked up the pot, poured the room temperature brew into a Superman mug, and handed it to Daniel.

"So, what should you let go?" Daniel asked Sonya as he took a sip.

"What?" she asked, trying to deflect the question.

"Shawn was telling you that it would be a good idea to just let it go. Let what go?"

"Our endless DC versus Marvel debate. Like you, she tried to argue, futilely I might add, that Marvel superheroes could defeat DC superheroes. I put aside some Elektra comic books for her and we started discussing who would win in a fight, Elektra or Wonder Woman. Even though it's obvious that Wonder Woman would wipe the floor with Elektra, there was no need to argue. I suggested that in light of our friendship, we should just let it go," Shawn replied on Sonya's behalf.

"Yeah right. Since it's clear that neither one of you are going to tell me, I'm not going to bother asking any further. I don't have the energy right now."

"How was your ride down?" he asked Sonya.

"It was good. Alexis just dropped me off. She is staying at the Star Light Inn tonight. She'll pick me up here tomorrow morning, so we have the whole night."

"Sounds good. What do you want to do?"

"I was thinking about that the whole ride down here. There is something that I have been wanting to do for so long. I can't get it out of my mind. It's been driving me crazy. Would you be willing to do it for me?" she asked seductively kissing him.

"Do what exactly?"

"I want you to go upstairs, take a shower, and…"

She kissed him again to tease him.

"… order pizza and wings from O'Scunizzo's."

Daniel's jaw dropped as Shawn and Sonya burst out laughing.

"You want me to order pizza?"

"And wings. I like mine mild," Shawn said with a big grin.

"I like mine hot, but you already knew that," Sonya joked.

"You guys are killing me," Daniel said.

"Oh, sweetheart. Don't worry. We will have plenty of time for other activities. I promise that you won't be disappointed, but right now I'm starving. I've been dreaming about O'Scunizzo's. It's been so long since I've been home. You don't mind, do you?"

"No, I don't mind. I'm pretty hungry myself. I'll go upstairs, take a very cold shower, and call for delivery."

"Don't forget the celery and blue cheese," Shawn added.

Daniel shook his head and walked away. Shawn and Sonya waited until they were sure that he was out of earshot before they continued their conversation.

"That was close," Shawn whispered.

"Do you think that he knew what we were really talking about?" Sonya asked.

"I'm not sure, but I think we should avoid discussing it any further for now. He needs to put it out of his mind for a while. It's been so long since the three of us have hung out together. I think it will be good for him. Hopefully, it will take his mind off of things and remind him of better times."

Daniel walked into his kitchen and opened up a take-out menu from O'Scunizzo's Pizzeria. As he looked it over, he was reminded of all of the nights growing up that he spent with Shawn and Sonya eating pizza and reading comic books. He longed for those simpler times. Things were different now. He was different now. He would have to keep things from both of them. He wasn't sure if he would be able to do that. Aashirya told him that he possessed an inner strength. At that moment, strength was the last thing that he felt. He was consumed with self-doubt and fear. He couldn't lean on the people that he loved and trusted the most. He was about to celebrate a long-awaited reunion with his best friends, but he had never felt more alone in his life.

Chapter 12

Sonya awoke naked in bed to the sound of the shower running. When she rolled over, she found the other side of the bed empty. She sat up, rubbed her eyes, and looked around the room for her clothes. It took her a few seconds to recall taking everything off, with the exception of her underwear, in the living room the night before. She and Daniel were downstairs until 5:00 am with Shawn reading comic books and reminiscing about old times. When they finally made it upstairs, they couldn't keep their hands off of one another. She was surprised that they made it into the bedroom at all. She stood up and found her underwear lying on the floor on top of an old Wolverine T-shirt. She casually slipped into both articles of clothing. The T-shirt smelled like Daniel, which brought a smile to her face.

She made her way into the kitchen and began making coffee. After she flipped the switch to start the pot, she opened the refrigerator to look for some cream. All she found was a few beers and several half-empty condiment bottles. She searched the cabinets for sugar with the same result. When the coffee maker beeped, she resigned herself to the fact that she would be drinking it black. She made a mental note to take

Daniel shopping the first chance that she got. She loved him with all of her heart, but not enough to live on black coffee, Bud Light, and Frank's Red Hot.

She took a seat on the living room couch and sipped her freshly brewed cup of black coffee. The bitterness of it overwhelmed her. She immediately spat it back out into her cup and decided that she would make Daniel take her out for coffee when he got out of the shower. She also added fresh coffee to her mental shopping list.

On the coffee table in front of her were the stack of Elektra comic books that Shawn gave her when she arrived. She managed to read through most of them the night before. When she and Daniel were finally alone, she had a fleeting thought of continuing to read them in lieu of having sex with him, although she could never admit that to him. She knew that he would never let her live it down. Once they began kissing and ripping each other's clothes off, comic books were the last thing on her mind. However, now that their night of passion was over, she couldn't wait to get back to it. She picked up an issue from 1996 and dove right in.

Several minutes later, Daniel walked out of the bathroom with only a towel wrapped around his waist. She didn't notice. She was too caught up in her comic. He walked over to the couch and took a seat next to her. He kissed her on the cheek. Still, she didn't acknowledge him.

"I think you might have a problem." he joked.

"The only vegetable in your refrigerator is a bottle of relish, and you think that I am the one with the problem?"

"Actually, I think that's a bottle of ketchup. I might have left it in there slightly past its expiration date."

"That's disgusting."

"In my defense, those dates are only a suggestion. The dates on the packages are much earlier than the dates when the food actually goes bad. It's a conspiracy engineered by the corporate food industry to keep getting you to buy new products. It's my little way of fighting the man."

"So, starving yourself and getting food poisoning is your way of fighting corporate greed?"

"It's more of a byproduct of my inherent laziness. The fighting corporate greed part is just a bonus."

"It's a miracle that you are even alive right now."

"You sound a lot like my Aunt Deanna."

"She sounds like a very wise woman. She will be happy to know that I will be taking you grocery shopping today. That is, after you take me somewhere to get a decent cup of coffee."

"That reminds me, the coffee in the cabinet might be a little past its prime as well. Also, I can't remember the last time I cleaned that pot."

"Thanks for the warning," she said cringing.

"I appreciate the offer to take me shopping, but I thought that you were heading back to Syracuse today with Alexis."

"I was, but I was thinking that I could stay longer. After all, I haven't finished reading all of my comics yet. I still have several years to catch up on. You don't mind, do you?"

Daniel didn't mind at all. In fact, he wanted her to stay permanently. He was going to bring up the subject, but he didn't want to seem as if he was moving too quickly. He decided that the best way to proceed was to let things happen naturally and to let her decide for herself what she wanted to do. Extending her visit was a good first step in his mind.

"I don't mind. It's a win-win for both of us. You can finish reading your comic books and I can enjoy a few meals that aren't served in a paper bag or a Styrofoam container."

"I also plan on buying you a vacuum cleaner. I assume that you don't currently own one?"

"That would be a safe assumption. Are you going to call Alexis to tell her not to pick you up?"

"I'll just let her know when she gets here. I was going to ask her to hang out for a bit. I promised Shawn that I would introduce them. I owe him for the comic books."

"I see. Do you think that she will go for him?"

"Let's put it this way. Compared to some of the guys that she has been with, hooking up with Shawn will be like hooking up with Brad Pitt."

"Shawn Lewis. Brad Pitt. Yep, I've been saying it for years. They are practically twins separated at birth. What time is she coming by to meet her leading man?"

"She said that she would be here at noon. What time is it now?"

"It's almost 4:00 pm."

"Seriously? I didn't know it was that late."

Sonya searched the room for the jeans that she was wearing the night before. She found them in a large pile of clothes, some of which were Daniel's. She pulled out her cell phone and checked to see if she had any text messages or missed calls. To her surprise, there were none. She pulled up her contact list and pressed the call icon next to Alexis' name. The call went straight to voicemail.

"Is everything OK?" Daniel asked.

"I don't know. Alexis hasn't called or texted me. She was supposed to be here four hours ago. Now she is not picking up."

"You said that she was going to see her boyfriend/drug dealer. That doesn't strike me as a quiet, in bed by nine, type of evening. She was probably out late and overslept."

"Maybe. She can certainly party with the best of them. It's just that she has never left me hanging before. We always let each other know where the other one is at, no matter what the circumstances are. It's our way of looking out for one another."

"What about her boyfriend? Do you know his phone number or where he lives? She might still be with him."

"All I know is that his name is Jake and he lives in Cornhill. I only met him once, briefly. I don't have his number and I don't know his address or last name."

"The Star Light Inn is just a few miles away. Why don't we get dressed and I'll drive you down there?"

"OK, maybe she is just asleep in the room and didn't hear the phone. It would make me feel a lot better to just know. Thank you. I'll be ready in a few minutes."

Twenty minutes later, they pulled into the Star Light Inn parking lot. It was a two-story motel located just off of exit thirty-one on the New York State Thruway. Most of the guests were people passing through for the night on business, or teenagers looking for a place to party.

There were six cars in the parking lot. None of them belonged to Alexis. Sonya recognized that fact immediately. It gave her a slightly queasy feeling in her stomach. Daniel parked in front of the main lobby. When they walked in, there was no one behind the front desk. The décor looked as if it hadn't been updated since the earlier eighties. Despite the no smoking sign, there was a pungent aroma of stale menthol cigarettes in the air.

Sonya rang the bell on the counter. A heavy-set woman with red hair and a perm walked out from the back room. She was wearing a white collared button-down shirt and a dark blue blazer with matching slacks. She had a gold metal pin on her lapel with the name, *Dianne*, printed in black letters.

"Can I help you?" she asked

"Yes, I'm looking for my roommate. She checked in yesterday. Would you be able to tell me what room she is in? Her name is Alexis Nesmith," Sonya replied.

Dianne looked up her name on the computer.

"Let's see here. It looks like she checked in yesterday afternoon at 4:30 pm. She paid for one night. Her scheduled checkout time was 11:00 am this morning. She was in room 207."

"Did she check out already?"

"It doesn't look like it. Our guests can check out from the TV menu in their room, or they can come to the front desk. It doesn't look like she did either one. Let me call the room to see if she is still in there."

She picked up the phone and dialed Alexis' room. She let it ring six times before she hung up.

"No one is picking up. Sometimes people are in a hurry and leave without formally checking out. I'm sorry. There is no other way for me to know when she left."

"Has anyone cleaned her room yet? If her things are still in there, she might be coming back to get them," Daniel asked.

"Let me call housekeeping."

She picked up the phone again and dialed housekeeping.

"Hi, this Dianne at the front desk. Has room 207 been cleaned yet?"

There was a brief pause.

"OK. Thank you."

She hung up and then looked back up at Daniel and Sonya.

"There is a maid in the room cleaning it right now. If you want to go take a look, take a left out of the lobby and go up the staircase. Room 207 will be the second room on your left."

"Thank you very much. We appreciate your help," Daniel said.

"No problem. I hope you find your friend."

Daniel and Sonya followed Dianne's directions and made their way up the stairs to the second level. When they arrived at the room, the door was open and there was a maid's cart parked outside. As they entered the room, they found the maid uniform vacuuming the floor. She turned off the vacuum when she saw them enter.

"Hello. Did you come back for your things? I haven't had a chance to gather them up and take them to the office yet. Everything should still be where you left it," the woman said.

"My roommate was staying here. We are looking for her. These are her things. Did you happen to see anyone come in or out of this room?" Sonya asked.

"No. I'm sorry. I haven't. My shift started about an hour ago. I cleaned two rooms on this level before this one and I haven't seen anyone up here. It doesn't look like your roommate spent much time in here. Both beds were still made when I came in. There is a make-up bag in the bathroom and a small suitcase by the bed. You can take them to her if you would like."

Sonya didn't respond. She stood silently in the middle of the room contemplating all of the possible explanations for why Alexis hadn't slept in the room or called her yet. When she couldn't come up with one that satisfied her, she turned and walked out onto the concrete walkway to try calling Alexis again. The call went straight to voicemail for the second time. This time, she left a message after the beep.

"Hey, where are you? You were supposed to pick me up hours ago. Daniel and I are at the motel looking for you. If you are on your way to the comic book shop, just wait there. We will be back there soon. Please call me as soon as you get this. I'm worried."

"She is still not picking up. I don't know what's going on. I have a bad feeling that something has happened to her. I don't know what to do," she said to Daniel as he joined her out on the walkway.

"Ok, try to keep calm. We shouldn't jump to any conclusions. It could be anything. Maybe her car wouldn't start and her phone died. Like I said before, she could have been out late last night and is still sleeping at her boyfriend's house. The point is that we don't know. We shouldn't start worrying just yet. She could be on her way over to 315 as we speak, so we should go back there and wait for her for a little while longer."

"I can't just wait around and do nothing. I'll go crazy worrying about her. We should try to find her boyfriend."

"I understand that you are worried, but I don't think it's a good idea for us to start driving aimlessly around Cornhill looking for a drug dealer. It's going to be dark soon."

"Daniel, I grew up in that neighborhood. I don't care if it is dangerous. I need to find her."

Seeing how determined she was, he realized that he was not going to change her mind.

"Ok, how about we compromise then? Why don't we go down to the police station and talk to my cousin, Nick? We don't know anything about this guy other than his first name and what neighborhood he lives in. Nick is a detective. He has a lot more resources at his disposal than we do, so he has a much better chance of finding him. What do you say?"

"OK, as much as I don't want to wait any longer, you are probably right. Let's go see him."

Sonya grabbed Alexis' makeup bag from the bathroom and Daniel picked up her suitcase. They thanked the maid for her help and walked back down to the car. They put the bags in the trunk and drove off in the direction of the Utica City Police Department.

Nick was at his desk filling out some paperwork for a drug bust that took place earlier that day. A local nurse practitioner had been stealing prescription drugs from the hospital where he worked and then selling them out of his grandmother's house in Rome, NY. The grandmother was eighty-seven years old and confined to her bed.

Six months earlier, Nick got assigned to a joint task force that included the FBI, the New York State Police, and six other local police departments. Their goal was to target and take down drug rings in Central New York.

Over the last year, law enforcement agencies began noticing a significant increase in the amount of illegal opioid sales. Dealers were trading in Ecstasy and Marijuana for Oxycodone and Heroin. While all illegal drugs carried risks, opioids were particularly dangerous due to their highly addictive nature and higher likelihood of overdose. Overdoses were becoming a serious problem. It wasn't just the number of people that it affected, it was also who it affected. The problem wasn't relegated to one particular group of people. Everyone from gang bangers, to high school students, to adult professionals were using the drugs. No one seemed to be immune from the clutches of addiction. Most of the drugs that were turning up on the streets came from China. They were shipped into Mexico and smuggled over the border into the United States. From there, they were distributed all throughout the country. That was the reason that the FBI was involved.

Nick had been working on the arrest report for three straight hours and wasn't even halfway done. Paperwork was his least favorite thing about police work. His fingers started cramping up and he was beginning to see spots. He looked at his watch. He only had twenty minutes left on his shift. He was planning on meeting Karen for drinks at the Hotel Utica after work. He reserved a suite for the two of them for the night. The plan was to unwind at the bar and then head up to the room. They recently decided that they were going to try and have a baby. Nick figured that a romantic night out of the house would be a good way to begin trying. He'd been looking forward to it all day. Since it was clear that he was not going to finish his report in the time that he had remaining on his shift, he decided to cut out a few minutes early. Just as he was about to leave, he heard someone call his name.

"Detective Morello."

He looked up and saw the desk sergeant escorting Daniel and Sonya over to his desk.

"I'm sorry to bother you, detective. This young man said that he is your cousin and that he needs to speak with you."

"Thanks, sergeant."

He stood up and greeted Daniel with a hug.

"This is a bit of a surprise. I don't think I can ever remember you coming down here to see me. I'm glad you are here though. I was a little worried about you after you took off the other night. Is everything OK?"

"I'm fine. There is something else that I need to talk to you about."

"Ok. Why don't you guys have a seat?" Nick said as he shifted his gaze towards Sonya.

"What's going on?"

"It's about Sonya's roommate, Alexis. She is missing."

"Missing? For how long?"

"She was supposed to pick me up at Daniel's place today at noon. She never showed up. I tried calling her, but her phone kept going to voicemail. We went to the motel where she was staying while she was in town. She wasn't there, and it looked like she hadn't been back to her room since she checked in yesterday afternoon," Sonya replied.

Nick pulled out a legal pad and a pen from his desk drawer to take notes.

"Alright, why don't we start from the beginning? Your roommate's name is Alexis. What is her last name?"

"It's Nesmith."

"How long have you been roommates?"

"Five years."

"I'm assuming that you came into town to visit Daniel. What was her reason for coming into town?"

Sonya turned to Daniel before answering. Daniel nodded to her as a signal that Nick could be trusted.

"She comes to Utica once a month to dance at Peepers," she replied.

"Is dancing her part-time job or her full-time job?"

"She works full-time at Fantasies in Syracuse. I work there too."

Nick had no idea that Sonya had been working as a stripper, but it was not the first time he heard something that surprised him in the course of his duties as a police officer. Over time, he learned to suppress his emotions when he was interviewing witnesses and suspects. In order to maintain the upper hand as a cop, he had to keep people from knowing what he was really thinking. He decided to continue his line of questioning without acknowledging her revelation.

"I'm wondering why she would make the trip from Syracuse to Utica just to dance at Peepers. Peepers is less than half the size of Fantasies. I would assume that she makes more money dancing at Fantasies. Why would she go to all that trouble to make less money?"

"The main reason that she makes the trip is to see her dealer, who also happens to be her on again, off again boyfriend. She dances at Peepers to break even while she is here."

"This boyfriend, do you know his name? Where he lives? What he looks like?" Nick asked as the situation became clearer to him.

"I only met him once. His name is Jake. I don't know his last name. He stopped by our apartment in Syracuse once for a few minutes, two years ago. Alexis introduced him to me, but he didn't say very much while he was there. He lives somewhere in Cornhill. I don't know the exact address. He is about five-foot-ten and has an average build and light brown hair. When I met him, his face was unshaven, but he didn't have a fully-grown beard. He had on jeans, a black sweat-shirt, and one of those green Vietnam-style army jackets. I'm not sure if that is helpful."

"It's very helpful. You would be surprised how much the little details end up mattering. Did Alexis ever mention if Jake was ever violent towards her, or if he had a temper?"

"No. She didn't talk about him that much. I know she never came home with any visible cuts or bruises after visiting him, and she never seemed upset afterwards."

"How about her? Has she ever taken off like this? Does she party a lot?"

"Like I told Daniel, she is a party girl, but she has never taken off without letting me know about it first. We watch out for one another. You have to when you do what we do. She has always been a loyal friend to me. She's not perfect, but she is a good person."

"She sounds like it."

Nick could sense the worry in Sonya's voice as she answered his questions. He decided to shift the questioning to Daniel to give her a break.

"What motel was she staying at?"

"The Star Light Inn in North Utica," Daniel replied.

"And when you were at the motel, what gave you the impression that she hadn't been back to the room since she checked in?"

"When we got to the room, the maid was vacuuming. She told us that the beds were still made up when she came into the room to clean."

"What about family or friends? Is there anyone that she might have called or gone to see for any reason?" Nick asked turning back to Sonya.

"No. Her mom took off when she was born. She doesn't know who her father is, and her grandmother died when she was ten. She grew up in the system. She took off on her own when she was fifteen and has never mentioned any other family. The only friends I know about are girls from the club. I can't think of any reason why she would take off to see one of them without telling me."

"OK. I think I have what I need for now. Just so you are both aware, I can't file an official missing persons' report for an adult until they have been missing for at least forty-eight hours. The only exception would be if we had clear evidence that the person missing was forcefully abducted or in harm's way. However, I can do some unofficial poking around in the meantime. I'll swing by Peepers and talk to the staff to see when they last saw her. I have a few informants that I can reach out to that might be able to help identify this boyfriend of hers. If I find anything, I will let you know. If we haven't found anything in forty-eight hours, I will file the missing persons' report, but hopefully it won't come to that. Sonya, will you be staying in Utica, or were you planning on going back to Syracuse?"

"She is staying with me. If you need to get a hold of us, just call my cell," Daniel replied for her.

"OK. If you hear from her, give me a call as well."

"Thanks, Nick. I appreciate it, man," Daniel said.

"No problem. You're family."

"Yes, thank you. Your help means a lot to me," Sonya said.

"Try not to worry too much. It's only been a few hours. There could be any number of reasons why you haven't heard from her yet."

Daniel and Sonya said goodbye to Nick and walked out of the station. Daniel put his arm around her as they made their way out of the building and into the parking lot. When they arrived at the car, he walked her around to the passenger side door and opened it for her. Once she sat down, he closed the door and walked back around the front of the car to the driver's side. His phone vibrated just as he was about to open the door. He pulled it out of his pocket and saw a text message from an unknown caller.

It read, "Proctor Park, Park Street, Starch Factory Creek."

It was sent just as Aashirya had told him it would be. He knew instantly what the message meant. A member of his flock had reached their designated time of death.

Chapter 13

In the early hours of the morning, Daniel gazed up at his bedroom ceiling with his eyes wide open. Sonya lay in bed next to him, sound asleep. She had finally passed out thirty minutes earlier. She'd grown increasingly worried since they left the police station. For each hour that passed without word of Alexis, she became more convinced that something terrible had happened to her. Daniel persuaded her to take a sleeping pill. He had a prescription from the VA, which he only took on occasion, so he had plenty to spare. His motivation for urging her to take it was two-fold. He wanted her to get some rest, but more importantly, he wanted to ensure that she would not wake up when he was out of the apartment. Aashirya warned him that he could not reveal the nature of his duties to anyone. As he sat up and looked down at her sleeping, it occurred to him that he would have to find a better way of concealing his work from her in the future. He couldn't give her a sleeping pill every time that he had to sneak out in the middle of the night. However, at that moment, he couldn't think of a viable alternative. He decided to table that thought for a later time.

He glanced over at the alarm clock on the nightstand, which read 2:00 am, as he picked up his clothes and walked into the living room to get dressed. He wanted to avoid making even the slightest sound, fearing that it could wake her up. Once he was dressed, he opened the closet door in the entryway and pulled out a black North Face jacket, a pair of fleece gloves, and a ski hat. He also pulled out a military-style tactical backpack. It was the same one that he'd carried throughout his combat tours in Iraq and Afghanistan.

He placed the backpack on the couch and unzipped it. It had been sitting in the closet since he was discharged. He hadn't had any need or desire to use the contents in it until that night. It contained a Mini-Maglite flashlight with a red lens, a GPS device, a pocket knife, and an entrenching tool. The entrenching tool was primarily used to dig fighting positions. He wasn't sure if the person that he was looking for would be buried or not. He thought that it would be a good idea to bring it with him just in case. His military training instilled in him a sense to be prepared for any situation.

When he was done inventorying his gear, he put on his coat, hat, and gloves, and made his way down the stairs and into the parking lot. The temperature had dropped significantly since he was last outside. He could see his breath in the air and there was a thick layer of frost now covering his Jeep. He quickly got into the vehicle and turned on the heater. While he was waiting for it to warm up, he input the location that had been texted to him earlier into his GPS. The location was Proctor Park, Park Street, Starch Factory Creek. Proctor Park was a large area. Based on his reading of the digital map on his GPS, he surmised that the person he was looking for would be located somewhere in the southeast corridor of the park. That still left a significant amount of land to search. It would be difficult to cover all of that ground during the day, let alone at night. Park Street ran parallel to the creek. He decided that the best way to search the area would be to start on the street and walk in a straight line towards the creek. Once at the creek, he would walk ten meters south, turn, and then walk in a straight line back to the street. He would repeat the process while continually moving in a southerly direction until he found the person he was looking for. It would be time-consuming and he wasn't sure if he would have enough time to search the entire area before the sun came up. He also had to make it back to his apartment before Sonya woke up.

As the car began to warm up, the frost started melting off the windshield. He flipped on the wipers to clear away the remaining frost and drove out of the parking lot towards the park. The streets were eerily quiet at that time of night. It was almost the end of December. At that time of year, the chilling temperatures kept most people indoors, especially at night.

He arrived at his destination fifteen minutes later. He turned off his headlights as he pulled onto Park Street. If somebody was passing by, it might seem suspicious that someone was driving through the park at that hour. He didn't want to attract any undue attention to himself. The moonlight was bright enough to guide him along the road. He slowed his speed to five miles per hour and drove to a clearing at the end of the road, which separated the northern section of the park from the southern section. He pulled over a few meters off the road into the woods. He wanted to make sure that his vehicle was concealed while he was searching the area. The last thing that he needed was someone to see his license plate number and report it to the police. He would have a hard time explaining the reason for his being there.

When he was satisfied that it was sufficiently hidden, he turned off the engine. He grabbed his backpack and stepped out into the darkness to begin his search. He pulled out the flashlight from his backpack and switched it on. The red lens provided him with an area of visibility of just a few feet. It was designed to be used in tactical situations to avoid detection from enemy combatants. Even though he had a lot of ground to cover, he would have to move slowly and search methodically. If he moved too quickly, he could easily miss his objective.

He began moving east. He rotated three hundred sixty degrees with each step that he took, carefully surveying the small area within the confines of the red beam of light. It took him more than thirty minutes to reach the creek for the first time. He looked at his watch. It was now 3:15 am. He estimated that he had between two and a half and three hours before the sun came up. It was not nearly enough time to search the entire area. Unfortunately, there were no shortcuts available to him. He would have to continue walking the line between the road and the creek. He knelt down in front of the creek and cupped his hands to scoop up some water. In all of his meticulous planning, he forgot to pack the most basic of survival items, fresh water. After a few handfuls, he continued his search.

As the night went on, the temperature continued to drop dramatically. His extremities began to go numb and feel like pins and needles. It was a familiar sensation, but one he hadn't felt in a while. In Iraq, the temperatures during the days could reach well into the one-hundreds. At night, they could drop into the thirties and forties. The extreme shift could cause one's body to feel as if it was much colder than it actually was. He remembered thinking that some nights felt more like a deployment to the arctic than to the desert. Those experiences made him resilient. They taught him to never give up and move forward, no matter how difficult things might seem.

He continued to focus on searching every square inch of the ground that he covered. He lost track of the time, but he knew that it was running short. He stopped for a moment to check his watch when heard the sound of leaves crackling. He stood still and shined the flashlight in the direction of the sound, but he didn't see anything. He started shifting the light to his left, when he heard it again. This time, it didn't stop, and it was getting closer. He realized that the sound he was hearing was footsteps and they were heading straight towards him. A few seconds later, a pair of glowing red eyes pierced through the blackness in front of him. Based on their height from the ground, he could tell that it was some type of animal. As it moved further into the light, it took shape. It was a wolf. He stood still for a few seconds and then slowly stepped backwards, hoping to avoid provoking it. As he moved back, he felt something catch his left heel. Before he could steady himself, he fell onto his back. Luckily, he fell into a large pile of leaves, so he didn't hurt himself. He did, however, lose his grip on his flashlight, which fell out of his hand. He spotted it on the ground a few feet to the right of where he was lying. He crawled over to pick it up. As he grabbed it, he felt a cold, wet nose brush up against his cheek. When he looked up, he saw the wolf standing over him. He remained frozen in place on all fours, staring directly into its eyes. It didn't make any sudden movements. It just stood there lightly panting with its tongue hanging out. After a few more seconds, it licked him on his cheek. He didn't know much about wolves, but he was sure that they weren't that friendly. He got up onto his knees and looked the animal over. He saw a collar around its neck with a gold oval-shaped pendant hanging from it. It had the name Riley engraved on the front of it. On the back, there was an address. He recognized it. It was only a few miles from the park. It wasn't a wolf after all. It was a dog. More specifically, it was a Siberian Husky, which could easily be mistaken for a wolf.

Once his heart stopped pounding, he started laughing.

"What are you doing out here at this time of night, girl? Did you sneak out of your house to meet your boyfriend?"

The dog barked in response. She then lightly bit down on the arm of his jacket and tugged at it. It seemed as if she wanted him to follow her. When he stood up, she turned around and started walking. He followed close behind her. She stopped after fifty feet. He knelt down beside her and petted her head.

"Ok, I'm here. What do you have to show me?"

This time, she let out three quick barks in response.

He shined the flashlight in the direction that she was barking, but he didn't see anything. He started to wonder if she thought that they were playing a game. Suddenly, she jumped up and batted the flashlight out of his hand.

"Hey, that's not funny. What are you trying to do to me?"

"Come to think of it, what I am trying to do to me? I'm in a park in the middle of the night, in December no less, looking for a dead body. This is nuts! I think it's time to go home. What do you say, Riley? Do you want to get out of here? I'm sure your owners will be worried about you when they wake up and see that you ran off. Why don't you let me give you a lift home? What do you say? I'll just pick up my flashlight, that you decided to knock out of my hand for some unknown reason, and we will be on our way."

As he bent over to pick it up, he saw a dull greyish glow emanating from the ground just to his left. When he moved in closer, he saw a person's arm sticking out of a pile of leaves. His heart felt like it came to a dead stop. He could feel drops of perspiration forming on his forehead. His instincts were to run away as fast as he could and not look back. He fought back those instincts. He had a job to do. He had to see it through, no matter how frightening it might seem. He took a deep breath and moved next to the body. Except for the arm, it was completely covered in leaves. It took him a minute to remove all of them. As he brushed them off, he could see that the dull greyish glow was emanating from the entire body. It was just as Aashirya had described it to him. He removed the leaves from the face last. He recognized the person immediately. It was Alexis. The unexpected sight made him jump back.

He wondered how this could have happened? Someone had to have killed her and left her there. There was no other explanation. How was he going to tell Sonya? She would be devastated. He quickly realized that he couldn't tell her. He couldn't tell anybody. He would simply have to wait until her body was discovered by someone else. He wasn't there to solve her murder. He was there to release her soul. Still, the thought of knowing that she was dead and leaving her there while Sonya continued to worry, made him nauseous.

At that moment, he had no other choice. The sun would be up soon. He had to work quickly. He would have to worry about the consequences later. He tried to calm himself down and remember what Aashirya told him to do. He had to place his hand over her chest and concentrate so that he could connect with her light energy. He closed his eyes and put his hand in place. He cleared his mind. After a few seconds, he began to feel a surge of energy flow up through his hand, into his arm, and then throughout his entire body. Once his body was immersed in the energy, he noticed the presence of a second consciousness in his mind, separate from his own. It was Alexis. He didn't know how it was possible, but he was sure that it was her. He felt her try to pull away from him. He could sense that she was afraid. He pulled her in closer until she stopped struggling, and then he removed his hand from her chest. When he looked down, the dull greyish glow was gone. All that was left was a pale corpse.

"Where am I?" he heard a woman's voice say from behind him.

He turned around and saw Alexis standing in front of him. He then looked back and saw that her body was still on the ground. He had done it. He released her soul from her body. He stood up and faced her. It took her a few seconds to recognize him.

"Daniel? Is that you? Is Sonya with you? What's going on?"

He searched for the right words. He didn't quite know how to explain the situation to her.

"I'm here to help you, Alexis."

"Help me? Help me with what? What is this place? How did I get here?"

"This is Proctor Park in Utica. I don't know how you got here. There is no way easy way to say this. You were killed. Your life has come to an end. I'm here to help you cross into death."

"Stay away from me. I don't know what you are up to. If you come any closer, I will scream," she said backing away from him.

He took a few steps back himself to assure her that he wasn't there to harm her.

"I know how this sounds, but I am telling you the truth. You died, and it appears that someone killed you. I'm not sure who it was, or why they did it. The only thing that I was told was that there was a soul waiting for me at this location. That's why I'm here. I'm what's known as a Shepherd. I have been chosen to guide you from life into death. I found you on the ground under a pile of leaves and I released your soul from your body. While you are standing there talking to me right now, your body is still on the ground. See for yourself."

He turned and pointed towards her body. She approached it slowly. She didn't know how to explain what she was seeing. Lying before her, was her. She wondered how it could be possible. She didn't want to accept it. She tried rationalizing it and told herself that she had been drugged and was hallucinating. She wanted to run away, but she couldn't. Her own fear paralyzed her.

"I'm not sure if you will believe me when I tell you this, but everything will be OK. Death is a part of life. Once you cross over, all of the pain that you have felt in your life will be taken away. You will be at peace."

"Why did this happen? I know I'm no saint, but why would somebody do this to me?" she asked as she began to cry.

"I'm sorry. I don't have that answer for you. Do you remember anything that happened?"

She closed her eyes and tried to think back. Her memory felt clouded. She was only able to recall a few details of where she was before she found herself in the park talking to Daniel.

"I can't remember much. The last thing that I remember was getting into my car outside of the club. I felt something tight around my neck. I couldn't breathe. Everything went black. That's it. That's all I can remember before I found myself here."

"It's OK. You don't have to worry about that now."

"What happens now?" she asked as her voice shook.

"You will leave this life and enter into death. Before you do, you will be given the chance to see one person from your life for a few moments, if you wish. It will be your opportunity to say goodbye, although they will not be aware of your presence."

She was silent for a few minutes while she thought about who she wanted to see.

"Can it be anyone, even someone that I've never met before?"

"Yes."

"Then, I would like to see my father. My grandmother never told me who he was when she was alive. I don't think she knew herself. I'm not even sure if he is alive, but if he is, that is who I would like to see."

"Close your eyes and concentrate. Clear your mind and then think only of your father. When you open your eyes, you will be with him."

Alexis followed Daniel's instructions. She closed her eyes and tried to picture her father in her head. Having never met him, she pictured the image of him that she created for herself as a child. When she opened her eyes, she was no longer in the park. She was in a child's bedroom. The room was dimly lit with a night light. She could see a white crib and a matching changing table. The walls were decorated with pink teddy bears and balloons. It was a young girl's room. She heard a man's voice. She turned around and saw him sitting in a rocking chair, holding a baby. He was reading her a story. She recognized the book immediately. It was *Good Night Moon*. Her grandmother used to read it to her when she was little. She still knew the whole thing by heart. The baby fell asleep as the man read the last few lines.

"Good night stars. Good night air. Good night noises everywhere."

He then closed the book and carried her over to the crib, where he gently laid her down and covered her with a pink fleece blanket.

"Goodnight my sweet Emma. Your Daddy loves you very much."

Finally, he turned and walked out of the room. Alexis stared down at the sleeping baby. She was overcome with emotion as she realized that she was staring down at her baby sister. She hadn't had any family in her life since her grandmother died. She had felt so alone for so long. She regretted not trying to find her father. She thought that if she only knew he was out there, and that she had a baby sister, things might have turned out differently for her. She felt tears streaming down her face as she closed her eyes once again. When she opened them, she found herself back in the park with Daniel.

"It's time," Daniel said.

A bright light appeared behind them, which illuminated the entire area.

"Please, I'm not ready. Can you let me stay? I saw my father for the first time. He has a baby daughter. She's my sister. There's so much I want to do. I want to get to know them both. I want to see her grow up. I know I've done some stupid things in my life, and I've wasted a lot of time, but if you give me another chance, I'll make my life count for something. I promise," she said, pleading with him.

Daniel recalled what Aashirya told him about people not being ready to accept that their lives were over.

"I'm sorry. I can't do that. It's not up to me. I'm simply here to guide you to the other side. We all have a designated time of death. This is yours. You must go forward into the light now."

Realizing that there was nothing further she could do to convince him, she gave up fighting the inevitable.

"OK, I understand. I will go, but before I do, could you promise me something?"

"Of course."

"I don't know if my father even knows about me. Could you try to find him and tell him about me? I just want him to know that he had another daughter. I want his daughter to know that she had a big sister. It would mean a lot to me."

"I will try my best."

"Also, take care of Sonya. Neither one of us had anyone that we could really count on before we met each other. We looked out for one another. Now that I'm gone, she is going to need someone to be there for her. I know how much she loves you. It's going to be hard on her when she finds out what happened to me."

"I will."

"Goodbye, Daniel. I'm glad that I got a chance to meet you. You are a good person and Sonya is lucky to have you in her life."

With that, she turned and walked into the light. She disappeared along with the light itself. Daniel looked up into the sky and saw the beginnings of daylight creeping into night. He knew he had to get back to his car and get home before Sonya woke up. There was nothing left for him to do there.

"Come on, girl, it's time to go home," he called out to Riley.

She barked and ran off. He didn't want to leave her in the park, but he didn't have the time to chase her down. She wasn't that far from home. He figured that she would make it back there on her own or her owners would find her walking through the park eventually. He tightened the straps on his backpack and jogged through the woods to the road. He made it to his car just as the first beams of sunlight started shining over the horizon. He looked around to make sure that no one else was around. It was still early for walkers and joggers to be out. When he was convinced that it was clear, he turned on his engine and drove off as fast as he could.

Chapter 14

For the second morning in a row, Sonya woke up in an empty bed. Unlike the previous morning, she was fully clothed. Still groggy from the sleeping pill that Daniel gave her the night before, she staggered into the living room, expecting to find him. To her surprise, he wasn't there. She looked around for a note but didn't find one. She also checked her phone, hoping that there would be a message from him, but again, there was none. It seemed odd to her that he would have gone out somewhere without telling her with all that was going on.

A few minutes later, he walked through the door. He was carrying two cups of coffee and a small white paper bag. She could smell the distinct aroma of fresh baked goods. Before he could say a word, she rushed over to him and wrapped her arms tightly around him. He tried to hug her back, but he couldn't because both of his hands were full.

"Is everything OK? Did something happen when I was gone?" he asked.

"No. I'm sorry. I didn't mean to alarm you. I was just worried when I woke up and you were gone. I know it's stupid. I'm just a little on edge with Alexis still missing."

"It's not stupid. You have every right to be upset. You were still sound asleep when I woke up. I ran across the street to get some coffee and croissants so that you would have something to eat for breakfast since we didn't get a chance to go grocery shopping yesterday. You were up so late last night. I figured that you would still be asleep when I got back. I'm sorry if I made you worry," he said as he handed her one of the cups of coffee.

"Don't feel sorry. It was very thoughtful of you to get breakfast. I'm actually pretty hungry. Are their croissants any good?"

He handed her one from the bag. They were still warm.

"They are the best. They bake them fresh every morning. Also, their coffee selection is slightly better than what I currently have on hand. I had them put in three creams and two packets of Splenda for you. I assumed that you still took it that way."

"Yes, I do. I can't believe that you remember how I take my coffee after all of this time."

"What can I say? I'm the perfect guy," he said blushing.

"Yes, you are, and you are all mine. I love you."

"I love you too."

"What time is it anyway?" she asked as she sipped her coffee.

"It is 11:30 am," he replied looking at his watch.

"It's that late? I guess that sleeping pill really knocked me out. I needed it though. I was exhausted."

"I'm glad that you got some rest."

"Have you heard from Nick yet?"

It took Daniel a few seconds to answer. He hadn't heard from his cousin yet, but he obviously knew what the news would be when he finally did. He wondered how long it would take for someone to find Alexis' body. She was a fair distance into the woods and was relatively far away from the normal walking and jogging paths. It could be days or weeks before anyone found her. If it snowed, she could be out there for much longer. He couldn't bear the thought of Sonya being tortured day after day, not knowing what's happened to her. As much as he wanted to tell her, he couldn't let on that he knew anything. He did what he was supposed to do. He guided Alexis into death. She was no longer in any pain. He would have to let the rest play out naturally.

"No. He hasn't called me yet. I'm sure he will call as soon as he knows something."

At that moment, Daniel's phone vibrated. Even before he pulled it from his pocket, he knew that it was Nick calling. Sonya could see his name on the screen when he held it up to answer it. She felt the muscles in her forehead tense up.

"Hey, Nick," he answered.

The conversation only lasted a few seconds. Sonya could tell that something was wrong before he hung up. Tears began to well up in her eyes. After Daniel hung up, he moved towards her to comfort her, but she stepped away from him.

"Just tell me. What is it? Did they find her? Is she dead?"

"Nick said that they found the body of a woman in Proctor Park who matches Alexis' description. They didn't find any ID on her. He said that he can't be sure whether or not it's her. He asked me if we could meet him down there to identify her."

Sonya dropped to her knees and began sobbing. Daniel knelt down next to her and held her tightly.

"I'm so sorry. If it's too much for you, I can go by myself. You can stay here with Shawn. It's not for an official ID. Nick just wants one of us to confirm that it's her so that they can start the investigation as quickly as possible."

"No. I'll go. I have to. She would do it for me. Nick might need to ask me some more questions. I want to do everything that I can to help catch whoever did this," she said as she wiped the tears from her face.

"OK. We will go together then. I will be with you every step of the way. I will do whatever you need me to do."

"Thank you. Just give me a minute to clean up and get dressed, and then we can go."

Forty-five minutes later, Daniel pulled into the park at the same entrance that he had earlier that morning. This time, there was a police cruiser and two uniformed officers blocking it. He could see a much larger police presence scattered throughout the rest of the park. There were dozens of personnel investigating the crime scene. Several areas were cordoned off with yellow police caution tape. Daniel rolled down the window as one of the officers walked up to the side of his Jeep.

"I'm sorry, folks. The park is closed. It's currently an active crime scene. You'll have to turn around and drive back the way you came," the officer said.

"Hello, officer. My name is Daniel Jefferies and this is my girlfriend, Sonya Alvarez. We are here to see Detective Nick Morello. He is my cousin. He called and asked us to come down here to help identify the victim."

"OK, stand by, sir."

The officer reached for the radio microphone clipped to his uniform on his left shoulder. Daniel heard Nick's voice on the other end. A brief exchange between the two of them followed and then the officer looked back down at Daniel.

"Sir, I will need you to park your vehicle on the side of the road. Detective Morello instructed me to escort you and Ms. Alvarez to his location."

"No problem. Thank you, officer."

Daniel pulled onto the grass, a few feet off of the road.

"Are you sure that you want to do this? I can take care of it. You can wait in the car," he said to Sonya.

"She is my friend. I'm going. Please stop trying to talk me out of it. Trying to avoid the situation is not going to make it any easier."

Sonya didn't say another word. She got out of the car and walked towards the officer. Daniel turned off the engine and joined her. They walked across an open grass field in a diagonal direction towards the woods. They passed several other police officers along the way. Daniel noticed two officers interviewing a middle-aged woman wearing an over-sized knee length winter jacket and a knit hat. She had a dog with her. She was holding tightly onto its leash. The dog was a Siberian

Husky. Daniel was sure that it was Riley. He was happy to see that she had been reunited with her owner.

Once they reached the tree line of the woods, they had to walk single file in order to navigate through the thick brush. The officer took the lead and Sonya followed quickly behind him. Daniel could see how determined she was. He knew how strong of a person that she was. Still, he wondered how she would react to seeing her friend's dead body. From his own experiences, he knew that seeing death up close and personal was never easy, especially when it was someone that you cared about. He thought back to all of the friends that he lost during his time in Iraq and Afghanistan. Those memories still haunted him.

It took them ten minutes to reach their destination. When they finally arrived, they saw Nick standing just to the right of a large blue tarp. In addition to Nick, there were four other investigators taking photographs and searching the area for evidence. The four investigators were wearing navy blue jackets with the words, *Crime Scene Investigation*, in yellow letters on the back.

Nick saw the group emerge from the trees. He waved them over and was taking notes on a small pad inside a leather carrier. He had a somber look on his face as he greeted them.

"Thank you for both coming. I know how difficult this must be for you. We received a 911 call approximately three hours ago. A woman who lives a few miles away from here was in the park looking for her dog, Riley. She said that Riley got out of the house last night. She doesn't know how. She was walking down Park Street when she spotted her by the tree line. She said that Riley stood still as she approached her. When she took out her leash to try to attach it to her collar, Riley barked loudly and ran into the woods. She ran after her. Riley finally stopped running at this spot. That's when the woman discovered the body.

The body is of a woman in her mid to late twenties. She is petite and has blonde hair. Based on a preliminary review, it seems as if she was strangled to death. She has been dead anywhere between twenty-four and thirty-six hours, which is only a rough estimate. We won't have a more exact time of death until an autopsy is done. Still, that timeframe does line up with when Alexis was last seen. I compared this woman to a few recent photographs of Alexis. Having never met her in person, I can't be one hundred percent sure that it is her. That's why I asked you to come down here. The first forty-eight hours are crucial in crimes like this. With every hour that passes, the chances that evidence disappears and the crime goes unsolved increases dramatically. We need to start the investigation as soon as possible. I need a positive ID before we can move forward."

"I'll do it," Sonya said without hesitation.

At that point, Daniel knew that trying to stop her from seeing what lay under that tarp was futile. Given her current state of mind, he believed that it would make the situation worse. He elected to stay silent. He stood behind her as Nick knelt down and pulled back the tarp, revealing Alexis' face. Sonya stared straight down at her. She began to cry, but she didn't turn away.

"It's her," she said shaking her head.

Nick pulled the tarp back over the body and stood up.

"Thank you. I'm very sorry for your loss. If you don't mind, I would like to ask you a few questions."

"Yes, whatever you need. I want to find who did this."

Daniel continued to stand silently behind Sonya as Nick began his line of questioning.

"I do too. Before we begin, I want to let you know that I identified her boyfriend. His name is Jacob James Cooper. He is known on the street as J.J. He is a small-time dealer who sells mostly marijuana and ecstasy. He is not connected to any gangs or major drug organizations. Most of his clients are college kids and it seems like he sells just enough to pay his bills and feed his own habit. I pulled his record. He had two misdemeanor arrests for possession when he was a teenager, but nothing since. He got probation for the first arrest and court-ordered treatment for the second. He hasn't served any prison time. He has also never been implicated in any violent crimes or burglaries. My sources on the street say that he is quiet and keeps to himself. He stays out of the way of the real bad guys and doesn't cut into their business, so they leave him alone.

He rents an apartment in a duplex in Cornhill. I went by there last night. He wasn't there, but I talked to his landlord, who lives in the other apartment. He told me that he paid his rent for next month two weeks early. J.J. told him that he was going out of town to visit family for the holidays. The landlord didn't know where he was going. All he could tell me was that he has lived there for the last five years and has never had a problem with him. He always pays his rent on time, keeps the place clean, and doesn't throw loud parties. Basically, he is a model tenant."

"What does that mean? Does that mean that you don't think he did this?"

"No, it doesn't mean that. At this stage, he is definitely a person of interest. We just don't have enough evidence to consider him a suspect yet. We will track him down and bring him in for questioning. That will give us a better idea if we should pursue him as a suspect or not. I also stopped by Peepers last night. I talked to one of the owners. He said that Alexis was working there until around 2:30 am Thursday morning. He said that she left alone and that he doesn't remember seeing anyone matching J.J.'s description being in the club that night. At this point, we don't know if she met up with him or not. Do you happen to know if they were supposed to meet at a certain time or place? Do they have a usual meeting place when she comes into town?"

"I don't know. All I know is that she would come home fully supplied from her trips. I got out of rehab six months ago and haven't used drugs or alcohol since then. Alexis respected that. She didn't bring up drugs and alcohol around me. She wanted me to be sober, even though she wasn't. I was hoping that she would see how well I was doing with it and go that way herself at some point. I guess it's too late for that now."

Seeing how much Sonya was struggling, Nick waited a minute before he asked her his next question.

"Is there anybody else that you know of that might have wanted to hurt her for any reason? Another ex-boyfriend perhaps? An obsessed customer at the club?"

Sonya took a few minutes to think about it before she answered.

"I don't know. We all deal with customers that can get overzealous from time to time. The security at the club is pretty good about keeping those types from being let back in once they cross the line. We also all have regular customers that can get too attached. They convince themselves that they are in love with us. It's usually just some lonely guy or girl. For the most part, they are harmless."

"Did she have any regulars that didn't seem harmless, that you know of? Did she ever mention anyone in particular to you?"

"No, but Alexis was a pro. She is the one who taught me how to handle myself around difficult customers. She was better than most at dealing with them. We talked about work like any other co-workers, but I don't remember her telling me about anyone who made her nervous. I would have remembered if she did. I'm sorry. I feel like I'm not being very helpful."

"No, Not at all. You are doing amazing. You are doing better than most people do under these types of circumstances. The fact of the matter is that the person who did this could have been intentionally unassuming. They probably went out of their way not to be noticed. For all we know, they could be hiding in plain sight. I'll need to get a list of names of her regular customers."

"The best person to talk to about that is Tommy. He works the door at the club. He looks intimidating, but he is actually a really nice guy. He is engaged to one of the other dancers. Her name is Darya and she came to the United States from Russia. He is very protective of her and all of the girls who work there. He keeps track of all of the regulars in case they get out of line. I'm sure that he will be glad to help you out. He should be working later this afternoon."

"That's a big help. Thank you. I will take a ride out there and speak with him later today. I think that is all I need from you for now. CSI will be working the crime scene for the next several hours. Once they are done, Alexis' body will be transported to the coroner's office for an autopsy. We will need one of you to sign paperwork officially identifying her when the autopsy is complete. Also, I will probably have more questions for you as the investigation progresses. For now, you two should go home. I have your phone numbers if I need to get a hold of you. If there is anything else that you think of, even if it seems insignificant, don't hesitate to call me, day or night."

"Thanks, Nick. We really appreciate everything that you have done," Daniel said.

"Don't mention it. I promise that I will do everything in my power to find the person responsible for this and bring them to justice. Again, I'm very sorry for your loss."

"Please take them back down to their car," Nick said to the officer who escorted them to the crime scene.

They walked back through the woods the same way that they walked in. When they reached the open grass field, Daniel put his arm around Sonya. They continued on in silence with the officer in the lead. They reached the parking lot at the same time that Riley and her owner did. Riley's owner was removing her collar so that she could climb into the car. When she saw Daniel, she barked and ran up to him. He knelt down and petted her head. Her owner ran over to retrieve her.

"I'm sorry. She seems to have gotten into the habit of running off lately."

"It's OK. She is a beautiful dog," Daniel said.

"Thank you. Her name is Riley. I woke up in a panic this morning when I realized that she had gotten out of the house. I felt so relieved when I found her in the park, only to have her run away from me again. I followed her all the way into the woods. She stopped right in front of that poor girl. She has never run away from me before. She must have known that she was out there and wanted me to follow her."

The woman saw tears in Sonya's eyes.

"I'm sorry, dear. Please forgive me. I didn't mean to upset you. She was a friend of yours, wasn't she?"

"It's OK. If it wasn't for Riley, she might not have been found at all," Daniel said as he stood up.

"Yes, well, it's getting cold out. I should really be getting her home. She has been out all night. I'm truly sorry about your friend."

"Thank you," Sonya said.

They parted ways. The woman and Riley got into their car and Daniel and Sonya got into theirs. Sonya sat silently. Daniel wasn't sure if he should say anything or just let her be. He decided to give her some time to absorb all that had happened. He didn't want to push her to talk before she was ready. Surprisingly, she broke the silence.

"Why would somebody do this? They killed her and left her in the woods like she was nothing, like she wasn't even a human being? Who could be so cruel and evil?"

"I don't have an answer for you. I wish I did. I've asked myself those questions more times than I would care to remember. I have never been able to come up with an explanation, other than there is evil in the world. It exists in people, some of which you would never know to look at them. I don't know how it gets inside of them. It's just there. There is no rhyme or reason to it."

"I can't go back to my life the way it was. Alexis was all that I had. I can't do it by myself."

"You are not by yourself, not anymore. You don't have to go back. You don't belong there. You belong here with me. This is your home. This is our home. Stay here with me in Utica for good. I'll take care of you now."

She kissed him with tears still streaming down her cheeks.

"Yes. I will stay with you. Take me home."

They arrived back at 315 and entered through the back door. Shawn heard them come in and greeted them by stairs. He could tell that something was wrong.

"Is everything OK?" he asked.

"No. We just came from Proctor Park. Sonya's roommate, Alexis, was found murdered. Her body was left in the park. Nick is handling the investigation. He needed us to go down there to identify her," Daniel replied.

"Oh my God! Sonya, I'm so sorry. I don't know what to say. Is there anything that I can do? Is there anything that you need?"

"No, but thank you, Shawn. I'm just going to go upstairs and lay down for a while," Sonya replied.

"I'm going to go up with her. Can you handle the shop alone?"

"Yeah, no problem. Take all the time that you need."

They started walking up the stairs when Shawn stopped them.

"Daniel, before you go upstairs, there is somebody here to see you."

"Who?"

"I didn't get his name. He said that he knows you from Iraq. He came in a few minutes before you arrived and is waiting for you up front."

Daniel tried to think of who it could be. Other than Keith, he hadn't stayed in contact with anyone from the military. He walked to the front of the shop and found the man standing by the sales counter. It was someone that he hadn't expected to see again. It was Amir Rashid, the police chief from Al Diwaniyah, Iraq.

"Amir? What are you doing here? How did you know how to find me?"

"Hello, Daniel. I apologize for dropping in unannounced. I tracked you down because I need your help."

"My help? With what? I'm not in the military anymore."

"It's not a military matter. I need your help to find someone."

"Who?"

"The person who killed Nella Kassab."

Chapter 15

Like a chess player contemplating his next move, Daniel stared silently at Amir from across a table inside Sweet Escapes Café. Their table was by the front window overlooking the street. Daniel agreed to speak with Amir, despite his reservations about leaving Sonya by herself at such a vulnerable time. Still, he felt that he owed it to Nella to hear him out. Shawn assured him that he would sit with Sonya until he returned.

"What can I get you gentlemen today?" a waitress asked.

"I'll just have a house blend, black," Daniel replied.

"And for you, sir?"

"I'll have an espresso please," Amir replied.

"Sounds good. I'll get those right over to you."

Amir hadn't offered any further explanations of his reasons for seeking Daniel out. He hadn't said a word since they walked over from 315. Daniel decided to initiate the conversation.

"Are you planning on keeping me in suspense here? What is it that you think I can do to help you find Nella's killer?"

"I've been investigating her death on my own for the last three years. I didn't mention it before, but her parents and I were close friends. We were all in grade school together. When they were killed, I felt that I owed it to them to look after Nella. When she was killed, I couldn't accept the fact that her killer was out there somewhere walking around free. It's taken some time, but I believe that I know who the killer is now. The reason that I came here is because he lives close by."

"I still don't understand how I can help. I'm not a cop or a private investigator. I work in a comic book shop. Why don't you go to the police or the FBI?"

"I don't have enough evidence yet. What I have gathered is largely circumstantial. I need to gather more conclusive evidence before I can bring it to the authorities. The person that I suspect as the killer is someone that you know. That is why I need your help."

"Someone that I know? Who?"

"Captain Andrews."

"Keith! That's insane. Why would he kill Nella? It doesn't make any sense. What makes you think that it's him?"

"I apologize for just coming out with it like that. I understand that you must have a number of questions for me. I assure you that I did not expect to come to this conclusion when I began my investigation. I simply followed the evidence and it all pointed in the same direction. If you will allow me, I will walk you through it. You can draw your own conclusions. If you are not convinced when I have finished, then you can walk away. I promise that I will not bother you any more than I already have. I'm just asking you to hear me out."

The waitress returned to the table with their order. She placed their coffee in front of them.

"Is there anything else that I can get you?" she asked.

"No, thank you. That's all for now," Daniel said with his eyes firmly fixed on Amir.

Daniel wasn't sure if he should hear him out or not. His instincts were telling him to get up and walk away. He didn't want to believe what Amir was telling him was true. Keith was one of his few close friends and he'd only known Amir for a short time, years earlier, but based on his personal experiences with him, he believed him to be a man of integrity. He was reasonable and pragmatic. It would be out of character for him to travel as far as he did on a whim. Daniel hadn't worn the uniform of a soldier in years, but he still felt a sense of duty to the people that he served alongside, both dead and alive. Nella was one of those people. He decided that he would hear Amir out.

"Ok. I will listen."

"Thank you, Daniel. I truly do appreciate it."

"I just said that I would listen. It's going to take a lot to convince me that what you are saying is true. Keith and I have been through a lot together. He can be a bit of an asshole sometimes, but that is a long way from being a killer. He has always been a loyal friend to me. He saved my life. If it wasn't for him, I would have died outside of your city. And that wasn't the first time that he got me out of a tough spot over there. I just don't see how it's possible for someone who has put their life on the line for one person, to be capable of murdering another person in cold blood."

"I don't have an answer to that question. I have contemplated it myself many times. I was the first on the scene after the explosion. I saw him tending to your injuries when I arrived. Based on my personal experiences with him, I wouldn't have suspected him either."

"So, what changed your mind?"

"I first became suspicious of him a few months after the attack. Your battalion commander visited the city. He was there to with meet the city's leaders to discuss future collaboration efforts between us and the military. The increased combat operations across the country seemed to be working. The number of insurgent attacks were trending downward. Orders were given to start the process of resuming non-combat operations that had previously been halted. That included the rebuilding efforts in Al Diwaniyah. After the meeting, I pulled him aside and asked him how the two of you were doing. I was pleased to learn that you were both making good progress. I also asked him whether or not it would be possible to get any assistance from CID to help with the investigation into Nella's murder. I mentioned that Captain Andrews had informed me that he made a request through the battalion before your team pulled out that day, and that it was turned down due to a lack of available resources. He told me that it was true that CID was stretched very thin. It did not have the resources available to assist me. He also told me that Captain Andrews never made such a request. He surmised that he likely intended to make it, but never got a chance because of the attack."

"That makes sense. We had a lot going on. We had to pull out of the city with very little warning, so he probably didn't get the chance to put in the request. We were headed to battalion headquarters. He could have been intending to put it in once we arrived."

"That's very possible. However, he distinctly told me that he put the request in the night before you left and that it was denied."

"I understand how it might seem, but that doesn't prove anything. In our line of work, we had to hold back the whole truth sometimes. It was nothing personal. We had limited resources. The people that we worked with didn't always accept that as an explanation for why things couldn't get done. The battalion commander told you himself that there weren't any resources available. As a team leader, Keith would have also been aware of that. He could have looked into it informally and realized that the request would have been denied. By telling you that the request was formally denied, it would settle the issue as far as you were concerned. He had a lot on his plate to deal with at the time and he made a decision in the moment under difficult circumstances. It doesn't mean that there was anything nefarious behind it."

"I agree with you. I thought about it and came to the same conclusion. I didn't really think about it again until several weeks later when it was Nella's birthday. The staff and the children at the shelter decided to hold a vigil in her honor. They put together a photo collage of her. One of the photographs caught my eye."

Amir took out his phone. He pulled up the photo and showed it to Daniel.

"I don't understand. This is a picture of our team and the volunteers outside of the school. What is this supposed to mean?"

"Nella is in the picture."

"Yes. She was one of the volunteers. So what?"

"Do you see who is standing next to her?"

"Yes. It's Keith. Again, so what?

"When your team arrived at the site where Nella's body was found, Captain Andrews claimed not to recognize her. Sergeant Nayar explained to him who she was, but he still claimed not to know her. This photograph would suggest otherwise."

"Amir, I'm sorry to be so skeptical, but that doesn't prove anything either. Keith and I have worked with hundreds of people in cities and towns just like yours. I would be hard-pressed to remember every person that I have encountered. There is no way to prove that he wasn't being truthful. Taking a photo with a group of people doesn't mean that you know every one of them."

"That's true. This isn't proof of his guilt and your explanation is plausible. However, he made two statements that could be false. As an investigator, I have to question that. If they are false, the question becomes, why would he make such statements?"

Daniel began to understand Amir's thinking.

"I am assuming you have more."

"Yes. There is one more thing that aroused my suspicion, the break-in at the motor pool on the night Nella was killed."

"I'm not following."

"As I said at the time they occurred, I believe that the two crimes are connected. I believe the person who killed Nella stole one of the pick-up trucks to transport her body out to the dump site after he killed her. I also believe that the vandalism of the other vehicles was done for the purposes of making it seem like it was a separate and unrelated crime. When I investigated the scene, I noticed something strange. The thief broke into the motor pool shed to get the key to the stolen vehicle. The keys to all of the vehicles were stored in a hidden lock box inside the shed. Although the key was missing, nothing else was out of place. Everything was as I had left it when I locked it up that night. That tells me that the thief knew exactly where to find the keys. If it was just a random burglar, they might have guessed that the keys were in the shed, but they wouldn't have known exactly where to find them. They would have had to search for them, leaving behind a significant mess. Given the fact that they slashed all of the tires on the vehicles, I doubt that they would have taken the time to clean up the shed after rummaging through it. There were only three people who had access to the motor pool shed and knew the location of the lock box. Those three people were myself, my deputy chief, and Captain Andrews. At the time of the crime, my deputy was attending a law enforcement training course in Turkey. I was on duty at the station all night along with two of my officers. That only leaves Captain Andrews. Can you vouch for his whereabouts that night?"

Daniel racked his brain trying to remember if he saw Keith at any point during that night. He had a hard time recalling much of anything from that period of time since the attack. He could only remember being up most of the night with Aashirya going over the inventory list of construction supplies for the school. He couldn't remember seeing Keith until the next day.

"No, I can't, but I also cannot be sure that I didn't see him. My memories from that time are a little fuzzy as you could probably imagine," he replied reluctantly.

"I understand. I will admit that all of this evidence is highly circumstantial. Still, I believed that it was enough to dig further. I was very limited in what I could do from Iraq. Three years ago, an opportunity presented itself that would allow me to continue my investigation in the United States. A former United States Army Colonel, whom I worked with during the invasion, was now working for the FBI on a joint terrorism task force. He was recruiting contractors who spoke fluent Arabic and understood the Iraqi culture. He asked me to apply. I agreed to do so and he recommended me to the Bureau. After a year of interviews and background checks, I was offered the position. I moved to Washington D.C and have been living there ever since. In my spare time, I have been gathering information about Captain Andrews' past. I've come across some troubling facts in my research. I don't believe that Nella was his first victim, or his last."

"What? Are you saying that you think he has killed other women? Are you telling me that you think he is a serial killer?"

"If proven true, then yes. His crimes would fit the definition of a serial killer."

"Who are these other victims? How did you find them?"

"It took some time. There weren't any obvious connections. I first had to locate Captain Andrews' service records so that I could establish his whereabouts over an extended period of time. I also had to do it in a way that wouldn't arouse any suspicions within the FBI.

I told my supervisor that he had contacted me about applying for a contractor position on our team. I told him about our work together. I asked him if he would look over his military records to see if he might be a good fit for us. He contacted the Department of Defense and asked them to send us his records. When they arrived, I told him that Captain Andrews informed me that he would need to undergo surgery related to the injuries he sustained in Iraq, and then require several months of rehabilitation afterward. I said that he was still interested in applying at a later date, but it wouldn't be feasible at that time. He asked me to file his records away and let him know if he became available in the future. I filed the records away after I copied them. I took the copies home and constructed a timeline of his whereabouts over the last twenty years."

"Don't get me wrong, Amir, but it seems that the only one who has committed a crime so far is you. The United States Government tends to frown on foreign nationals walking out of the FBI offices with their records. You could get into some serious trouble if you get caught."

"I assure you, Daniel, that I am well aware of the risks. One thing that I have learned in my life is that doing what is right often comes at great risk to yourself and those around you. I am willing to accept those risks to do what must be done."

"That's very honorable of you. I would also like to thank you for including me in this little quest of yours. I've always wanted to be an accessory to a federal crime. On the bright side, if I go to jail, the cell will probably be nicer than my apartment."

"Daniel, please forgive me. My intention was not to make you an accessory to any crime. I assure you that I would never implicate you in any of this. No one will be able to prove that you had any knowledge about the actions that I have taken to gather this information."

Daniel laughed it off.

"Don't worry about it. I'll be fine. I've been in bad situations before. What is one more in the grand scheme of things? Why don't you just tell me what you found?"

"Once I established his whereabouts, I started searching the internet for unsolved murders and suspicious deaths in the areas where he was living. It was a long and tedious process. After several months, I found a case that stuck out to me. A woman by the name of Katherine Lyle was found strangled to death in Sierra Vista, Arizona. There is a United States Army base in Sierra Vista called Fort Huachuca. Fort Huachuca is the home of the Army's military intelligence training center. Captain Andrews began his Army career in military intelligence. At the time of her murder, he was a second lieutenant and attending the military intelligence officer basic course. Ms. Lyle was a waitress at a local bar outside the base, which was frequented regularly by base personnel. According to news articles, Ms. Lyle was originally from Houston, Texas. She moved to Sierra Vista the year before she was killed. She shared an apartment with a childhood friend and her friend's husband, who was also stationed at the base. She was last seen on Sunday, April 11, 2004 around 3:00 am. She was working the late shift and left the bar at the same time as the manager and another waitress. The three of them were the last people in the bar that night before the manager locked up.

The manager and the other waitress both said that they watched Ms. Lyle get into her car and drive off. After that, they never saw or heard from her again. Her body was discovered by hikers at the base of Miller's Peak in the Huachuca Mountains four days later. I found orders in Captain Andrews' personnel file which shows that his tour at Fort Huachuca ended on April 11. There is also a leave form which shows that he signed out at 8:00 am on that day. He signed back into duty five days later at Fort Bragg. As far as I can tell, he was never a suspect in the crime or questioned about it. Ms. Lyle was strangled in a similar manner to Nella. Her body was also left in a remote location."

"I will admit that the timing is coincidental and the crime is similar, but there doesn't seem to be enough evidence in the articles to link that woman's murder to Nella's. Were you able to get access to any police records through the FBI computers?"

"No, not in this case. However, I did find a more direct connection between Captain Andrews and the death of another young woman, years earlier."

"Was that woman strangled as well?"

"No. Her death was ruled an accident, but I have conclusive evidence that Captain Andrews was in the immediate vicinity when the accident occurred."

"How did you find that?"

"After 9/11, the government realized that there was a need to more quickly share information across agency and police department lines to more effectively investigate potential acts of terror. The FBI created a crime database, which provided access to other federal agencies, the military, and state and local police departments across the country. Violent crimes, among others are logged into the database on a daily basis. When the database first came online, it was limited to state police departments and major metropolitan area police departments such as New York, Los Angeles, and Chicago. As time went on, more smaller departments began to participate. Unfortunately, the Sierra Vista police department was not one of them. However, all branches of the military log every crime that falls under their jurisdiction into the database. In addition to that, they also logged in crimes that were committed as far back as 1985."

"When did this girl die?"

"May 3, 1997"

"1997? Keith would have only been sixteen at the time. What did you find?"

"As I said, I was searching for murders and suspicious deaths in areas where Captain Andrews was living. I wanted to be thorough. I came across an article from a newspaper in Watertown, NY. A girl by the name of Elizabeth Masterson was tragically killed at Fort Drum during a land navigation training course. Ms. Masterson was a student at Chittenango High School, the same school that Captain Andrews attended. In fact, they were in the same class. She was a cadet in the school's JROTC program, as was Captain Andrews. They were both attending a weekend-long field training exercise at Fort Drum. Since her death occurred on base, the Army CID and the military police conducted the investigation. All of their records were logged into the crime database. According to the reports, the cadets were sent out on their own to test their land navigation skills. The training was supposed to last four hours. After five hours passed, all of the cadets had returned except for Ms. Masterson. A search party was sent out to find her. The party consisted of five people, two of the adult instructors and three of the cadets. One of the cadets who volunteered was Captain Andrews.

The search party made their way to the center of the course and then branched out individually to cover more ground. Twenty minutes after they split up, everyone heard a loud scream. One by one, they each made their way to the source of the scream. Ms. Masterson had fallen from a small ledge on the side of a thirty-foot cliff onto some rocks. She died instantly. The coroner's report revealed that she broke her left ankle, likely before she fell to her death. Based on his assessment of the terrain, the investigator concluded that she initially broke her ankle and slipped off the cliff onto the ledge on the rock face. It had been raining on and off all day, so the conditions were slippery. It was the opinion of the investigator that she fell off the ledge when she tried to climb back up the cliff after being stranded there for an undetermined amount of time. The members of the search party all provided signed statements to the investigator. Each one of them were alone when they heard the scream. None of them claim to have seen the fall. Of note, Captain Andrews was the last to arrive on the scene."

"Do you think that he pushed her off and then made it seem like she fell by accident?"

"There is no way to know for sure, but that is my suspicion. I've continued to search for further evidence of additional crimes over the last several months, but I have come up empty until this morning."

"What did you find this morning?"

"In addition to searching past crimes, I keep an eye on current crimes that are being logged into the database. Each morning, I start with New York State and then move onto the surrounding states. This morning, the Utica Police Department logged an entry. The body of a young woman was found in a local park here in Utica. She has yet to be identified, but the police entered it as a homicide. The most likely cause of death was noted to be strangulation, pending an autopsy. I knew as soon as I read it that it was him. I jumped in my car and came up here as fast as I could. We have to stop him before he kills again."

Daniel felt his stomach twist up into a knot. As much as he didn't want to believe it, he couldn't ignore the evidence. The person who saved his life, and whom he considered to be a close friend, could really be a coldblooded killer. He wondered how he could have missed it. He began to worry that if he did kill Alexis, that he might go after Sonya next. He didn't know how he was going to stop him if it was true, but he was determined to do whatever it took.

"I have a key to his apartment. He has a physical therapy appointment at the VA in about an hour. If we leave now, we can get there and search it before he gets back."

Chapter 16

For the fifth time in as many minutes, Keith glanced up at the clock on the wall in the waiting room of the physical therapy and rehabilitation clinic at the Syracuse VA Medical Center, which now read 5:45 pm, forty-five minutes past the scheduled time of his appointment. He was reading a three-month-old issue of Sports Illustrated to pass the time. For the last three years, he visited the clinic on a weekly basis in order to build up and maintain the strength in his leg after losing his foot. Visiting the clinic week after week had become burdensome. He questioned whether or not it was benefiting him in any meaningful way. In his mind, it had simply become a waste of time. The only reason that he continued to go was because he needed periodic adjustments to his prosthetic. He didn't have the money to pay for those services at a private facility. The VA would only do the adjustments for him if he attended weekly physical therapy appointments.

He felt trapped by his situation. He hated being reliant upon the VA for anything. He looked upon other disabled veterans who sought care from the VA as weak. He resented them, even though they were all there for the same reasons that he was. In his mind, he was above them. To him, they were nothing more than lambs walking towards their own slaughter. He viewed himself as a lion, a predator on the prowl, who was both powerful and cunning. That sense of self-aggrandizement and superiority began when he was very young. He felt that other people were beneath him, unworthy of his understanding and compassion.

He felt his phone vibrate in his pocket. When he pulled it out, he saw an alert from his home security app. When he first moved into his apartment, he installed a security system with a hidden camera and a motion sensor. The system was linked to his phone. Once the phone was outside of the apartment, the system would switch on. If anyone entered the apartment when the phone wasn't there, it would trigger an alert. When he tapped on the alert icon, a live video feed from inside his apartment appeared on the screen. He saw Daniel and Amir standing in the middle of his living room. Another alert popped up on the screen. It asked him if he wanted to alert the police. The app would automatically alert the police of an intruder if the user tapped yes. Keith tapped no. A few minutes later, his physical therapist entered the waiting room.

"Keith, I'm ready for you. I apologize for the wait. It seems that the system overbooked my appointments today."

Keith stood up and scowled at him.

"I won't be needing your services any longer. Give my appointment to one of these poor bastards, clinging to their last bit of hope that you can make them whole again. I have more important things to attend to," he said as he walked out of the waiting room.

Daniel and Amir began searching Keith's apartment as soon as they entered it. They didn't know how long he would be away, so they had to work quickly. There were no obvious hiding spots where evidence could be hidden. They only found clothing in his closets and drawers. There were no holes in the walls, or signs that any had been covered up. Keith didn't have many personal items either. After twenty minutes of searching, it became clear that if he was hiding anything, it wasn't there.

"This is a dead end. I don't know what I was thinking. I've been over here dozens of times. Homeless people have more possessions than Keith. What was I expecting to find, a signed confession?" Daniel said.

"Investigative work is long and tedious. I've been working on this case for more than three years now. You can't expect evidence to just appear out of thin air and crack the case in an instant. In most cases, there isn't a single piece of evidence that indicates the suspect's guilt. More often than not, the evidence is cumulative in nature. On its own, one piece of evidence doesn't reveal much of anything. It is only when it is pieced together with other corroborating pieces of evidence, does the truth of the matter start to become clear. If we are correct in our assumptions, Captain Andrews has been hiding his true nature from the world for quite some time. He has committed these murders in the shadows. He is a very intelligent individual. He commits these acts only after a careful analysis and the crafting of a detailed plan to cover his tracks. Vandalizing the other vehicles in the motor pool, with the intent to give the appearance that theft of the single vehicle was unrelated to the murder, is evidence of his level of sophistication. He also took great care to ensure that none of the individual murders could be connected to one another. I had very low expectations that we would find anything of significance here. Still, we have to chase down every lead."

"I don't know. Maybe we are just seeing things that aren't really there. I will admit that there are several coincidences, but that could be all that we are talking about here. Any one of those murders could have been committed by any number of people. Alexis came to Utica on a monthly basis to get drugs from her dealer boyfriend. My cousin, Nick, said that he is currently out of town and hasn't been seen since the murder. There are dozens of people or groups that could have killed Nella. The killing of innocent people in Iraq was not exactly uncommon at that time. You said yourself that you don't have access to the police records in Arizona. There could be other more likely suspects that the police are still investigating in that case. The death of the girl from his high school was investigated and ruled as an accident. She was young and inexperienced in the woods. The conditions were wet and slippery. She fell off of a cliff. It's tragic, but that doesn't make it murder."

"Everything you said is true, Daniel. The evidence we have now can be viewed in a variety of different lights. We are no closer to the truth now than we were before we entered this apartment. However, I saw the look in your eyes when I mentioned the murder of Ms. Nesmith. Something inside your brain clicked into place. You arrived at the same conclusion that I did. Admittedly, I talked you through the evidence, but you made the final leap on your own. Sometimes all you have is your own intuition. It is easy to discount it or doubt it. It is not something that is tangible. You can't see it or touch it. You can only feel it. All you can do is move forward, trusting that it will guide you in the right direction."

Amir's words refocused Daniel's attention.

"Ok, fair enough. Intuition aside for the moment, we still need a plan. There's nothing here. Where do we go from here?"

"Are there any other places that Captain Andrews spends his time, his family's home perhaps?"

"I know he goes to the strip club where Alexis worked. That's how he knows her. Going there won't tell us anything that we don't already know. He is just another regular customer. His parents still live in Chittenango. I don't know how often he visits their house. They also run a family owned sporting goods store. Keith has been working there since he got out of the Army. There's a large storeroom in the back. It's possible that he might have hid something in there. I don't know how we would get back there without drawing attention to ourselves. We don't even know what we are actually looking for."

"That is true. It stands to reason that if he would go to such lengths to conceal these crimes, that he would not keep any evidence that could prove his guilt. If he did, at the very least, he would ensure that it was extremely well hidden. He would hide it in a spot that would not be obvious to anyone. For now, we should operate under the assumption that we won't be able to find any hidden evidence. We will have to find another way to prove our theory."

"Why don't we go to my cousin, Nick? He is the detective that is investigating Alexis' murder. His father, my uncle, is also the police chief. They have resources that we don't. He was already able to track down Alexis' boyfriend with only partial information about him. I'm sure that he would help us. He said that he would be going to the strip club today to get a list of names of Alexis' regular customers. Keith will be on that list. He is sure to connect the dots back to me anyway. It might be a good idea to tell him what we know now."

"I am not opposed to alerting the authorities. However, as you have already pointed out, I have obtained some of my information illegally. I am willing to accept the consequences of my actions, but not before I have proven my theory. If we tell your cousin what we know now without solid proof, I could be charged with a crime and deported back to Iraq. That would give Captain Andrews the opportunity to further conceal any possible evidence that he is hiding. It would also effectively eliminate me and all of the evidence that I have collected in Iraq from the investigation. I should remind you that it was the details surrounding Nella's murder that initially sparked my suspicion. Her murder is the key to linking all of the rest of them together. For the moment, I am the only one who can connect those dots. We would be better served to let your cousin conduct his own investigation for now. If Captain Andrews becomes one of his suspects and he questions you about him, you can lead him in that direction naturally. Has he ever met him? Does he know that the two of you are friends?"

"I always go to Syracuse to visit Keith. He has never come to Utica. I've mentioned my friendship with him a few times. Nick knows that he was injured in the same attack as I was, but he has never met him."

"Your cousin sounds like a competent investigator. If he plans to speak with all of Ms. Nesmith's regular customers, he will inevitably speak with Captain Andrews. Once he makes the connection between the two of you, it will undoubtedly raise questions in his mind. Perhaps we should closely monitor the investigation from a distance and take a step back for the moment."

"That seems like the safe move, but if we are right about him, he could kill again. I don't think we have the luxury of waiting. I don't think I could live with myself if another innocent woman is murdered, knowing that I could have stopped it."

"I understand your frustration, Daniel. The feeling of helplessness is not an easy one to accept. I've witnessed many atrocities in my life. I've seen horrible things happen to innocent people more times than I can count. I want nothing more than to forget those events, but they are seared into my brain along with that same feeling of helplessness that I felt when I watched them occur. I wish that I could say it gets easier, but it does not. When I read about Ms. Nesmith's murder on the database, it was particularly jarring for me. I must admit that I felt a great deal of guilt. I questioned every one of the actions that I took since I first suspected Captain Andrews and I still can't help thinking that I could have done more. Perhaps I could have pushed myself harder to find more conclusive evidence and stopped him before he killed her. At the same time, I also had to acknowledge the reality of the situation. I am doing everything that I can do to stop him. He was the one who committed those crimes, not me. All I can do is continue to be vigilant in my pursuit of him."

"Thanks for the pick me up, but my feelings are not really what matters right now. We have to draw him out. We have to get him to slip up somehow and reveal something that can lead us to the truth."

"That is a sound strategy. How do you propose we do that?"

Daniel stood silently in thought for several minutes before he proposed a plan.

"What if we wait here for him to come home?"

"I don't see how that helps. If he sees me, he might become suspicious."

"Exactly. We want him to be suspicious. He won't know for sure whether you are here because you suspect him of Nella's murder or because you had a genuine desire to visit old friends. It will keep him off balance and might make him nervous. He might let something slip, another lie perhaps, like when he told you that he requested assistance from CID. In fact, you could bring that up. Don't tell him that you know that he lied about it, just that you talked to our battalion commander about it. It will keep him guessing. It will also force a discussion about Nella's murder, a topic that he was probably hoping would never come up again."

"How do we explain the fact that we are in his apartment while he was not home?"

"He gave me a key to his apartment. I drop by on a regular basis. If he is not here when I arrive, I let myself in. There is nothing suspicious about that. We can explain your presence here as visiting old friends, just as I said. You have been working in the United States and you had some personal time off. You decided to look me up. I then decided to bring you to Syracuse to visit Keith. When he gets home, I will suggest that we go out for a bite to eat to catch up. After some initial small talk, I'll ask you about the rebuilding efforts after we left. That will give you the opportunity to bring up the fact that you got a chance to meet our battalion commander, and that you made another request for CID assistance to help investigate Nella's murder."

"I don't know. I'm not confident that it will yield the result we are seeking. It might heighten his awareness and make him nervous, but I doubt that he will reveal anything of any significance to us. If anything, it could force him to be even more careful about concealing his actions. He might take additional steps that could make it even more difficult for us to find any evidence that he could be hiding."

"That might be a good thing."

"How so?"

"If he takes additional steps to hide evidence that he has already hidden, he could lead us right to it. After we eat, we can drop him off and say our goodbyes. For all he knows, I will be heading back to Utica and you will be heading back to DC. We can park our car across the street somewhere where we can see him, but he can't see us. We wait for him to get into his car and then follow him. It's a long shot, but it seems to be all that we have at the moment."

Amir thought it over for a few minutes.

"I would have to agree. It seems to be our only move at the present time. I think it is worth the risk of revealing ourselves to him. However, I should stress that we must act naturally and seem completely calm at all times. Do not seem over-eager about getting him to talk. Based on the meticulousness of his crimes, we must assume that he observes his victims for long periods of time before he kills them. In all that time, he has undoubtedly developed a keen sense of awareness of human behavior. He will likely be able to pick up on even the slightest inconsistency in your behavior. If he discovers the truth, it could give him the advantage."

"Understood. He should be home soon. When I let myself in, I usually help myself to a beer while I'm waiting. Since we are supposed to act natural, I think I will have one or six to calm my nerves. Can I get you one?"

"No, thank you. I don't drink alcohol."

"Suit yourself. Why don't you grab a seat on the couch? If you want to watch TV, the remote is on the coffee table."

Daniel grabbed a beer from the refrigerator and then took a seat on the couch. They waited in the apartment for the next four hours. Keith's physical therapy appointments typically lasted between an hour and an hour and a half. Daniel didn't know if he had any other plans that day. He could have been out running some errands, but it seemed unusual that he would be gone for that length of time. He assumed that if Keith was planning to be out for an extended period of time, he would have stopped home to shower first. His physical therapy sessions could be intense and he was usually drenched in sweat afterwards. It felt odd that he hadn't shown up yet. Daniel decided to call him to tell him that he was waiting for him in his apartment. As he was about to dial, his phone vibrated. It was Keith calling him.

"Keith, I was just about to call you."

"You don't say. What's going on, Danny?"

"I'm actually sitting here in your apartment right now. I've been waiting for you to come home. I remembered that your physical therapy appointment got rescheduled for today and I figured that you would have been home hours ago. I'm with an old acquaintance of ours from Iraq. He looked me up today and I thought that you might want to see him too."

"You don't say. An old acquaintance. Let me guess, Amir Rashid."

Daniel knew something was wrong. He didn't want Amir to know that he suspected anything. He continued on with the conversation as if everything was normal.

"It's Amir Rashid, the police chief from Al Diwaniyah. He is a contractor with the U.S. government now. He came by the comic book shop today to say hi. I thought that it would be fun for all of us to catch up."

"Government contractor, and for the FBI no less. I must say, that is pretty impressive," Keith said sarcastically.

Daniel grew more worried as the conversation continued.

"So, when are you planning on coming home? I thought that we could all grab dinner together."

"Sorry, Danny, no can do. It was a nice try though. I must say that I am impressed with your investigative instincts. You really should talk to your uncle about joining the force. They could use a guy like you. You are really wasting your time in that crummy comic book shop with that loser friend of yours. Speaking of which, he is here with me. He can't come to the phone right now. He's a little indisposed at the moment. Don't worry about him though. He has some company. Your girlfriend is here too. I must say, Danny, she is one fine mamma-cita. I have to admit that I'm jealous. She is something special, not like that drugged out skank roommate of her hers. You should hold onto her, if you can."

Daniel's worry turned to absolute terror.

"I didn't know that you were going to be in the area. Did you want to meet up in Utica then?"

Keith laughed as he continued to taunt him.

"You know what, that sounds like a good idea. Why don't we all get together? We really have a lot to talk about. Why don't you head back down the Thruway and give me a ring when you get back to the comic book shop? There is something that I'm going to need you to do for me before we see each other. And make sure to keep our nosy Haji friend in the dark about our plans. I want this to be a surprise party. See you soon, Danny."

Keith hung up and Daniel put down his phone.

"What's happened?" Amir asked.

Daniel didn't respond. All he could think about was Sonya and Shawn.

"What's happened? Is something wrong, Daniel?" Amir asked again.

Daniel refocused his mind before he replied.

"No. Nothing is wrong. He is just not coming home tonight. He is on a business trip with his brother. They are traveling east to meet with some of their suppliers. He was in Utica and called to see if I wanted to grab a quick drink before they headed to their next stop. They are heading out to Albany now, so it seems as if we will have to do this another time."

"I see. Did you get the impression that he was at all suspicious when you told him that we were waiting in his apartment for him?"

"No. It didn't seem that way. He said that he was looking forward to seeing you. He said that if he had the time that he would swing by the shop on his way back home tomorrow," Daniel said, trying his best to maintain his composure.

Daniel wanted to change the subject before Amir became suspicious.

"Why don't we head back? There is nothing more that we can accomplish here tonight."

Daniel and Amir arrived back at 315 an hour later. They walked in the back door. When they got to the front of the store, they found it empty. The door was locked. Sonya and Shawn were nowhere to be found.

"Business must have been slow. Shawn probably locked up early. I'll give him a call to find out where he is. Why don't you just hang out for a bit?" Daniel said.

Daniel called Keith's number. It rang four times and then went to voicemail.

"I'm back at the shop. Let me know where you are at," he said after the beep.

A few seconds later, he received two text messages, one after the other. The first one was a photo of Sonya and Shawn tied up and gagged. The second was a message that read, "If you want to see them alive again, kill Amir. I left you a present behind the counter. Put one right between his eyes. When you are done, text me a picture. If I don't hear from you in five minutes, they are both dead."

Daniel rushed behind the counter and found a Glock 9mm pistol on the shelf below the register. He picked it up, moved towards Amir, and pointed it at him.

"Daniel what are you doing?"

Daniel moved to within a foot of Amir with the gun pointed squarely at his chest.

"I'm sorry, I have no choice."

He lowered the gun to his side. He then raised his free hand and placed it in the middle of Amir's chest. He felt the surge of light energy throughout his body and then Amir's consciousness within his own mind. When he pulled his hand away, Amir's lifeless body fell to the floor in front of him.

Chapter 17

Everything went black, followed by a sudden burst of light. As Amir regained his bearings and his vision came back into focus, he gazed down upon his own body, motionless, lying face up on the sales floor of 315 Comics. The last thing that he remembered was Daniel pointing a gun at him. While he didn't remember him firing it at him and killing him, he couldn't think of any other explanation for what he was witnessing. He wondered if he was in Barzakh. In Islam, Barzakh is an intermediary world between the current world and the one to come. It is similar to the Roman Catholic belief in purgatory, an intermediate state after death where souls can atone for their sins in life so that they may eventually enter the Kingdom of Heaven.

"I'm sorry. I didn't have time to explain. I know how confusing this must seem," Daniel said.

"Daniel? How is it that you can see me and talk to me? You pointed a gun at me and now I'm looking down at my own body. What have you done?"

"Give me a few minutes. There is something that I have to do first."

Daniel ran into the back room. He returned a few seconds later carrying a Halloween make-up kit. It contained pieces of skin-colored plastic prosthetics and a container of fake blood. He ripped open the package and began crafting what appeared to be a bullet hole in the middle of Amir's head. He glued down the pieces of prosthetic to give the appearance of a circular wound, and then filled it with the blood until it began streaming down his head. Finally, he poured a pool of blood onto the floor around his head and shoulders. When he was finished, he took a picture of the body with his camera-phone and texted the picture to Keith. Several seconds later, he received a text in response. After he read the message, he took a deep breath and turned back towards Amir.

"Keith knew exactly what was going on when he called me earlier. He already knew that you were with me before I told him, and he knew what we were planning. He must have had some type of hidden camera or listening device in his apartment that we missed. I lied to you. He wasn't on a business trip with his brother. He was here in Utica. He kidnapped Sonya and Shawn while we were waiting for him. He has them now. He told me not to tell you. He gave me instructions to drive back to the shop and contact him when we got here. I called him when we arrived. He texted me a picture of Sonya and Shawn tied up and gagged. He left a gun for me on the shelf underneath the register. He gave me five minutes to shoot you in the head and text him a picture of your body. He told me that if I didn't do it, he would kill them. I had to think quickly, and I didn't have time to explain myself."

"I still don't understand what has happened. If you didn't shoot me, how did you kill me?"

"I didn't kill you. I released your soul from your body, temporarily."

"I'm sorry, Daniel. I'm not following. How is that possible?"

"It's a little hard to explain. I'm not sure that I completely understand it all myself, but I'll do my best. When I was twelve years old, I started to feel as if I was different than other people. The night that my father died, he appeared in my room at almost the same time that he was found dead at work by one of his co-workers. I convinced myself that it was a dream, until I had another experience. After the ambush in Iraq, just before I passed out, I saw Nella. She stared right at me before she walked into a bright light and disappeared. I thought I was hallucinating. I even started taking medication for it. Over the last week, I began seeing Aashirya in different places around the city. I thought I was getting worse. The other night, I walked into my apartment and she was there waiting for me. I finally realized that my experiences weren't hallucinations after all. They were real."

"Are you telling me that you are some type of medium that is able to communicate with the dead?"

"No, not exactly. Aashirya explained to me that life and death are two separate but equal plains of existence. Souls continually travel back and forth between these plains at designated times. In order for both plains to exist, a balance must be maintained. I was chosen to help maintain that balance. I am what is known as a Shepherd. When a person has reached their designated time of death, I am responsible for releasing their soul from their body and guiding them into death."

"Are you saying that I have reached my designated time of death?"

"No. I released your soul prematurely. It was the only way that I could think of to convince Keith that I killed you. He texted me a location of where to meet him in two hours. He told me to bring your body. I might be able to get away with that amateur monster make-up in a picture, but he will undoubtedly do a closer inspection in-person. Since you have not reached your designated time of death, I believe that I can return your soul to your body once he is convinced that you are dead. We might even be able to use it to our advantage."

"Daniel, how do you know if any of this will work? More importantly, what will happen if it doesn't? I'm not completely convinced that what you have told me is real, and I can't claim to be a very spiritual man, but you are dealing forces that you admittedly know very little about. This could result in any number of unintended consequences."

"You aren't telling me anything that I haven't already thought of myself. Unfortunately, I don't have the luxury of time to come up with a better plan. You were right. Keith is a killer. I don't know how I missed it, but I did. Now he is going to kill my girlfriend and my best friend. I can't let that happen. I'm prepared to live with the consequences of my actions, but I'm not prepared to live with the consequences of inaction. You understand more than most people that desperate times call for desperate measures. Right now, I'm extremely desperate and I need your help. You asked me to take a leap of faith and trust you against my better judgment. I'm just asking you to return the favor."

Amir thought it over for a few minutes before responding.

"OK, I will help you. I am responsible for pulling you into this. I am therefore responsible for the current predicament that you and your friends find yourselves in. I will do whatever you ask of me. What is your plan?"

"We have to meet Keith in two hours. The location that he texted me is an industrial area that used to house several factories. There are a few businesses that still have offices there, but most of the buildings have been abandoned. It's highly unlikely that there will be anybody around at that time of night, which is probably why he chose it. We never accused him of being unintelligent. I'll put your body in the trunk. Once he checks your pulse and is convinced that you are dead, I will return your soul to your body. I'll keep the trunk open and try to get him to turn his back to you. I'll keep him talking. When you hear me say the words, "It's not too late for redemption," that will be your signal that his back is turned. You will need to get out of the trunk as quickly as you can and try to surprise him from behind. Go for his weapon first and then tackle him to the ground. I'll get Sonya and Shawn out of the line of fire and then help you subdue him. Hopefully, we can accomplish this without anyone getting hurt. Once we have him restrained, we will call my cousin, Nick. We have more than enough evidence to turn him over now. We can even leave out the part about you stealing government documents."

"It could work, but there is also much that could go wrong. Perhaps I was wrong earlier. Maybe we should alert your cousin and the police department. We have no idea what we are walking into. He could have any number of things planned for us. We simply can't be prepared for all of the possibilities in such a short amount of time. The police have hostage negotiators. They are much better equipped to handle situations like this. The chances of getting your friends back alive might actually be higher if we call them."

"It's too late for that. We don't even know where he is right now. He could be outside watching us for all we know. If he believes that we tipped off the police, he could kill them both and simply disappear. Any plan that we come up with will have some inherent level of risk attached to it. The fact of the matter is that we set off on our own to investigate him. If we called the police before we made that decision, we might not be in this situation now. We made this mess and now we have to clean it up. If I thought calling the police would give us a better chance of getting Sonya and Shawn back alive, I would call Nick in a second. I just think that he is too many steps ahead of us at this point. He has the clear advantage. If we make one more mistake, he will kill them. He is in control now. We have to do what he says until we get our opportunity to take him down."

Amir nodded his head in agreement.

"I suppose you are right. He is in control. We shouldn't risk angering him any further by trying to deceive him. I will see this through with you until the end."

Two hours later, Daniel pulled into the parking lot of an abandoned factory in North Utica. All of the surrounding buildings were also abandoned. There were no lights coming from any of the windows. There were also no working street lights in the area. He felt as if he was in an industrial ghost town. He turned off his headlights and kept the engine running while he waited. He didn't see any sign of Keith. After ten minutes, he received a text message.

It read, "Drive around to the back of the building. Back your car into the loading bay with the open door. Once you are in inside, turn off the engine, open the trunk, and pull the loading bay door closed. Finally, walk five feet in front of your car, get on your knees, and place your hands on your head."

Daniel followed Keith's instructions. Once he was in position on his knees, the lights inside the building came on. Sonya and Shawn were thirty feet in front of him also on their knees. They were still gagged and their hands were bound behind their backs. Keith emerged from behind them with a 9mm Glock handgun pointed in Daniel's direction. From Daniel's vantage point, Sonya and Shawn seemed frightened, but unharmed. Keith moved towards Daniel. He came up behind him and told him to get on his feet. Once Daniel was standing, Keith patted him down and checked for any hidden weapons. Once he was satisfied that he was unarmed, he told him to stand by the open trunk and turn around.

"Danny, Danny, Danny. Always trying to do the right thing. Always trying to be a hero. I warned you about that shit in Iraq. I told you that it would get you killed some day. I have to ask. Why? Why would you put yourself and the people that you care about at risk? To avenge the deaths of strangers you barely know?"

"They were people. They were human beings. You took their lives from them. Who are you to decide who lives and who dies?"

"Who said that I was the one who decided. I killed them, but how do you know that I wasn't supposed to? How do you know that it wasn't their time to die?"

A harsh realization suddenly hit Daniel. Although Keith's actions were deplorable, he was right about one thing. It was their time to die. Everyone had a designated time of death. It was part of maintaining the balance. Keith, while not completely aware of his role, was just as much a part of it as he was. Still, he couldn't accept that murder was necessary to maintain it. He clung to the belief that while it did serve a purpose, it was still wrong and he had a moral obligation to stop him from killing any more innocent people.

"Whether it was or was not their time to die, ripping them out of their lives was wrong. What you did to them was evil, pure and simple. How did you get to the point where you could justify killing four innocent women?"

Keith burst out into laughter.

"Who said I was justifying it? People always try to justify or rationalize their actions in this world. I'm not one of them. I simply accept who I am. While I might seem like a monster to you, I see myself as nothing more than a predator who exists in nature hunting its prey. It's a hunger that needs to be fed. No more, no less. It's no different than a lion hunting a gazelle. I am who I am. I can't change what I am any more than you can. I honestly wish that we didn't end up here, although I'm not that surprised that we did. If it means anything, I really did consider you a friend. I never had any other friends, and truth be told, I've never wanted any. I guess you just grew on me."

"So, you are just going to kill me? Is that your definition of friendship? I saved your life. I pulled you out of that Humvee. If I hadn't, you would have been killed when the whole thing exploded."

"As I said, you always do the right thing. And just for the record, I also saved your life. You would have bled out and died in the middle of the desert if it wasn't for me. I would say that makes us even. Don't blame me for this. I'm not the one who made you go poking your nose around in places that it didn't belong. You made that choice. I'm only doing what I need to do to survive."

"So, what are you waiting for? I'm here. I'm unarmed. Amir is dead. Why not just kill me right here, right now?"

Keith laughed again.

"Is that your attempt at reverse psychology? You are a smart guy, Danny, and you are right. I am going to kill you and your friends. I don't have a choice. I can't let all of you go and expect to survive myself. I haven't killed you yet because I was telling you the truth. I consider you a friend. I'm not doing this to satisfy my appetite for killing. I'm doing this for self-preservation. Believe it or not, there is a difference. I wanted to give you the opportunity to say a proper goodbye to your girl. I know how much she means to you. I thought it was the least that I could do."

"You really are an asshole, Keith."

"I know, Danny. I know. I think we have said all that we need to say. Uncover Amir so that I can make sure that you did what you were supposed to do. Do it slowly and keep your hands where I can see them."

Amir had been by Daniel's side observing the whole time. Keith was unaware of his presence. Daniel covered his body with a sheet before they left the shop. He pulled it down to just below his waist. Keith waved him off and then checked for a pulse. He didn't feel one.

"I have to say, I'm impressed. I didn't think that you would really do it. You did the right thing, Danny. You can have a few minutes before we wrap things up."

In order to return Amir's soul to his body, Daniel had to make physical contact with him. He had to give Keith a believable reason to get close to him.

"Can I re-cover the body?"

"Seriously? Why? Do you think that he is cold?"

"No. It's considered disrespectful in Islam to leave a body uncovered after death."

"You have to be kidding me. I'm about to kill you and your friends and you are worried about offending a dead guy?"

While Keith was suspicious of Daniel's request, he was confident that he still had the upper hand.

"Fine. If it's that important to you. Keep your hands where I can see them. If I see you reach for anything other than that sheet, the party is over."

Daniel grabbed the sheet with one hand and placed his other hand over Amir's chest. He closed his eyes and concentrated. He channeled the light energy and re-connected with him. This time, instead of pulling his soul out, he pushed it back in. When he opened his eyes, Amir was no longer standing beside him.

"Ok, let's go. I don't have all night. You have two minutes to say your goodbyes," Keith said impatiently.

Daniel turned and walked over to Sonya and Shawn. He helped them both to their feet and removed their gags. He grabbed Sonya by the cheeks and pulled her in for a kiss. Her hands were bound behind her back with duct tape.

"Are you OK?"

She nodded her head.

"Are you OK?" he asked Shawn.

"I'm OK."

Keith moved towards them with the gun still pointed at them.

"I'm sorry, but this little love fest will have to come to an end. It's been real, Danny. I'm going to miss you."

"You don't have to do this, Keith. It's not too late for redemption."

As Daniel uttered those words, he felt his throat close up. He had no way of knowing whether or not he had successfully returned Amir's soul to his body. He stood there frozen with nervous anticipation as he waited for Amir to climb out of the trunk. Several seconds passed. To him, it felt like an eternity. His eyes widened when he saw Amir sit up.

"Danny, Danny. I really feel like you didn't listen to a word that I said. It doesn't matter though. Times up."

As Keith was about to squeeze the trigger, Sonya screamed and Amir jumped out of the trunk. Keith heard his feet hit the floor from behind. As he turned around, Amir nose tackled him to the ground. Once they were down, Amir quickly threw himself on top of Keith and tried to grab the gun. The hard fall disoriented Keith, but he managed to keep a firm grip on the gun.

Daniel pulled Sonya and Shawn off to the side of the warehouse floor. He looked around for something to cut the tape around their hands with. He found a rusted, jagged piece of metal on the floor. He picked it up and cut the tape around Shawn's hands first. He then handed it to him and told him to free Sonya while he helped Amir.

Amir was still on top of Keith. He was using most of his strength to restrain his right hand, which was holding the gun, but he was quickly losing his grip on him. With his left arm free, Keith began elbowing Amir in the face. Daniel raced over and leaped on top of Keith just as he was able to free himself from Amir. Shawn cut the tape around Sonya's hands. She saw Daniel struggling and ran over to help him. Keith was able to squeeze off a shot at Daniel. Daniel deflected Keith's hand with his arm and the bullet missed him. The shot went off right next to his ear and disoriented him. Keith took advantage of the situation by forcing himself on top of Daniel and subduing him. Suddenly, Keith felt a hard punch to the left side of his face. It knocked the wind out of him and he dropped the gun. Amir had managed to get back up and hit him. He also picked up the gun and held it on him. Keith held up his hands in surrender. Daniel got to his feet and moved away from Keith as he caught his breath.

"Daniel, we need to get some help," Shawn said with his voice cracking.

Daniel turned around and saw Shawn holding Sonya in his arms on the floor. He was holding his hand tightly over the middle of her abdomen. Blood was pouring out of it. The bullet that missed him, hit her. He ran over to her. Blood was seeping out of her mouth. She couldn't speak. She could only cough. She lost consciousness almost immediately. He checked for a pulse and didn't feel one. He looked down in horror as he saw a dull greyish glow begin to emanate from her body, just as it had from Alexis' body. He knew instantly that it was her designated time, and that he had to guide her into death.

He turned back around and saw that Keith was now on his knees with his hands over his head. Amir was standing behind him holding the gun on him. In a moment of rage, he charged at Keith. He threw him on his back and began punching him in the face repeatedly. Amir pleaded with him to stop, but he didn't listen. He just kept hitting him. The barrage of punches finally ended when he lost feeling in his knuckles. Keith looked up at him. With his face beaten to a bloody pulp, he smiled up at him with a menacing grin. Without thinking, Daniel reached down for his chest. He felt the surge of light energy and instinctively ripped Keith's soul from his body.

Like Amir had earlier, Keith stood over the sight of his own body in utter disbelief. Daniel briefly acknowledged him, but he didn't say a word to him. Instead, he made his way back over to Sonya. He started sobbing. He knew what he had to do, but he couldn't bear the thought of losing her. He held her in his arms for several minutes before he laid her down on her back. He gently placed his hand on her chest and proceeded to release her soul. When he pulled his hand away, he heard her voice from behind.

"Daniel, what's happened?"

He stood up and faced her. His eyes were red and swollen and his clothes were covered in her blood.

"I'm so sorry. This was all my fault. You died because of me. You were shot and killed by Keith. I tried to stop him, but I failed. I failed you. I have to help you cross over into death now."

"I don't understand."

"You have reached your designated time of death. It's now time for you to leave this life and cross over into death, where you will wait for a new life to begin. I have been chosen to help you with this step of your journey. It's my job to help guide you from life into death. Before you cross over, you have the chance to say goodbye to one person in your life. It can be anyone that you choose. You will have a few minutes to say goodbye, although they won't be aware of your presence. Do you have anyone in mind?"

She looked down at her body and the blood pouring out of her stomach. Tears began running down her cheeks as the reality of the situation sank in.

"Oh, Daniel. I love you so much. You are the only person that I have left. If you are the last person that I get to see before I die, that is fine with me. I will miss you so much."

"I will miss you too. I'm so sorry that I broke my promise. I told you that I would never let anything keep us apart again. I let you down again. I hope that you can forgive me."

"There is nothing to forgive. I'm just grateful that we got to be together again, even if it was only for a short time. Goodbye, my love."

A bright light appeared behind her. She blew one last kiss to him and walked towards it, but just before she was about to enter, Daniel called out to her.

"Wait, stop!"

Sonya turned around. Daniel placed his hand back over her chest. He re-channeled the light energy and pushed her soul back into her body. Her soul vanished from sight and the light disappeared. He pulled her up into his arms and lightly shook her. A few seconds later, she opened her eyes and smiled up at him.

Chapter 18

"Daniel!" Sonya cried out as she sprung up into consciousness.

The sun was shining down on her face and she was in an unfamiliar place. As she looked around, she realized that she was in a hospital room. She didn't know how she got there. She vaguely remembered walking towards a bright light. Before she reached it, Daniel called out for her to stop. Her last memory was of him holding her in his arms.

"It must have been a dream. It seemed so real, but how could that be possible?" she thought to herself.

She felt a soreness in her abdominal area. When she placed her hand over the center of her stomach, she felt a thick layer of bandages. The memory of being shot suddenly returned to her. She could remember it clearly at that point.

"How long have I been asleep? Where is Daniel? Where is Shawn? Were they also injured?" she wondered.

She wanted answers. She began looking around the room for a nurse's call button when the door opened. Daniel walked in with a cup of coffee in hand. He looked like he hadn't slept in days, but he was alive and appeared to be uninjured. She felt an instant sigh of relief.

He was equally relieved to see her awake. He tripped and nearly spilled his entire cup of coffee trying to rush over to her bedside. He put the cup down on the nightstand and leaned in to kiss her. He was careful not to pull out any of the tubes or wires that were hooked up to her.

"What happened? Are you OK? Is Shawn? My mind is so fuzzy right now," she asked after she kissed him back.

"I'm fine and so is Shawn. We have been worried about you. You got shot and lost a lot of blood. You had to have surgery when you arrived at the hospital. You have been asleep for two days."

"I remember being shot by Keith. His gun went off when the two of you were fighting. I still don't understand why he kidnapped us. I thought he was your friend."

"I thought the same thing. I guess you never truly know people. Keith was a bad guy. He murdered a young woman in Iraq. She lived in the city that our unit was assigned to help. My friend, Amir, was the city's police chief. He became suspicious of him a few months after we left. He picked up on few inaccurate things that Keith had said to him when we were there, so he began investigating him on his own. Eventually, he made his way to the U.S. and tracked me down to help him.

We went to Keith's apartment to see if we could find any evidence to back up his theory. It turns out that he had a small hidden camera in his apartment, which was linked to an app on his phone. He grabbed you and Shawn while we were waiting for him to return home. Amir thinks that he might have killed two other women before he killed the woman in Iraq. You should also know that he killed Alexis. I'm so sorry. I had no idea who he really was."

The thought of Alexis brought tears to Sonya's eyes.

"It's not your fault. You shouldn't blame yourself for what happened to her, or to me. He is the one who is responsible. Where is he now? Did the police arrest him?"

"He's dead. I killed him. He can't hurt anyone anymore."

"Don't feel guilty about that either. He got what he deserved."

"I suppose," Daniel said stoically

"I need to ask you something else about what happened. I don't want you to think that I'm crazy."

"You don't need to worry about that. I don't think you are crazy, I know you are."

"Asshole!" she said lightly slapping his shoulder.

"I'm just kidding. What do you need to ask me?"

"After I was shot, I remember standing up and looking down at my own body on the floor. I thought that I was dead. You could see me and talk to me. You told me that I had been killed and that you had been chosen to help me cross over into death. A bright light then appeared and I began walking towards it. You called out for me to stop. I turned around and the next thing I knew, I was in your arms looking up at you. It felt so real. Was it?"

He took her hand into his, looked deep into her eyes, and spoke softly to her.

"No. It wasn't real. It was just a dream. I did hold you in my arms, and you did look up at me, but that is all that happened. After you were shot, we called an ambulance. They rushed you to the hospital. The doctor said that if you had arrived any later than you did, you would have died. They operated on you for almost seven hours. You lost more than half of your blood. They told me that it's common for patients who experience that level of trauma to be disoriented when they first wake up. Memories and dreams can blend together. It can be hard to tell the difference between the two. The important thing is that you are awake now and you are going to be OK."

After he brought Sonya back, Daniel decided that he could not reveal the truth to her. Aashirya warned him how dangerous it could be. He already revealed himself to Shawn and Amir. Shawn witnessed him release her soul, only to pull it back in before she could cross over into death. He didn't want to put anyone else at risk, especially her. She had already been through too much already.

There was a knock at the door.

"Come in," Sonya said.

Nick walked into the room. He was dressed in a dark blue suit and a grey overcoat. His badge was displayed in a custom black leather wallet, hooked onto the front breast pocket of his overcoat. Seeing Sonya awake brought a smile to his face.

"It's good to see you awake. How are you feeling?"

"I'm a little banged up, but I'll be OK."

"Well, you look better than this guy."

"You look like you could use a long nap and a hot shower," Nick said to Daniel.

"I'm so glad that you could find time in your busy schedule to come down here and insult me."

"What are cousins for?"

"In all seriousness, he hasn't left this place since you got here. He refused to leave your side. It took my mother to convince him to even change his clothes. He was really worried about you. We all were. I'm glad to see that you are going to be OK. Just FYI, Mom is planning on cooking you the biggest Italian feast in the history of Utica when they let you out of here. She might even drop by with some samples of the menu beforehand. She can't bear the thought of you having to recover on hospital food." Nick said to Sonya.

"That sounds great. I can't wait."

As they were talking, Sonya's nurse entered the room. It was the first time that she had seen her awake. She began examining her and then turned to Daniel and Nick.

"Would the two of you mind stepping out of the room for a few minutes? I will have to call the doctor. She needs to examine her now that she is awake. You can have a seat in the waiting room if you would like. I promise that I will come and get you just as soon as we are done. It shouldn't take too long."

"It's OK. I'll be fine," Sonya said to Daniel.

"OK, I'll see you in a little bit. Do you need me to get you anything?"

"No, I'm fine. Just bring yourself back."

"I love you," he said as he leaned over and kissed her forehead.

"I love you too."

Daniel and Nick walked out into the hallway.

"I was just on my way down to the coroner's office to get Keith's autopsy report, but if you have a minute, I need to talk to you," Nick said.

"Sure, what's up?"

"I got a call this morning from an agent with the FBI. It seems that there is a pissing contest going on in Washington right now over who is going to have jurisdiction over the investigation into Keith's activities. In addition to the FBI, the Department of Defense and the State Department are also involved. Since Nella Kassab was an Iraqi citizen and Keith was a U.S. military officer at the time that he allegedly killed her, it's stirring up a firestorm. It's only been two days since all this has come to light and the Iraqi government is already demanding answers. This could even get visibility all the way up to the White House. Your friend managed to create an international incident. He's lucky that he's dead."

"I'm sorry, Nick. I know I fucked up. Everything happened so quickly. I just reacted to the situation as best I knew how. I didn't mean to drag you into the middle of this."

"Don't worry about it. I don't think anyone is going to blame you. If it wasn't for you and your friend, Amir, nobody would know anything about this. Keith could have killed more women. For all we know, he has. It will be off my desk soon anyway. The Utica Police Department isn't exactly equipped to handle an investigation into an international serial killer. That being said, the agent asked me to get all of the paperwork in order so that we can turn the case over to the Feds when the jurisdiction issue is settled. He said that somebody should be heading down here in about three or four weeks. Shawn and

Amir put in their formal written statements yesterday. I know it's been a rough couple of days, but I need you to do the same as soon as you can. Dad's even breathing down my neck about it."

Daniel knew that is was inevitable that he would have to make a statement to the police. He also knew that he would have to leave out certain parts of the story. He hid the truth from Sonya to protect her, but he couldn't do the same for Shawn and Amir. They all agreed to keep the full truth from coming out into the open. If it did, the consequences could be disastrous. Before the ambulance and the police arrived, they crafted a version of events that would be believable. Amir took the lead because of his experience in law enforcement. He told them that as long as their statements were consistent with each other, there would be no reason for anyone to believe that they were hiding anything. He also insisted on being truthful about his methods in obtaining Keith's military personnel file. He didn't think that it would be wise to hide it from the investigators. He was confident that they would discover the truth on their own anyway, and in doing so, it might make them question other aspects of their story. He told Daniel to include that part of the story in his statement as well.

"Yeah, no problem. Do you think that it could wait until tomorrow morning though? I'm pretty beat and Sonya just woke up. I don't want to leave her alone right now. I promise that I will be there first thing in the morning."

"Sure. Twenty-four hours isn't going to make much of a difference. Just do me a favor, take a shower first," Nick said, seeing how run-down Daniel was.

"It will be my first order of business. I appreciate it. Thank you."

"Don't mention it. One more thing. In all of the chaos, I never took your cell phone. I need it for evidence. We'll need to download the pictures and messages that Keith sent you."

Daniel reached into his pocket and handed it to him.

"Here you go."

"Thanks. I don't know when I'll be able to get it back to you, but we have some extra burners lying around the station that aren't being used. I can probably get you one of those to use in the meantime if you want."

"Don't worry about it. I'll live. Thanks again."

"Anytime. Take care, Danny-boy."

Nick entered the coroner's examination room on the basement floor of the hospital. The coroner was a short, heavy set bald man with glasses. His name was Elton Donaldson. He was thumbing through some papers when Nick entered the room. There was a body on the examination table covered with a dark grey sheet.

"Detective Morello. I'm glad that you stopped by. I was getting ready to call you. I've completed the initial autopsy on Mr. Andrews and was starting to write up my report. I was going through some reference materials when you walked in. I must admit that I'm not stumped that often. It's rather exciting for me when I am. It seems that we have a genuine medical mystery on our hands."

"I'm not following. The guy looks like he got hit by a Mac truck and my cousin's knuckles are the front end of that truck. What is the mystery?"

Elton lifted the grey sheet, uncovering Keith's body on the table. He had massive bruising on his face and both of his eyes were swollen shut.

"It's true that he did receive quite a lashing, but that didn't cause his death. Aside from the obvious bruises and lacerations on his face, the only other evidence of trauma that I found was that of a mild concussion. It certainly wasn't what killed him. His brain shows no evidence of the level of trauma that would be required to cause death."

"Ok, so what did cause his death?"

"Hence, the mystery detective."

"What are you saying? You don't know what killed him?"

"To put it simply, no. He certainly is dead, but I can't determine the cause. I've run all of the normal tests on all of his major organs. There is no sign of failure in any one of them. There is also no evidence of a stroke or a heart attack. Aside from the facial wounds and the concussion, he is perfectly healthy."

"Perfectly healthy? The guy is dead."

"Well, there is that one minor detail, yes. I can say for sure that he is in fact dead. I just don't know why."

"Are there any other tests that you could run? What about his toxicology screens? Were there any signs of drugs in his system?"

"There are a few more tests that I could run aside from the standard ones that I usually complete. Still, I'm not optimistic that they would reveal anything. As far as drugs in his system, I did send out for a full blood panel. It will take a few more days before we have the results, but I don't think they will tell us anything either."

"Why not?"

"If someone overdoses on drugs or is poisoned, there is usually some type of physical evidence that would indicate that. In this case, as far as I can tell, all of his organs simply stopped working at the same time for some unknown reason. He could have ingested some type of chemical that I'm not aware of. Unfortunately, not being aware of it, makes it rather difficult to test for it."

"Perfect. So much for getting all of the paperwork done before the Feds show up."

"Am I to understand that the FBI will be involved in this case?"

"Amongst others, yes."

"That could be beneficial for us. They will undoubtedly have higher levels of access to the Centers for Disease Control's database than I do. If we are dealing with some type of mystery drug, they would be the ones who would have the best chance of finding it. In the meantime, I will continue on and conduct those additional tests. If I find anything, I will let you know immediately."

"Thank you, Elton."

Nick walked through the hospital parking lot and got into his car. When he sat down, his phone vibrated. He reached into his jacket pocket to pull it out but pulled out Daniel's phone by mistake. He placed Daniel's phone on the dashboard and reached back into his pocket for his own phone. Karen was calling him.

"Hi, honey, what's up?"

"Not too much. I just wanted to see how Daniel was doing."

"He's doing better. Sonya woke up. It seems like she is going to be OK."

"That's great! I'll stop by the hospital later this afternoon to see her. While I have you on the phone, I wanted to ask you if you think that you will be home for dinner tonight? I was going to make a pot roast in the crock-pot."

"Yeah, I should be home around 5:30 pm. I'll call and let you know if I get tied up."

"OK, I'll throw it in. If worst comes to worst, I can re-heat it if you are running late. I'll let you get back to work. I love you."

"I love you too, sweetheart."

After he hung up, Nick stared at Daniel's phone on the dashboard. It dawned on him that he should put it into an evidence bag so that it wouldn't get lost. He reached into his center console and pulled one out. He always kept a few handy. Before he placed it into the bag, he decided to look through the messages on it. He looked over the pictures and read through all of the texts that Keith sent to Daniel.

Just as he was about to put the phone into the bag, he noticed a strange text. The sender was unknown. The text read, "Proctor Park, Park Street, Starch Factory Creek." It was sent on Thursday, December 22 at 5:30 pm. He recognized the date as the same one that Daniel and Sonya came to the police station to report Alexis missing. He also recognized the location as the scene of Alexis' murder. That meant that Daniel had knowledge of her location the night before her body was found.

Chapter 19

One Month Later

Jacklyn's time was running short, a fact that Daniel was painfully aware of as he was walking down the hallway towards her room at the Masonic Care Community. She was scheduled to be transferred to the hospice facility in Rome the following week. Her condition had deteriorated substantially over the last month. With everything that happened, he hadn't had much time to visit her. He knew that he wouldn't have many more opportunities to spend time with her, and he wanted to make the most of the time that she had left. When he arrived at her room, he found Karen organizing her dresser drawers, dressed her in her scrubs. Karen greeted him with a hug while Jacklyn lay asleep in bed.

"It's good to see you. I've been meaning to stop by and check in on Sonya. I ran into her yesterday when she was at the hospital for her follow-up appointment. She seems to be doing a lot better."

"She is. She's been healing well. She's just been a little rundown lately. I guess it's to be expected, under the circumstances."

"It takes time to heal. You can't force it. She'll get there. I know being with you makes all the difference to her. Speaking of which, how are you feeling?"

"I'm doing OK. I got a call from the hospice this morning. They will be here Monday morning to transport Mom to their facility. It seems like a nice place. Hopefully, she will be comfortable there."

As Daniel talked about his mother, the pain in his voice was palpable. It reminded Karen of how she felt when her mother was dying.

"I know what it's like. You see her in pain and you want to take it away, but there is nothing you can do about it. You feel helpless and alone. Just remember, you are not alone. You have all of us and Sonya now too. Don't be afraid to lean on the people who love you."

"Thank you, Karen. It means a lot. I know Mom appreciates it too."

"It's nothing at all. You are both family."

Karen looked at her watch and realized that she was running late.

"I'm sorry to run, but I have to be at work in fifteen minutes. Do you need me to do anything else before I leave?"

"No, I'll be fine. Thank you though."

"OK, tell Sonya I'll give her a call soon. You guys should come over for dinner this weekend. The four of us really haven't gotten a chance to hang out together. It would be a nice change of pace for everyone. What do you say?"

"Sounds good. I'll let Sonya know."

"Take care, hun," she said as she gave him another hug and a peck on the cheek.

When Karen left the room, Daniel picked up a chair and placed it beside Jacklyn's bed. He sat down and watched her sleep. She seemed peaceful, although he knew it was only temporary. When she woke up, she would be in terrible pain again. It was true what Karen had said. He did want to take her pain away. What she didn't know was that he actually had the power to do it.

A woman entered the room and interrupted his thoughts. He didn't recognize her. She appeared to be in her late twenties or earlier thirties. She had shoulder-length reddish-brown hair and piercing dark brown eyes. She was fair skinned with delicate, yet strong facial features. He found her extremely attractive. She was wearing a grey turtle neck, black dress pants, leather healed-boots, and a knee-length leather jacket.

"There is nothing more painful than watching someone you love suffer in pain. Most people would do anything to ease that pain. Some people would even be willing to take their loved-one's place and endure it for them. It's remarkable, don't you think?" she said with an Irish accent.

"What is?"

"Human empathy. It's amazing the lengths that some people are willing to go in order to protect the ones that they love, even if it means harming themselves or others in the process. It's admirable, don't get me wrong, but it's short-sighted. Most people are too focused on themselves and the lives of the people close to them. They don't understand the big picture and the true consequences of their actions. You can't blame them really. They unaware of the true nature of existence. After all, that knowledge is only shared with a select few individuals."

"Who are you?"

"My name is Fiona Murphy. At least, that was my name at one point. No one has called me Fiona in quite some time. I would like it if you did, Daniel. I'm not fond of formal titles. I've always been a simple girl."

"What are you doing here? What do you want from me?"

"I will admit, I don't usually like to meet with subordinates like this. That's why I have others who speak on my behalf. I'm sure that Aashirya explained all of this to you, did she not?"

"Aashirya? Then, you are...the Reaper?"

"As I said, Daniel, I'm not fond of titles. Even after all these years, I've never been able to get used to one. It must be the commoner in me. I grew up in Shannon Ireland. I lived in a small two-bedroom farm house with my parents and four sisters. My father was a sharecropper. We were very poor, but we were a close-knit family. We never felt as if anything was lacking in our lives. In many ways, it was the happiest that I've ever been.

I was married at the age of seventeen. Marrying that young was a common practice in those days. My husband was a lieutenant in the British Army. He was assigned to Thomas Gage's regiment not long after he was named the military governor of the Massachusetts Bay colony. We traveled to live in Boston. I'd never been more than twenty miles away from home before. Suddenly, I found myself living halfway around the world across an entire ocean. As nervous as I was, I found life in America quite agreeable, at least for a little while. The tensions between the colonists and the military hit a natural boiling point and fighting broke out. My husband fell at Breeds Hill. I continued to live in the city after his death. I probably should have gone home, but I didn't want to return and become a burden on my parents. Three days before the British evacuation of the city, a group of men grabbed me when I was walking home at night. They claimed to be members of the Sons of Liberty. They told me that they were taking their revenge on British loyalists for the atrocities committed against their fellow countrymen. I can't tell you if they were really members of the Sons of Liberty. What I can tell you is that they were drunkards, looking to take their boredom and frustrations out on a defenseless woman. They beat me and then took turns raping me. They even brought a few bottles of ale along with them to enjoy in between turns. When they were finished, they threw me down on the cold cobblestone ground and urinated on me. I was found in an alley the next morning, barely alive. I was brought to a doctor where I was cleaned up and my injuries were tended to. They put me on a ship and I sailed back to England with the rest of the fleet. I died halfway through the voyage. I never fully regained consciousness."

"I'm sorry. I can't imagine what that must have been like for you. What those men did to you was evil."

"Yes, Daniel, it certainly was. Evil really does exist in this world. However, what most people don't understand is that some degree of evil is necessary to balance out the good that also exists. Believe me, I don't enjoy reliving those memories. I wish that they could be erased along with that life, but I was chosen for a higher purpose, as were you. I came to understand that what happened to me was part of a much larger plan. I made my peace with it. Now you must do the same."

"What does that mean?"

"It means that you must sacrifice for the greater good. Sonya has already reached her designated time of death. As painful as that might seem, you have to accept it. By allowing her to live past her designated time, you have put the entire balance of existence in jeopardy. She must cross over, so that she can begin a new life when the time comes. This life for her is over."

"No! Please. Don't make me do it. I can't. I love her. I can't lose her again. There has to be another way. It's just one life," he pleaded.

"Yes, it is and every individual life matters. Each one affects the other. It's like a machine. It cannot run without all of its parts, no matter how small any individual part might be. A soul is needed to fill a new life."

"Wait, if it's just a soul that is needed, does that mean that another soul can take her place?" he asked, clinging to his last bit of hope.

"Technically, yes, but that means that another must be chosen, and then that person's life will end. Are you really willing to place one life above another and accept the consequences of that choice?"

"Normally, no, I would not. However, my mother is already near death and suffering in terrible pain. Everything that she was is already gone. Let me release her. She can take Sonya's place."

Fiona stared at him in silence before she responded.

"I would normally not consider such a request, but at the present time, there are matters of even greater importance that need to be dealt with."

"I don't understand."

"Sonya was not the only one who was supposed to cross over into death that night. Keith's life was also near its end, although his time was to be several hours after Sonya's. By releasing his soul prematurely, you allowed him to escape death. He now exists outside of both life and death. While allowing Sonya to continue to live is not inconsequential, it can be more easily rectified. The situation with Keith is much more precarious. He retains all of the memories and instincts from his former life but is no longer bound by it. He is now a lost soul, armed with the true knowledge of existence. Given his proclivities, the damage that he could cause is incalculable."

"I'm so sorry. I had no idea. This is all my fault. Tell me how I can fix this."

"Keith must be found. He must be brought into death, forcefully if need be, and by any means necessary. He must not be allowed to interrupt the balance any more than he already has. Time is of the essence."

"How do I find him?"

"It will be difficult. Aashirya will assist you. He must be found at all costs. As Aashirya explained to you, maintaining the balance is an extremely delicate and fragile process. While it can sustain some minor interruptions from time to time, a tipping point exists. Once that point is reached, it cannot be restored. Without the balance, all existence will end."

"I understand. I will do everything in my power to find him. I promise you that."

"I hope you can deliver on that promise, Daniel. The stakes could not be any higher."

As Fiona turned to leave, Daniel stopped her.

"Wait, what about Sonya and my mother?"

"I will grant your request, but before I do, you must commit to accepting the consequences of your decision. I will make no further concessions to the normal order. Too much damage has been done already. I will caution you. You might not be satisfied with the end result. You have already made decisions without fully understanding the consequences once. Do you really want to do that again?"

As he contemplated her words, he realized that Amir had been right. He didn't fully understand the forces at work of which he was dealing with. However, he also knew that sometimes there were no good choices and that you had to make the best decision that you could, based on the available information. He didn't know how everything would turn out, but he did know that he couldn't let Sonya die, and he could no longer stand by and watch his mother suffer in agony.

"Yes. I will accept the consequences of my decision."

"Then you may proceed. Aashirya will contact you soon. I'll wish you good luck, for everyone's sake."

Fiona left the room and Daniel was once again alone with his mother. He sat with her for several minutes, trying to remember all of the good times that they had together. He admired the strength that she had shown throughout her life, even in the direst of circumstances. Tears formed in his eyes as he relived those memories. When he was ready to begin, he stood over her and gave her a kiss on her forehead. He then placed his hand in the middle of her chest. He focused his mind and concentrated until he could feel the light energy within himself. Once he felt that he had a firm grasp on her soul, he released it. For the first time in recent memory, he heard his mother speak to him clearly. He turned around to find her standing in front of him.

"Daniel, is that you?"

"Yes, mom, it's me. I'm here," he replied, overwhelmed with emotion.

"This feels like a dream. I feel so light. I can't remember the last time that I felt this way."

As she stared back at him, she noticed the tears in his eyes.

"What's wrong, sweetheart? Why are you crying?"

Daniel was standing in between her and her bed. He stepped to the side so that she could see the person lying in it. Her reaction was different from that of Alexis and Sonya. Theirs were reactions of fear. Hers was one of relief.

"Oh, Daniel. Don't cry, sweetheart. This has been coming for a long time. I'm no longer in any pain. Don't feel sad. It's just my time. I have had a wonderful life. Being able to be your mother was the best thing that ever happened to me. I will always be grateful for that."

"Mom, this might be hard to understand, but I'm here to help you cross over into death. The night that Dad died, I saw him in my room at the same time that he was found at work. I thought I was crazy, but it turns out that I had been chosen to be what is known as a Shepherd. When someone dies, it is my responsibility to release their soul from their body and guide them to the gateway between life in death. Once they cross over, their memories from their life are erased along with all of their pain."

"I see. Well, I knew my time was coming, so I am grateful that my son gets to see me off."

"There is one more thing. You are allowed to see one person before you cross over. Since I'm already here, you can choose someone else. Uncle Vincent, perhaps?"

"No, I choose you. I love you so much, Daniel. You have been a wonderful son. I'm so proud of the man that you have become. I'm saddened that I won't be able to see you become a father yourself, but I know that you will be a wonderful one."

"I love you too, mom. I'll miss you."

"Just promise me that you won't waste too much time missing me. I want you to live your life to the fullest."

"I promise."

A bright light appeared in the hallway outside the room.

"It looks like it is time to go. Goodbye, sweetheart."

"Goodbye, mom."

With what felt like an out of body experience, Daniel stood back and watched as his mother walked into the light and disappeared.

Chapter 20

For three hours, mourners passed by Jacklyn's casket in the viewing room of the McArthur and Williams funeral home. They paid their respects to the family as they filed out of the room one by one. Daniel sat in the front row with Sonya by his side. Vincent, Deanna, Karen, and Michael also sat in the front row. Shawn and his parents were seated in the row behind them. Several other family members and close friends were scattered throughout the room for the duration of the calling hours. The funeral director walked to the front of the room to address the crowd.

"On behalf of the Jefferies and Morello families, I would like to extend their appreciation to all those who attended this afternoon. The funeral will be held tomorrow morning at 9:30 am at St Mary of Mt Carmel Church. Immediately following the funeral, there will be a procession to the Mohawk Street cemetery where Jacklyn will be laid to rest next to her late husband, Donald. All are welcome to attend. The viewing room will be closing in five minutes. Please convey any final thoughts or prayers that you may have for the family at this time. On behalf of the McArthur and Williams funeral home, I would like to extend our deepest condolences to all of Jacklyn's family and friends. Thank you for coming and have a pleasant evening."

After the announcement, everyone remaining in the room began to file outside. Daniel was the last person out of the room. When he arrived outside, he found the family congregated together, discussing plans for the following morning. Nick walked up to the group and kissed Karen.

"I'm sorry I'm late. I had to tie up some loose ends on a case. I couldn't get away," Nick said.

"How are you holding up?" he asked Daniel.

"I'm good, thanks."

"I promise that I will be there tomorrow."

"Don't sweat it, man. It's OK. I understand."

"Thanks."

"Do you have a minute, Dad? There a few things I need to talk to you about," Nick asked Vincent.

"Sure. Excuse me, everyone. I'll be right back."

Vincent followed Nick away from the group. Nick waited until they were out of earshot to speak. He didn't want anyone to hear what they were about to discuss.

"I just got off of a conference call with the FBI, the DoD, and the State Department. They formed a joint task force to investigate the Andrews case. The FBI was granted jurisdictional authority to lead it. They asked me if I could work with them as it relates to the murder of Alexis Nesmith. You will be contacted shortly by the agent in charge regarding my participation. I told them that I would do whatever I could do to help and that you would also welcome the UPD's participation. I hope I didn't overstep."

"No not all. You did the right thing. We want to be as open and as transparent as possible. A case this high profile is bound to become very political, very quickly. We don't want to give anyone the impression that we are holding back, especially since Danny is so close to this thing."

"That's what I thought you would say."

Vincent could tell that there was something that Nick was not telling him.

"What is it?"

"We might have a problem with Danny. I just don't know how big of a problem."

"I don't understand. He gave his statement along with others. All of the evidence seems to corroborate their story. Did you find something else?"

"Maybe. I'm not sure yet."

"Out with it. This is not something that we can fuck around with. We are a city police department. We are out of our league when it comes to this type of case. If the FBI even thinks that we aren't being straight with them, they could crucify us."

"I know. Believe me, I do. I did find something, but I don't know what it means yet. I wanted to be sure before I brought it to you. I've been trying to run it down, but I've hit a dead end."

"Just give it to me then."

"I talked to Danny at the hospital the day that Sonya woke up. I told him that I needed him to come down to the station to fill out a formal written statement. I also remembered that I never took his cell phone into evidence. When I asked him for it, he handed it right over. Before I put it into an evidence bag, I went through the messages. Everything that we got off of Keith's phone, including the pictures of Sonya and Shawn, were in there. However, I saw one other message that nobody ever mentioned. The sender was unknown. The text was one line, "Proctor Park, Park Street, Starch Factory Creek." That was the same location where Alexis Nesmith's body was found. It was sent twelve hours before that happened."

"What are you saying? Are you saying that Danny was involved in her murder somehow?"

"No, I don't think so. I did some digging around. According to the coroner, Alexis was definitely killed sometime early Thursday morning, between 3:00 am and 5:00 am. Danny was with Shawn and Sonya during that time. I also checked the cell tower logs in the area. Keith's phone was definitely in the vicinity of the park. Danny's was not. I also checked Keith's complete call history. There were some calls to Danny earlier in the week, but those were most likely regarding their scheduled visit, which he told us about. There were no other calls, texts, or emails sent to Danny from Keith before the murder. The next call wasn't until Friday when Danny was at Keith's apartment and he had already kidnapped Sonya and Shawn. Danny and Sonya came to see me at the station early Thursday evening. They both seemed genuinely worried about Alexis. I didn't get the impression that either one of them were hiding anything at the time. They were with me for about twenty minutes or so. I typed up a report and logged it into the computer. I checked my own call history. I called Karen just after they left to let her know that I wasn't going to be able to make it out for our date night. I placed that call at 5:20 pm. The message that was sent to Danny was sent at 5:30 pm. Presumably, that means that he wasn't lying to me when we spoke that night. In addition to that, the message might not have meant anything to him at the time it was sent. The only thing that I can't figure out is why he didn't say anything about it after the fact? It had to have occurred to him when he arrived at the park that he received a message with that same location from an unknown caller, twelve hours earlier."

"Have you been able to identify the caller who sent that message?"

"No, that's my dead end. The message was probably sent from a burner phone. I don't have any way of finding out who it belonged to. It could have been Keith's, but we searched his entire apartment, as well as his parent's house and the sporting goods store. We didn't find any other cell phones or computers. We also didn't find any evidence that he had a storage facility where he might be stashing things away. It also doesn't make sense that he would tip someone off about the murder. He went to great lengths to cover his tracks. He didn't even keep any type of trophies from the murders, as many serial killers tend to do. If I had to guess, it was sent by someone else. I just have no way of knowing who that someone else is right now."

Vincent stood silently in thought for a few seconds before he spoke again.

"OK, first off, did you log Danny's phone into evidence?"

"No, not yet."

"Good. Don't do it. At some point, we will have to talk to Danny about this, but now is not the time for that. Keep digging. See if you can find out who sent that text."

"What about the FBI? They tend to be pretty thorough. At some point, even without the phone, they might pull Danny's cell phone records. If they do, they are going to see that message and then they will have the same questions that we do."

"We'll deal with that when the time comes. It is still a small detail, so it will take some time before it comes up. We will just have to solve this little mystery before it does."

Daniel stood silently at the edge of the group as everyone else continued to chat. He felt a strong desire to step away and clear his head after such a long service. In an attempt to sneak away discretely, he grabbed Sonya's hand and silently began to walk in the opposite direction of everyone. When he turned around, he saw Aashirya walking up the sidewalk towards the funeral home. She stopped walking once they made eye contact. Sonya also noticed her.

"Who is that, Daniel?"

"It's an old friend. Would you give me a minute? I'll be right back."

"Sure, no problem."

Daniel met Aashirya on the sidewalk while Sonya hung back on the grass.

"I'm sorry about your mother, Daniel," Aashirya said.

"Thank you. I appreciate that."

"I assume you know why I'm here."

"I have an idea. I just want to say that I'm sorry for everything that happened. You warned me about all of this and I didn't take it seriously enough. I'll do whatever it takes to make things right."

"Oh, Daniel, it's not that simple. There is still so much that you don't know. It's probably my fault. I should have explained more, but I felt that you needed to be brought along slowly. I didn't want to overwhelm you any more than I already had."

"I don't understand. I know I messed some things up and Keith got away, but we can still find him, right?"

"It's going to be difficult. I've been trying to locate him ever since you released his soul. So far, he's managed to evade me. That's why Fiona came to you."

"What exactly can Keith do without his body?"

"As I've already explained to you, if the knowledge about the true nature of existence were to fall into the wrong hands, it could be manipulated towards other ends. Keith never crossed into death and he has all of the knowledge from his life, including an idea of how the light energy works now. If he figures out how to use it, he can enter another body and assume a new identity."

"How can he do that?"

"A soul can enter a body as long as the body has not been without a soul for more than forty-eight hours. It's just a matter of finding one in time. All he would have to do is find a person who recently died and crossed over. He could enter a new body in much the same way that Amir and Sonya were returned to their own bodies."

"What happens if he has already entered another body?"

"Then our job is that much more difficult. We will just have to hope that we can locate him before that happens."

"I understand. We should start at St Elizabeth Medical Center. Karen works there and I know my way around. It's also the same hospital that his body was brought to. It would make sense that he might go back there. I'll drop Sonya off at home and meet you there in an hour."

"OK, then that's where we will begin our search."

"Listen, I know that I broke the rules, but I did it so that Sonya could live. I can't live without her. I know that's not an excuse. I just hope that you can understand why I did what I did."

"I understand all too well, Daniel, but unfortunately you do not".

"What do you mean?"

"Your mother took Sonya's place, which means that Sonya took her place. You mother's chosen time of death was set to take place six months from now. Once that time arrives, Sonya will have to cross into death. I'm sorry to tell you this, but you didn't prevent Sonya's death, you only postponed it. As painful as it might seem, you are still going to have to let her go. There is nothing more that can be done."

With that stunning revelation, Aashirya turned and walked away, leaving Daniel alone on the sidewalk. Fiona warned him that he might not be satisfied with the end result of his decision, and he now knew what that meant. Sonya came up behind him and tapped him on the shoulder.

"Is everything OK?" she asked.

"Yes, everything is fine," he replied instinctively, not knowing what else to say.

"What did your friend want?"

"She...she wanted to tell me that she was sorry about my mother. She was in a rush, so she had to leave," he replied, quickly thinking of an excuse to explain her visit.

"I see. There is something that I need to talk to you about. I was waiting for the right time, but I'm not sure if there will ever be one."

"What is it? Are you feeling OK?"

"No. I mean, yes. I feel fine. Actually, I'm a little more than fine."

"I'm not following."

"I got a call from my doctor this morning. He ran some blood work at my appointment last week, just as a routine follow-up. The results came back over the weekend. One of the tests that he ran was a pregnancy test. It came back positive. Daniel, we are going to have a baby."

Epilogue

For the past month, Keith had been conducting careful reconnaissance, and he had finally honed in on his target. He was waiting patiently in the fifth-floor waiting room of the St Elizabeth Medical center. The hospital's intensive care unit was located on that floor. He watched as an elderly janitor walked past the waiting room and into one of the patient rooms. Several minutes later, a bright light appeared at the end of the hallway. The janitor re-emerged from the room along with a middle-aged man dressed in a hospital gown. The janitor pointed towards the light. The man walked into the light and disappeared. No one else on the floor seemed to notice anything.

Keith waited until the janitor was out of sight and then he entered the room. He found the man whom he had just watched disappear into the light, lying in bed. He was unconscious and not hooked up to any monitors. He stood next to the bed and placed his hand in the middle of the man's chest. He focused his mind until he felt the surge of light energy within himself. It was similar to what he felt when Daniel released him from his own body. There was only a slight difference this time. His was the only consciousness present. He felt a connection with the man's body. It was a strange feeling. It felt as if he was walking through an unfamiliar door. A sudden flash of light temporarily blinded him. When his vision came back into focus, he was no longer staring down at the man. He was looking up at the ceiling. As he got his bearings back, he realized that he was now lying in the same bed that he had been looking down upon just a few seconds earlier.

He got out of bed and closed the door to the room. He then went into the bathroom and looked at himself in the mirror. The face that he saw staring back at him was not his own. He could hardly believe what he was seeing. The gravity of what he had just accomplished began to sink in. The extraordinary accomplishment brought a huge smile to his face.

The precariousness of his situation also began to sink in. He knew that he had to get dressed and get out of the hospital before anyone discovered him. There was a wooden wardrobe unit next to the bed. When he opened it, he found a dark blue suit, a light grey button-down shirt, and a pair of black dress shoes with matching socks. He also found a small plastic bag, which contained a wallet and a set of keys. Once he was dressed, he cracked open the door and peered out into the hallway. To his delight, it was empty. He seized the opportunity and exited the room. He walked to the end of the hallway in the opposite direction of the waiting room. He walked through an emergency exit door, which led to a stairway. He made his way down the stairs to the bottom floor, where there was another door that opened up into the main lobby. He casually walked past the reception desk towards the front entrance. He made it to within ten feet of the entrance when the automatic doors opened up.

Daniel and Aashirya entered the lobby and walked straight towards him. He didn't panic or stop moving. He continued walking and passed right by them. They had no idea that it was him. That brought another smile to his face.

He made his way over to the patient parking lot on the left side of the building. He pulled out the set of keys that he found in the room. The keychain had a BMW logo on it. He walked up and down the rows of cars pressing the electronic unlock button. After a few minutes, he heard the sound of a horn and saw the flash of tail lights. It came from a silver 2011 BMW 750i that was just a few feet in front of him. He quickly got into the car, started the engine, and sped away from the hospital.

Ryan Young

The Saga Continues In…

THE SHEPHERD'S DUTY

Made in the USA
Middletown, DE
11 September 2021

47388635R00175